TOWER OF FIRE

PARALLEL MAGIC: BOOK 3

EMMA L. ADAMS

To be notified when Emma L. Adams's next novel is released and get a free prequel short story, sign up to her author newsletter.

"Natural one?" I looked at the die on the table in disbelief as it clattered to a halt next to the game board. "No way."

"It happens," said Liv.

Devon leaned forward, her spiky blue hair sticking up in all directions. "You take aim at the monster, but at the last second, you trip and fall flat on your face."

"Wonderful." I tapped on the painted miniature which represented my character—an elf, naturally—with my knuckles until it fell over. Devon, our DM, had loaned it to me for the session, since I'd only recently become a regular member of their group. Things were off to a somewhat rocky start for my adventurer, to say the least.

Across the table from me, Liv grinned, while Ryan gave her a disapproving look. "We can't all have lucky dice."

"My dice are luckier when I use them to knock people out," said Liv. "Not so much when I'm actually in a campaign."

I'd never thought I'd find myself joining my once-adversary's Dungeons & Dragons group, but the unlikely collection of allies I'd amassed over the last few weeks was the least of the recent changes in my life. Our current group consisted of Liv, a spirit mage; Devon, a magical practitioner and cantrip expert; Ryan, the Death King's Air Element; and Trix, an elf. There were a few others who showed up intermittently, but tonight it was just us, plus Dex, a fire sprite whose main goal was to fly above the table, making sparks dance across the game board for special effects.

Admittedly, I'd mostly come here for the chance to talk to Trix, but I'd have to wait until the session was over unless I wanted word to get out that the Death King had told me to find the elves and ask for their help in the upcoming fight against a group of rogue spirit mages who happened to be allied with my own family. Liv and the others didn't know anything about the people who'd raised me, and it was easier to avoid the subject.

Frankly, I didn't know if the elves would even *want* to speak to me, given what the Family had done to them. Even though I was half elf myself, I'd grown up human, and even now I wore a cantrip that hid my pointed ears and elven features. I had three rules for living in the Parallel, the first of which was to always be ready to run at any time, followed by doing whatever might be neces-sary to survive and adapting to my surroundings when possible. Hiding my true identity had been necessary in order to keep all three of those rules, since there weren't a ton of elves in Elysium and even fewer who'd run around on the wrong side of the law like I had. Add in my fire magic and it was a wonder I'd managed to fly under the radar for as long as I had. If I *did* find the elves, I could say farewell to keeping a low profile as far as that half of my heritage was concerned.

I did my best to keep my focus on the game, but my attention kept drifting to Trix. He looked like a typical elf, with symmetrical features and silky dark hair framing his pointed face, and his mild temperament stood in contrast to the fierceness with which elves were capable of fighting when pushed into a corner. Ryan caught me staring and frowned. Trix and Ryan had been growing closer and I knew they liked one another, but I wasn't trying to flirt with the elf, just get his attention. One did not get on the bad side of the Death King's Air Element, so I held my tongue until the gaming session came to an end.

While Devon and Liv stayed at home, the rest of us returned to the Parallel via the node which lay on top of their house. A flash of light engulfed our group, depositing us on the other side of a high fence circling the Court of the Dead. I waited for Ryan to head in through the gates to the castle, wondering how to broach the subject. I assumed Trix knew the elves were the first beings who'd lived in the Parallel—before the mages had taken their territory for their own—but I didn't know the extent of his knowledge. I assumed he knew more than I did, at the very least, since the town where I'd been born had burned to the ground long ago and taken what remained of my elven history with it. Trix had told me himself that the elves had lost most of their strongholds, but he must have an idea about how to find someone who might give me a sense of direction. When Ryan was out of sight, I approached Trix before he could turn away.

"Oh, hello, Bria," he said, in his usual pleasant tone. "Something up?"

"Can I talk to you?" I asked. "You offered to teach me elf magic once, right?"

"I did, yes," he said. "Did you want to start now?"

"Not yet," I said, seeing Ryan give me a disgruntled look from the other side of the gates. "I just wanted to ask for a few more details about what kind of magic you can teach me."

"I can teach you how to heal, but only if you already have the gift," he said. "It usually works on autopilot if you get hurt."

"I think I do have that gift." Unfortunately, the Family did too, which meant they were functionally immortal. They died and got straight up again, which made it damn tricky to figure out a way to permanently be rid of them. Even after I'd burned them to cinders, they'd managed to recover and walk away in one piece, and I had little doubt they'd pay me back at the first opportunity. I'd been on tenterhooks waiting for retaliation ever since. "What about the mind-control thing you did on the wyrm?"

"That, I can teach you," he said. "Most of us can enact control over animals, but larger ones like the wyrm are trickier, and humans and other elves are the hardest of all."

Hmm. Adair's mind-control worked even on humans—and elves, I assumed—but his ability was unique even among people like us. I assumed most elves didn't have the ability to mind-control anyone they encountered, and I didn't particularly want that skill myself, but if I could convince Neddie the zombie horse to obey me for once, I was all for it.

"Good," I said. "I know nothing about the elves' history, either. Do you know any other elves in the Parallel?"

"Oh, lots," said Trix.

"Seriously?" I didn't know why his admission surprised me, but elves were a rarity in Elysium, and I could count the number I'd met on one hand. "Do any of them have knowledge of the elves' history? I mean, from before the war?"

"It depends," he said. "The older ones will, but not anyone who was born after the strongholds were destroyed. Any reason?"

"The Death King asked me to find any elves who might be willing to fight alongside him," I explained. "I figured they might have an incentive to help out, given what the Family did to them already, but it depends how much they know of their history."

"Oh," he said. "That might be tricky. We're quite scattered, and so is our knowledge."

I thought so. The Family had engineered their current scattered statue, along with the mages who'd run the council before the war. "Do you know anyone in particular who might be willing to talk to me?"

"I can think of a couple of people," said Trix. "I planned to check in with them anyway, so I'll drop by tomorrow and give you an update if they tell me anything you might find useful."

"Thanks," I said. "It's appreciated."

Trix glided away, while I studied the dark shape of the castle behind the fence, wishing I could be certain I was making the right call. If I started contacting all the elves in the Parallel, I ran the risk of the Family finding out my intentions to seek out the history they'd made me forget. On the other hand, I remained short on ideas of how to find a permanent way to be rid of the Family, and the elves might be my last shot at thwarting them.

I walked between the pair of shadowy liches guarding the spiked gates in front of the castle, unsurprised to find Ryan had waited for me at the foot of the stone staircase leading up to the front doors. "Why were you talking to Trix?"

"I wanted to ask him how to contact the other elves," I admitted, figuring it was better to go with the honest approach when it came to the prickly Air Element. Even without the armoured uniform typical of an Elemental Soldier, they towered over me, their shaved head and stern expression emanating hostility even though they'd had us all in stitches earlier that evening by doing a pitch-perfect impression of one of Dex's NPCs.

Ryan arched a brow. "You're an elf?"

"I thought you knew." Maybe it wasn't so obvious after all. "I'm half elf, half mage."

Suspicion filtered through their expression. "I thought all non-humans were eliminated in the first round of the Death King's trials."

Oops. I'd forgotten that slight detail. "I showed up late, remember? I really thought you knew."

"How did you expect me to figure that one out?" said Ryan. "I'm not a vampire. We can't all sniff out a person's magical species from a distance."

"Vampires can do that?" I hadn't known, though it explained why they always seemed to be able to zero in on any magic-related trouble. I knew even less about vamps than I did about elves, though.

"They can sniff out spirit mages, at any rate," they said. "I take it the Death King knows what you are?"

"Of course he does," I said. "He's the one who told me to find the elves and ask if they're willing to form an alliance with him. That's why I spoke to Trix first. He has contacts."

"I don't know why I'm surprised." Ryan sighed. "If Trix finds someone with information, I'm coming with you."

I gave an eye-roll. "So I have to play third wheel again."

"You're the one dragging Trix into this."

"He volunteered," I said. "Besides, I don't exactly know any other elves to ask, do I? My family is dead. My real family, I mean, not the dickheads who raised me."

Ryan's expression softened a fraction. "I didn't know."

"That'd be because I didn't tell anyone."

Except Miles. I'd told him too much, if anything. I should know better than to be that trusting, not with the Family still alive and searching for me. After all, they'd killed the last person I'd grown close to. Admittedly, Tay had been slaughtered by an assassin and not directly by the Family, but she wouldn't have been there at all if the Family hadn't manipulated her into doing their bidding. They'd had their claws in her life from the start, the same way they had with mine.

I shoved the unpleasant memories away, with difficulty. "Never mind. I'm going to bed."

As I turned towards the castle, the shadowy figure of the Death King loomed out of the darkness at the foot of the stone staircase. I managed to refrain from jumping—barely. While his usual dark armour covered his body from head to toe, he also wore an illusion of a human face instead of a mask, a surprisingly young one with dark curly hair. You'd think it would make him look less scary, but someone who could rip out my soul at a touch was not to be trifled with.

"How is your progress with the task I gave you?" he asked.

"Trix is going to talk to the elves tomorrow," I told him. "He'll bring me an update if he learns anything of use."

"And the Houses?" he said.

Out of the corner of my eye, I spotted Ryan walking back towards the castle's back entrance, leaving me alone with the Death King. That figured. "I've been at Devon and Liv's place for D&D night. I haven't had time to talk to anyone at the Houses."

"You've had all week."

Guilty. "I wanted to give them the chance to fix some of the damage before I showed up."

The whole city of Elysium had been in upheaval after the Family had unleashed cantrips laced with a lethal virus among the Houses, ordering the earth mages they'd lured onto their side to distribute them throughout the city for unsuspecting bystanders to pick up. It'd been a bloodbath, and I still didn't know how many members of the Houses had survived.

The Death King frowned. "You won't get many other chances before the Family makes another attempt to convince the Houses to join their side."

"I was waiting for an update from Miles, but it's not like he can get too close to them either," I said. "Besides, it sounds like Trix is going to have an update on the elves tomorrow. I can't be in two places at once."

"I'm aware of that," he said. "And yes, the elves should

be a priority. I don't, however, think we can give up on getting the Houses to ally with us yet."

No. You wouldn't, given that you used to belong to one of them.

I held my tongue. The Death King and his Court were no longer the House of Spirit in name, since they'd all been turned into liches after the last spirit war. Nevertheless, they'd once been one of the five Houses of the Elements, and for all I knew, there was still some loyalty between them and the others, however deeply buried it might be.

As for me, my relationship with the Houses had been rocky from the start. As an illegal mage with talents which they believed shouldn't exist, I'd been jailed no fewer than three times and I fit all their criteria for a troublemaker who deserved to be locked up for life. I wasn't convinced the Houses would ever change enough for me to see them as potential allies—and I was fairly sure the feeling was mutual. The Death King, on the other hand, was preparing for a second spirit war, and I understood why he didn't have time to stand around chatting to the Houses. Unless someone else volunteered to act in his place, it was all on me.

"I'll see what I can do," I told the Death King.

In my dreams, I watched the village burn.

Smoke caught in my lungs as I ran out into the narrow street, between crumbling buildings of brick and stone, with strident screaming echoing in my ears. The obsidian shape of the citadel was the only constant, standing in the centre of the torrents of orange flames and outlined in brightness which I now knew came from the transporter spell inside the upper room of the tower.

I halted before a pile of stone blocking the route ahead, and then veered into a side street. A roaring noise sounded in the background, and more flames bloomed over the rooftops. A pair of hands grasped my shoulders, cold and transparent.

My eyes flickered open to see Miles hovering above over me—in a literal sense—having astral projected into the castle from the outside. His body was transparent, his straw-coloured hair leached of colour and light, and his ghostly hands brought a chill to my skin. "Sorry I startled you. I didn't know how else to wake you."

I breathed in and out, my heart pounding in my chest. "What's going on?"

"Security breach. Rogue liches."

"Shit." I was on my feet an instant later, grabbing the round pendant which contained all my cantrips and looping it around my neck. I wasn't dressed for battle, but I shoved my feet into my shoes and ran out of the room in my pyjamas, while Miles floated behind me in his incorporeal form.

"Don't use your fire on them," he warned. "If they're killed, they'll just reform inside the castle and hide among the other liches."

"Scumbags." I picked up the pace. If the liches had been physical enemies, I might have stopped via the weapons room, but no sword could pierce the dead, and spirit magic was the only way to bring one of them to a permanent end. I followed the sound of shouting to the castle grounds, where the other Elemental Soldiers sprinted ahead of me towards a mass of dark confusion.

There, Liv faced off against the oncoming tide of living shadow, and as I drew closer, she reached into one of the liches' bodies with a glowing hand. After a brief flash of light, the lich's shadowy form collapsed in on itself, turning to nothingness.

Miles flew in to join her, blasting a second lich with a bolt of vivid white spirit energy. He then caught the lich's life essence in his hand, draining it in an instant and causing the shadow to dissipate. Spirit magic might look less flashy than my own fire magic, but it was regarded as the most lethal sort of magic for a reason. Even a lich had no resistance against it if the spirit mage was strong enough—which Miles certainly was. His lean form glowed around the edges, as ethereal and bright as the liches were dark and shadowy. It didn't hurt that he was able to draw power directly from the node near the castle, intended solely for the Death King's personal use—with one brief exception involving a transporter spell which I wasn't sure he'd entirely forgiven me for.

When the last lich evaporated beneath Miles's spirit magic, Ryan and Liv ran over to the gates separating the castle grounds from the rest of the swampland.

"How'd they get in?" I walked over to join them, my sock-less feet slipping around inside my shoes. "What happened to the liches on security duty?"

"Judge for yourself," said Ryan.

I squinted into the darkness and nearly gagged when I realised what I'd thought were bushes were two heaps of bones and rotting flesh lying in front of the gates. "Were those *liches*?"

"You remember I mentioned cantrips which can make the undead fall to pieces?" Liv strode forward, her mouth twisting with distaste. "The cantrips return the liches to life, only for their magic to eat them from the inside out."

"Fuck."

If Harper had been on guard duty, she'd have met a similar demise, but she wasn't one of the Death King's security liches. They never would have had the chance to defend themselves, not if the cantrip had been deployed by someone who'd then fled the castle's grounds before they were spotted.

"Those cantrips only work on the dead." Felicity, the Water Element, strode up to join us, her blue-lined cloak rippling behind her and the Earth Element, Cal, on her heels. "That means if humans had been on guard duty, they wouldn't have been affected."

"There are only four of us," Cal pointed out. "If we're going to take over security, we'll have to take long shifts."

"Then we'll do it," said Ryan.

Shit. How am I supposed to find the elves and guard the castle at the same time? The Death King already expected me to negotiate with the Houses as well as the elves, but he was as vulnerable to those cantrips as any other lich. Only now did it hit me how much of a threat they might pose to the Court of the Dead.

"It won't happen again," Liv said firmly. "Not if I have anything to do with it."

"Who even created those cantrips?" I asked.

"A vampire who got what was coming to him." Liv crouched beside the bodies, reaching past the piles of rotting flesh to pick up a coin-shaped cantrip, and then holding it up so we could all see the faded markings on its surface.

The Family's signature stared back at me. *No way.* "I thought all the cantrips with their mark on them were destroyed."

"Whose mark?" Liv said, as sharp as always.

"Long story." If the Death King hadn't already told her, then I didn't have the energy to relate my entire sorry history to her. "They're called the Family, and they like to put their signature on things."

"Hawker was using them before," Miles added. "Might be him."

"Exactly." But I didn't think so, somehow. This felt… personal. Maybe it was paranoia talking, but given the Family's flair for the dramatic, it wasn't too out there that they'd decided to remind me of their existence by leaving their signature outside the gates to my new home. As if I could ever forget.

Liv continued to glare at me, but I'd never been involved in the Family's cantrip creation schemes and hadn't even known about them until I'd met one of the victims of said schemes in the flesh. Still, I'd never expected the Family to openly target the Court of the Dead. Their usual method in times of conflict was to watch from the shadows and then swoop in to scavenge the ruins. Either they wanted to play a more central role this time, or they were mad enough at my spurning them that they didn't care if they angered the Death King. Unless someone else had used the cantrip and intended the Family to take credit. Whatever the case, I met Liv's stare until she shrugged and returned to the castle. Then I walked over to Miles, whose transparent form was almost invisible in the gloom.

"Those cantrips wouldn't have any effect on you, would they?" I asked him.

"Unless I ask one of my Spirit Agent friends to turn me into a lich, no," he said. "Which I have no intention of doing. I like being alive."

"Good." Liches were created by a spirit mage binding a person's soul to an amulet—either their own or someone else's—and turning them into a being which existed in limbo between life and death. Most were part of the Court of the Dead, which was open to any lich who agreed to surrender their soul amulet to the Death King. The Parallel was filled with enough dangers that even the dead tended to stick closely together, so almost all of them had opted to stay here in the castle.

One of said liches was my friend Harper. She'd been a fire mage before she'd died in battle, and Miles had offered to bind her soul to an amulet to give her a second chance at life. She'd said yes, and while she didn't yet know if she wanted to make that decision permanent, she didn't deserve to have the choice taken away from her again by some dickhead who thought it was funny to mark lethal cantrips with the Family's signature.

"I should head back before Shelley throws a bucket of icy water over my head while I'm astral projecting," Miles said.

"Is that likely?"

"Wouldn't be the first time." He stepped toward me and hugged me. His transparent arms passed through mine, leaving a faint chill in their wake, but his closeness helped to dispel my unease a little.

While he vanished back to his body, I re-joined the Elemental Soldiers in the castle's grounds. Liv had already gone back into the castle, perhaps to find the Death King and tell him the threat was taken care of. Why he hadn't come to fight himself was a mystery, but he hardly needed to fend off intruders when he had four Elemental Soldiers and an army of the dead at his service.

"Who wants to take the first watch?" asked Ryan. "We can trade shifts every six hours or so."

"I'll take the first watch," I said. "I have things I need to do tomorrow."

"I'll join you, then," said Ryan. "I think there should be two of us out at a time. Also, you might want to put some clothes on first."

Right. I looked sheepishly down at my pyjamas, which I'd forgotten, but the others were more or less dressed in full uniform as though they'd expected an attack. I should have, too, but I'd let my guard down.

I was halfway to the castle when it hit me how quickly Ryan had decided to partner up with me to guard the castle. Did they still not trust me not to run off if their back was turned? Maybe not, but it'd be reassuring to have someone's company through the rest of the night, in case the Family did show up in person.

If anything, this attack had reinforced my determination to find a way to be rid of them for good.

2

Dawn arrived without any more intrusions, which was a blessing. At the end of our shift, Ryan went for a run around the castle's perimeter instead of going to bed like a normal person, since not even an attack in the middle of the night would cause them to break from their workout routine. As for me, I returned to the castle for a quick shower and then went straight to bed, but I barely managed a short nap before Ryan woke me by banging on my door. "Trix is here."

"Give me five minutes." I changed into fresh clothes and tied my long dark hair into a ponytail. These days, I dressed better than I had as a rogue, in the armoured uniform of an Elemental Soldier and with my red-lined cloak marked with the Death King's emblem, which consisted of the symbols for the four elements surrounding a skull. Everyone always left out the fifth element, spirit, perhaps as an aftereffect of the last war.

I ran to the break room and grabbed a breakfast bar

before going to meet Trix beside the gates. Ryan was already there, presumably intending to keep their promise not to let us go off alone. In fairness, I wouldn't mind having the company of the Air Element, who looked a damn sight more intimidating than I did in their armoured uniform and green-lined cloak.

"Did you talk to your elf friends?" I asked Trix.

"Yes, and I found one who's willing to talk to you," he responded. "She lives in Arcadia."

"Oh, good." I'd hoped it wouldn't take too long to find an elf willing to share their history with me, because my new guard duty schedule at the castle would make it hard for me to get away for long periods of time for the foreseeable future.

The three of us used the node near the castle to transport ourselves to a street in the outskirts of Arcadia, near the large warehouses which housed the city's markets. In the distance, the dark form of the citadel towered over the rooftops, the only landmark I recognised in the unfamiliar city. I knew Elysium backwards, but Arcadia's winding streets confounded me, as did the labyrinth of tunnels underneath our feet. Trix led us to a brick terraced house at the end of a long street and knocked on the door.

A female elf with dark eyes and glossy hair answered. Her features were pointed and striking, and she wore simple cotton clothing with a pair of knives visible at her waist. Few people in the Parallel went around unarmed, even mages and elves, who came equipped with their own magical skills which outdid most weaponry.

"Hey," said Trix. "This is Drina. Drina, meet Bria and Ryan."

Drina eyed me suspiciously. "Who are you?"

"I'm Bria," I said. "The Death King's—"

"I know you're with the Death King," she said. "Both of you. You're wearing his uniform."

"Ah." Her hostile tone made me regret wearing my armoured clothing and cloak. "We're not here on his behalf."

"Could have fooled me," she said. "What do you want, then?"

I hadn't expected a warm reception from my fellow elves, considering how I looked more human than elf, but Trix hadn't forewarned me of her apparent dislike of the Death King.

"It's really not to do with the Death King." I reached for the pendant around my neck and deactivated the illusion cantrip. Her eyes widened a little as my pointed ears became visible, my features sharpening and turning elfin. "This is why I'm here."

"The Death King hired an elf as his Elemental Soldier?" she asked.

"I'm half-elf, half-mage," I clarified. "It's the elves I want to talk to you about."

"Oh?" Some of the hostility vanished from her expression. "You'd better come in, then."

Whatever I'd expected from an elf's home, it wasn't the sight that greeted us on the other side of the door. Plants filled the entire room, more than I'd ever seen in one place in the Parallel before. Vines covered the walls like spiked, writhing snakes, while toxic-coloured flowers bloomed in the corners. A a single chair made out of what looked like a tree stump stood in the centre. Drina sat upon it, while the rest of us hovered awkwardly around the edges of the room, trying not to knock into any of the lethal-looking plants.

"What's your issue with the Death King?" I asked. "He's got nothing to do with the elves."

"Do you have any idea what the spirit mages did to us?" she said.

Oh. The Death King had once been a spirit mage, before he'd died. "He's not working with the spirit mages who started the war. Or the ones who are trying to start a second one, either. He actually sent me here to ask if any of the elves would be willing to help us take a stand against the rogue spirit mages."

"He sent you to ask that, did he?" she said. "What gives you the impression I'm the spokesperson for all the elves in the Parallel?"

"I—" I looked at Trix. "Trix said you'd be willing to talk to me."

"Not about being a soldier-for-hire," she said. "I'm no fighter."

"That's okay," I said. "I just want to know who I should speak to if I want to find elves who *can* fight. Is there not a leader of the elves, like the vampire lords? Or the Houses of the Elements?"

Not all the mages belonged to the Houses, of course, but I'd assumed each of the magical communities had representatives. The Houses would have been happier to lock me up than fight on my behalf, but a small part of me had hoped the elves might be different. Frankly, I didn't know *who* they answered to, since the Family had taken care to avoid teaching me anything about how their communities worked. After all, they hadn't wanted me thinking I might find allies among them.

"None of us knows where our Elders are," she said. "They disappeared after the last war destroyed our forests, our relics, everything connecting us to our history. If any of them survived, they haven't contacted the rest of us since before the war."

My mouth parted. "Really?"

"What planet have you been on?" Drina gave me an eye-roll. "Did the elf side of your family tell you nothing?"

"My parents are dead." I fought to keep my tone free of my growing annoyance. I'd hardly *asked* to be raised by a pair of manipulators who'd buried my own history before I'd known it existed. "My parents died when I was a baby and I was raised by people who wanted me to stay ignorant of the elves and of my heritage. I know where they used to live, but their village was destroyed, and I don't know if there were any survivors."

She gave me an assessing look. "Don't you have an Akrith?"

I blinked. "What's that?"

"She doesn't know?" She gave Trix an incredulous look. "Does she know nothing about us at all?"

"I told you," I said heatedly, "I was raised as human, though the people who brought me up stretch the definition a little."

Trix glanced between us. "I thought she knew more than she did. I'll explain."

An exclamation from Ryan made all of us jump. Several spiky vines had detached themselves from the wall, pointing at the Air Element like spears.

They held their sword aloft. "One of your plants attacked me."

"Did you poke it with that weapon of yours?" said Drina.

"No," the Air Element insisted. "Look, if they stab me, then they can't expect me not to poke them back."

The plants rustled against one another with hissing noises that sounded disconcertingly like snakes, while several glistening spikes hovered close to Ryan's head.

"We should leave." I'd rather listen to Trix's explanation outside rather than risk us all ending up impaled by deadly plants.

"No," said Trix. "We can stay longer if you like. Drina won't mind."

"I'm more than happy to leave," Ryan said, with a disgruntled look at the offending plant. "Be seeing you."

Drina gave them a look which implied *I hope not,* ignored me entirely, and then gave Trix a friendly nod as the three of us left the house and walked out into the narrow street.

"How am I supposed to have learned my history when I grew up without any connections to the elves?" I remarked. "What *is* an Akrith, anyway?"

"Akriths are petrified tree carvings taken from the heart of our Elder Trees," Trix said. "Every elf has one, though our trees are all dead now."

I glanced backwards at Drina's house. "I don't know if I ever had one. I'm half-human, and as your friend heavily implied, I'm no more an elf than the Death King is."

"No, you would have had one," Trix insisted. "Your elf parent would have given you one on the day of your birth. It's one of our surviving traditions. You were still living with your birth parents as a baby, weren't you?"

"I was… but I don't remember anything from that

time." If I'd had an Akirth, had the Family taken it away from me when they'd captured me from my home? Or was it still in the house I'd lived in as a baby, reduced to a ruin along with the rest of the village? "I know where my old home is, but it's way out in the wasteland near the Family's house."

Ryan rounded on me. "That place? You never mentioned you grew up there."

"I was born there, but the Family burned the whole place down and took me away when I was a kid," I said. "Like I said, I barely remember. I thought the place looked familiar, but it wasn't until I asked them directly that they confirmed my guess. Anyway, if I had an Akrith, it might have been buried in the wreckage. Either that or the Family took it for themselves, but they might not have known it was important to the elves at the time."

"Do you remember the exact location of the house you lived in as a baby?" asked Trix.

I thought back. "No, but I do have a memory of the day the town burned, and I think if I went there, I could figure out the location. I remember seeing the citadel, which is the only building left standing."

"The Death King said there's nobody living out there at the moment," Ryan said, "but that doesn't mean the enemy won't return. The nullifying cantrips we used on the citadels aren't permanent."

"No, it's a risk, I'm not going to deny it," I said. "If having my own Akrith makes the elves more likely to trust me, though, it might be worth it. Besides, I wouldn't mind having a look in the place where I was born to see if my birth family left anything else behind. I doubt the

Family are spending every waking moment searching the ruins for me."

"They still have that wyrm of theirs, don't they?" said Ryan.

"I can deal with the wyrm," said Trix. "It won't harm us."

"You don't have to come," I insisted. "Either of you."

"You seriously think we're going to let you wander off into the wasteland alone?" said Ryan. "The Death King would kill you."

I rolled my eyes. "Careful or I might start to think you care if I live or die."

Ryan made a sceptical noise. "Look, I know the Death King wants the elves' help, and I know you want to learn more about your history, too. I bet if we head back to the castle, you'll sneak off at the first opportunity anyway."

Hmm. They had a point. "If we're going to look around the ruins, then I have to check in with Miles first. He'll be ticked off if we go without him."

"You mean in Elysium?" said Ryan. "You want to get that close to the Houses?"

"The Houses are pretty much in ruins after the battle," I reminded them. "The Death King wants me to go back and talk to them, too, but I'll deal with that later."

Ryan gave me an assessing look. "Did he tell you to go to the Houses today, instead of speaking to the elves?"

"No, he expects me to be in two places at once," I said. "Also, last time I went to the House of Fire, I ended up in a cell. Twice. The Death King is seriously overestimating my skills at negotiation. Anyway, Miles and the Spirit Agents live in Elysium, so they'll know if the Houses are up and running and if any of those lethal cantrips might still be in the area."

"I'd prefer not to take any detours," said Ryan. "Especially if you expect us to stand outside while you convince your friend Miles to let you risk your neck… or if you two otherwise get distracted."

I gave an eye-roll. "You two can get a head start on walking to the ruins, then. It's a long way if you don't have a transporter spell. Which I do, but I can't use it on all of us at once. I'll catch you up. Give it half an hour."

"I'll hold you to that," said Ryan.

Really, I was doing them a favour. Ryan and Trix would get to spend some quality time together while they walked, and I'd get to talk to Miles face to face for a few minutes without any pesky astral projection getting in our way. Whatever Ryan said, we wouldn't get to do much more than talk, especially with the number of Spirit Agents running around their house.

To start off with, we used the nearest node to transport ourselves into the city of Elysium, and parted ways near the Spirit Agents' house. The house itself was pretty swanky, with whitewashed walls and a neat, wide garden. It'd once belonged to a vampire and was consequently nicer than almost any house I'd been to in the Parallel. Those perks didn't come without a cost, though. Most spirit mages were estranged from their families, and since there was no House of Spirit like the other four Houses, the spirit mages had to group together for their own survival. Miles's own family was imprisoned in the Houses' jail for angering the wrong person, so he knew first-hand how keen they were to punish mages for the slightest perceived transgression. Yet the Houses were the one thing standing between the Family and domination over one of the Parallel's major cities. I knew *why* the Death King would prefer to make a deal with the Houses before that became an issue, but he might have picked a negotiator who wasn't intimately acquainted with the inside of their jail.

Miles answered the door when I knocked. "Hey, Bria."

"Hey." My heart lifted despite myself at the sight of him in person and not the monochrome transparency of astral projection. "No trouble in Elysium at the moment?"

"None that I've seen." He ran a hand through his straw-coloured hair. "Did the Death King send you to speak to the Houses, by any chance?"

"Yes, but I'd prefer to avoid a face-to-face meeting," I said. "How're they getting on, do you know?"

"The guards aren't coming outside much," he said. "They lost around a quarter of their members, and I'm surprised it wasn't worse."

"Damn," I said. "Sure the survivors aren't working with the rogue spirit mages?"

"No, unfortunately," he said. "I'm not as optimistic as the Death King that they'd be willing to work with you. Maybe he thinks the recent trouble might have changed their attitudes towards you."

"Considering I was at the centre of said trouble, I doubt it," I said. "Anyway, I have another dangerous trip I need to take today. Want to come?"

He cocked a brow. "Where to?"

"The town I grew up in." I gave a quick summary of what I'd learned from Trix's elf friend.

"You want to dig around in a pile of ruins to find a petrified tree carving?" he said.

"You don't have to come," I said. "Ryan and Trix insisted on joining me so I already have company."

His brow wrinkled. "What's in it for them?"

"Trix is an elf, so he'll know how to recognise this tree carving if I find it. Ryan thinks the Death King will be furious if I end up dying out there, so they volunteered to supervise me."

"How nice of them." Miles leaned towards me. "I have a better reason for coming, though. I like you."

My heart gave a flutter. "Like in what way?"

He kissed me in answer. "Like this."

I kissed him back, wishing I could always feel as grounded as I did when his arms were wrapped around me. While we'd mutually agreed to ignore the myriad reasons that getting involved with one another was a bad idea at best, we had yet to discuss the future of our burgeoning relationship. I knew developing feelings for anyone was dangerous as hell right now, but it wasn't like I had any control over where my heart lay, and it'd firmly planted its roots here in Miles's arms.

If we ran into the Family out there in the wilderness, though… I'd feel responsible for bringing him into danger with me. "Want to astral project? Ryan and Trix already have a head start on us already, and there aren't many nodes out there in the ruins."

His brow furrowed. "I doubt being transparent would deter a phantom from coming after me."

"Believe me, it's not the phantoms I'm concerned about," I said. "The more of us there are, the more likely we are to be caught by the Family, and… and I can't lose anyone else."

Tay's face came to mind as it always did, and Miles's

expression softened in understanding. "Okay. I'll astral project." He gave me another hug and kiss, then backed down the hallway of the house. "I'll tell the others, then I'll catch you up."

"Sure." I waved him off and left the Spirit Agents' house, walking to the node. It didn't take longer than a minute before Miles caught up to me, transparent again, and we left for the town in which I'd spent my earliest memories.

3

Once we emerged from the node at the northern point of the city, I broke into a sprint while Miles floated alongside me. Soon enough, we caught up to Trix and Ryan in the wilderness which comprised the main part of the Parallel, where the city's outskirts became barren ground littered with debris. Even Trix couldn't think of anything positive to say about our surroundings, and his usual optimism faded with each pile of rubble we passed. I deliberately steered our path as far as possible from the ruins of the Family's estate, using the pillar-like shape of the citadel as a guiding light to keep us on the right path.

Within minutes, we found ourselves surrounded by gutted buildings, formed of chunks of metal and wood and stone, and despite the absence of humanity, very little plant life aside from a few pernicious weeds rooted in the soil. The magic which had scorched the town to ruins had left few chances for life to spring up again.

"Keep an eye out for revenants," said Miles.

"Revenants are child's play," came Ryan's response. "Same with phantoms."

I had to agree. The Family were more dangerous than any other threat that might leap out of the ruins to feed on our blood or life force. They'd hidden a warehouse over by the citadel to manufacture illegal cantrips, so they'd definitely ventured into the town's ruins before, even if they'd then gone on to abandon said warehouse and leave their unpaid employees to face a grim death. But if I needed to get my hands on an Akrith in order to gain the elves' respect, then I had nowhere else to look except here. Unless I wanted to risk trespassing inside the Family's house, of course, but if I got caught, Tay wasn't around to save me this time.

A familiar wave of grief hit me at the thought of my former best friend, and I did my best to push it away as I walked through the dirt roads winding between ruined houses, Miles floating at my side. The others followed close behind, Trix lithely treading among the debris while Ryan steamrollered through without a care for how much noise they made. It wasn't like we'd be able to hide from a wyrm in flight regardless of how quiet we were, so I kept an eye on the skies as we walked on. Trix had the useful ability to make the wyrm obey his commands, of course, but if the creature brought the Family along with it, then it would become much more dangerous.

A stone tumbled from the nearest pile of rubble into the street, and the pale face of a revenant surfaced. Hairless and ugly as their vampire cousins were pretty, revenants fed on the energy from the nodes rather than drinking blood. Ryan raised their hands and blasted air magic at the revenant, blowing a torrent of debris into the air which exposed two more of them crouching in the shadows. I shot a fireball which disintegrated their fragile bones in an instant.

"Let's move." Hoping nobody had seen the flash of fiery light, I took the lead through the ruins towards the towering shape of the citadel. I hoped last night's dream had been accurate, or I'd have had a hell of a time finding the right house to search. Unless it had just been a dream… but it'd felt real enough I could still taste the ashes on my tongue.

I stepped around the crumbled wall of what might have once been a large garden, catching sight of scorch marks on the stone which hadn't come from my own flames. "This can't all have been the work of an inferno cantrip. There wouldn't be anything left."

"What makes you think it was an inferno cantrip that did this?" said Ryan.

"In my last memory of the town, it was on fire," I explained. "Also, Trix told me some kind of magic similar to the inferno cantrips wiped out the elves' strongholds, so it makes sense that they'd have been used on places like this as well."

Trix's eyes widened with horror. "How did you escape?"

"The Family took me away and left the others to burn, I assume," I said in bitter tones. "I *think* I was around three or four when I went to live with them, but it's not like they wanted me to remember my life beforehand."

"There's nothing left of this place," he said softly. "I doubt anyone else remembers."

My gut clenched. "I know. The citadel is the only

building left intact, and I guess that's because the spirit mages built it."

"The spirit mages didn't build it," he said. "The elves did."

My heart missed a beat. "The *elves* built the citadel? Are you sure?"

"I'm sure," Trix said. "It's not well-known, but my dad told me himself, before he died of a sickness when I was a child. None of our strongholds are still standing, but they used to look quite similar."

I didn't know what to say. The citadels had stood here for hundreds of years and dated back to the first inhabitants of the Parallel itself. For that reason, I'd always assumed the spirit mages had been the ones who'd created them—there was no disputing that they'd created the Parallel, after all—but given what the mages had taken from the elves already, who was I to assume they hadn't also taken credit for their creations?

I glanced at Miles and saw my own concern and shock mirrored on his face. He hadn't known either. Nor had Ryan, though their attention was on our surroundings. The street we stood on was wide open, exposed, and a chill breeze blew light pieces of debris across the barren ground. The citadel drew my gaze, its obsidian walls stark against the grey surroundings. Of all the different beings in the Parallel, the elves were the longest-lived aside from the vampires, so it made sense that they'd built their own monuments. Their extended lifespans hadn't prevented them from being almost wiped out in the war, though, and it seemed the spirit mages' last action against them had been to erase their most lasting achievements.

A flicker of movement stirred in the corner of my eye

and a ghostly figure floated into my peripheral vision. Not a human, but a phantom, the closest to genuine ghosts the Parallel had to offer. "We have company."

Ryan raised their hands. "I'll get rid of it."

Air magic blasted into the phantom, knocking over a pile of debris but not leaving a mark on the transparent beast. Miles moved in to finish it off, his hands aglow with spirit magic, but my firepower couldn't permanently get rid of something which had no physical form.

I took a few steps forward and swore under my breath. More phantoms hovered among the ruins ahead, drifting onto the road, and there was no way to get any closer to the citadel without walking right through their midst.

"Go on, move." Ryan advanced on them, hands splayed and a whirlwind dancing between their palms. "You have three seconds to run."

"I don't think they can understand you," said Trix.

"Get lost." Miles blasted spirit magic into the road ahead. The phantoms drifted to either side to avoid being hit, moving with quiet rustling sounds which seemed almost like whispers.

With the road clear, I ran ahead and paused at the end of the street to figure out my proximity to the citadel. From its position, I'd almost reached the area I'd been to in my dream. I picked up the pace, abandoning caution and taking on my elven speed as I turned down a side street and found myself faced with another wall of phantoms. They stood there, a silent barrier of flickering transparent shapes. "Go away."

They didn't move. I backed up a step, prepared to shortcut through the ruined houses if I had to, and the whispering sound resolved into something that sounded almost like words. Or one word, repeated over and over again. *Bria.*

I shook my head fiercely. I couldn't have heard my name from one of those creatures. They couldn't *speak.* Or so I thought.

Bria. The whisper sounded again, louder and clearer this time. Bria.

"What do you want with me?" I turned around to look for Miles and the others, but in my swift stride, I'd left them a couple of streets back. The phantoms drifted closer, surrounding me in a fog of icy cold which bit into the very marrow of my bones. Fire sprang to my hands, but even their heat didn't dispel the chill. Nor did the whispers fade, the sound of my own name spoken from mouths without tongues, voices without names.

Thoroughly spooked, I backed down the road and retraced my steps, but the whispers tailed me, relentless. I broke into a run, as though I could outpace the sound of a disembodied whisper which might as well have come from within my own mind.

A looming phantom cut off my path and I veered off the road and among the ruins, leaping from one pile of crumbled stone to the next. My foot struck something hard, and I tumbled head over heels into a heap of stone. Wincing, I straightened upright to find the citadel looming closer than ever.

I hopped from the pile of stones onto a bare patch of ground and I tilted my head at the citadel to get the angle right. My home, assuming that was where my dream had begun, was buried in this very street, but each side of the road resembled a wall of rubble from which distinguishing individual houses seemed impossible. Struggling to retrace the frantic steps of my dream, I picked my way through the ruins, already wondering how in the world I'd expected to find anything in here. Footsteps sounded nearby, the crunch of broken glass, and I raised my head.

"Hey!" Ryan's air magic slammed into the ruined wall of stone, driving a chunk of debris into the air.

I climbed upright, shielding myself from the dust with an arm. "Whoa. It's just me."

"Don't run off like that," Miles reprimanded, floating into view behind Ryan. "Bloody phantoms... is this the place?"

"I think it is, but I can't find anything in this mess." Glass and bits of broken furniture lay buried beneath pieces of stone too heavy to lift, even if my hands hadn't been shaking from my encounter with the phantoms.

I'd never heard of them knowing someone's name before. What if they were more than just echoes of the dead? What if they were the ghosts of those who'd perished in this very town? Did they remember who they'd been beforehand?

Miles floated down to hover at my side. "What am I looking for?"

"It looks like a petrified tree carving," I said. "Trix, is there a way you can track it down which doesn't involve lifting every stone in the street?"

"I know how to recognise one." Trix lithely climbed down the slope of stone wall beside me and picked his way forward with easy grace. Ryan followed close behind, not being nearly as careful, but I could hardly reprimand them for wrecking my house when it was already a pile of rubble.

What was I thinking? The place might have already been

looted if it contained anything valuable, though even a thief would be hard-pressed to navigate this mess. I suppressed a sigh, coughing on dust, and kept an eye on the citadel in an attempt to find the right house. Or heap of rubble.

A glow caught my eyes, signalling the phantom's return. Or rather, one lone phantom, floating above the nearby wreckage. I waved an impatient hand at it. "Shoo. I used to live here, you know. I have more of a right to be here than you do."

The phantom didn't move, but it didn't attack me either. I kept walking down the street, suppressing a shiver at the memory of the chorus of creepy voices tailing me. Phantoms might be ghosts, but they'd never really *scared* me before. I lived in a castle inhabited by liches, for the Elements' sakes. I'd never sleep at night if I feared the dead.

Doing my best to ignore my disembodied companion, I resumed my search. The phantom watched as I did so—though it didn't have eyes, so that was only an assumption—but I made no headway, unearthing nothing of note among the ruins.

Finally, I folded my arms and faced the phantom. "Did you live here, too? Is that why you're hanging around?"

The phantom said nothing. They weren't usually capable of speech, but they'd picked up my name from somewhere. Unless their whispers had been a figment of my imagination, of course.

"I don't suppose you know where I can find an Akrith?" I didn't expect a coherent answer, but I was desperate enough to try anything at this point. Even if the phantoms *were* the ghosts of living people, I had zero clue if they might have once been human or elf. It didn't really matter, since they were little more than echoes, less substantial than the recorded tape of a living person left behind following their death.

I spotted a flicker of light behind the phantom, amidst the ruins of the collapsed wall. With no response forthcoming, I walked that way, and a transparent small figure appeared before my eyes. Around eight inches tall, he resembled a humanoid male, and from the blue sheen around him, he must be a water sprite.

"Oh," I said. "Hi. Can I help you?"

"You're the one who saved us from the tower," said the sprite.

"I am." Relief struck me at the sound of a disembodied voice which *wasn't* creepily whispering my name. "I didn't know any of you were still here."

"You shouldn't have come back," said the sprite. "It's not safe out here."

"I had to," I said. "I'm looking for something important."

"There's nothing here but death," he said.

"And phantoms," I added. "Were they... I mean, were they once the people who lived here?"

"I don't understand phantoms any more than humans do," he said. "But I've seen worse here in the ruins. I've seen... *them.*"

My heart climbed into my throat. "The Family didn't build another warehouse, did they?"

They didn't necessarily need to, what with the number of cantrips already in circulation. The earth mages who worked with them had spread the damn things all over Elysium and possibly further afield, though it was entirely possible there'd been more than one manufacturer. They never let the people making their cantrips live near their estate. Understandable, given the risk that they might have ended up turning on the Family and setting the place on fire like I had. It wasn't like anyone had thoroughly combed the ruins in search of a second hidden warehouse, either.

The sprite didn't answer, shrinking into the shadows. I turned around and nearly jumped out of my skin when the phantom appeared nearby, now with two others at its side. The whispers returned, echoing in a single chilling note. *Bria. Bria.*

One word repeated over and over again, like a warning.

Then I saw him, a solid figure standing atop a pile of debris, and my heart dropped like a stone from a great height.

Adair was here.

4

From the outside, some might think my brother and I were related by blood. He was tall and lean, with inky dark hair and a pointed face and ears. He kept his elven features on display for the world to see, stalking out in the light where I hid in the shadows. He hadn't spotted me yet, but there was no use hiding when the slightest movement would make a sound that would alert his attention.

Ignoring the tension prickling at my skin, I walked until I was within his line of sight. When he saw me, his brows rose a little, then a smile broke out on his mouth. It was not a friendly expression at all. I swiftly dropped my gaze to avoid looking him in the eyes in case he tried using his persuasive magic on me.

Miles floated up to my side, facing Adair. "Hey, dickhead. Mind buggering off?"

Adair's gaze went to Miles. "Too cowardly to risk venturing out of your hidey-hole in person, were you?"

"Nah, you aren't worth getting out of bed for," said

Miles. "Why're you sniffing around here, then?"

"Hoped I'd get lucky and find a rat or two."

"Hilarious," I said. "Did Lex and Roth send you? Or are they hiding out here somewhere as well?"

"They wouldn't bother wasting their time on the likes of you."

So they'd sent him alone. It wasn't unusual for them to send him to run errands, but dealing with Adair and his mind-controlling power would be difficult enough. "Yet they have you wasting *your* time poking around these ruins. I guess nobody else was available, or they wanted you out of the way."

His face flushed. "You don't know shit."

"Keep telling yourself that."

I *did* know he desperately wanted to please Lex and Roth, because I'd wanted the same thing, back when I hadn't known any better. The Family's lies had wormed their way into my head, and it'd taken years for me to begin to shake off their conditioning. They'd had years longer to work their spell on Adair, as the eldest of the pair of us, but he'd always been crueller and more willing to hurt others, while I'd refused to do so even before I'd known the depths of the Family's depravity. All the same, their mild cruelties towards the pair of us when we were children were nothing compared to this.

"What made you come here, then?" he said. "Not the scenery, I assume."

"Maybe I just felt like a walk," I answered.

"I don't think so," he said. "You wouldn't risk your life, or your precious friends, unless you were doing some-thing important."

"Well done, Sherlock," Miles said.

Adair ignored him. "I could *make* you tell me."

Miles drifted closer to him, unafraid. "You'll have to go through me first."

Adair narrowed his eyes. "I can hunt you down at your hiding place, along with those spirit mage friends of yours. I'll make you beg me to spare their lives."

My chest tightened, though I felt doubly relieved that I'd convinced Miles not to come here in person. I'd guessed right that Adair couldn't use his powers on Miles when he was astral projecting. Ryan and Trix didn't have that advantage, though. I could take Adair on alone, no problem, but not if Lex and Roth showed up to join him. They'd sent a message to the Death King that was tantamount to a declaration of war already. Dammit, I should have stayed away from the ruins until I had more of a plan.

"Why are *you* here?" My fists clenched. "Building more warehouses? Or do Lex and Roth have *you* creating cantrips for them instead of the elves? Did they tell you about the one they left on the Death King's doorstep early this morning?"

Confusion momentarily crossed his features. "Huh?"

"I guess not, then," I said. "I suppose Lex and Roth only tell you what's absolutely necessary. If they'd sent you to deliver it in person, you'd have probably wound up getting yourself locked in a cell again."

"I seem to remember *you* were the one who let me out of the cell," he said. "Along with that friend of yours."

Don't you dare talk about Tay. Wanting to knock him off balance, I said, "As a matter of fact, I'm here because I was born in this town before the Family wrecked the place. Maybe you were, too. Do you remember?"

My words hit home, and he stared at me for a moment before his expression hardened with anger. "Does it matter? Lex and Roth did more for us than whoever gave birth to us, and you repaid them by throwing it back in their faces."

"Lex and Roth set my home on fire and then stole me from the ruins and left my family to die," I said. "They did the same to you, too, I'll bet. They didn't give us anything but trauma."

"Enough of your bullshit," he said. "The elves are a lost cause. They're going extinct, and we'll see to it that there won't be any left standing to challenge us."

What the hell was he talking about? "You're here to look for the elves?"

"Of course," he said. "Can't have them picking the wrong side, can we?"

The *Family* was looking for the elves as well? Dammit, I should have known. Despite my reluctance to admit we had anything in common, they'd shaped my way of thinking, and they knew that if they were in my place, they'd be seeking out the elves, too. "Since when were Lex and Roth even interested in recruiting elves?"

"Not those pathetic city elves," he said. "The *real* elves. We already have one Akrith, and we can get more."

"Am I supposed to know what that is?" *I did my best to keep my expression neutral, but alarm flickered within me at the mention of the word. They have an Akrith?*

Adair scoffed, but before he could say a word, Ryan fired a blast of air which slammed into Adair with the force of a speeding truck. He flew a good fifteen feet into the air and crashed to earth in a pile of stone and dust.

I grimaced at the sound. "Ryan, what the hell was that for?"

"I thought I should finish him off before his delightful adoptive parents showed up."

"That won't have killed him," I said. "He'll be back on his feet soon enough."

"Time for us to leave, then," Ryan said. "Come on, Trix. I'm done risking our necks for one morning."

"Hey!" I said, as they made to turn away. "We haven't even found what we came for. Trix, did you find any signs of an Akrith?"

"No." He lithely stepped over the ruins, his mouth turning down at the corners. "If a single trace of the elves was ever here, it was lost a long time ago."

"I bet it's in their house," I said. "The Family's, I mean. Adair *said* they have one. The fuckers scavenged it first."

"You can't go to their estate again," Miles said. "That's exactly what they want you to do."

"I know." Now they had the perfect bait to lure me back into their midst, but I wouldn't take it. I'd need to find another way to get to the elves instead.

"Don't you even think of going back to them," said Ryan, as though I hadn't already got the message. "However urgent you think it is, it's not worth your life or ours."

I looked at Trix, whose concerned expression suggested he understood the conflicting thoughts in my mind. Not that knowing he understood made it any easier for me to deal with the knowledge that in walking away, I might have given the Family the chance to get to the elves first. "The Death King is the one who told me to get in touch with the elves, but if the Family has one of the

Akriths, that doesn't mean they have all of them. We still have a shot at finding one, if not my own, right?"

"Of course," said Trix.

"Come on," *the Air Element insisted. "We're walking targets out here."*

At Ryan's urging, we began to retrace our steps out of the ruined town. As we walked, I said, "I think we can safely say we're chasing the same goal, and the Family is ahead of us."

"Bastards," said Miles. "I'd be happy to throw that dickhead around for a bit, but I don't think you'll find what you're looking for out here."

No. We wouldn't find anything but trouble, but the fact that the Family had decided to recruit the elves was bad news all around. I kept both eyes open for any signs of Lex or Roth, certain that if they *did* have an Akrith, at least one of them would be back at the house. Waiting—or hoping—for me to walk into their trap.

"How widespread are these Akriths?" I asked Trix. "I mean, what are the odds of the one Adair has belonging to my birth family?"

"Depends where they got it," said Trix. "It's unlikely they dug it out of the ruins on their own, though. Most likely they stole it from another elf or bought it from a trader."

I pulled a face. "Thieving bastards. Adair implied the Family is looking to get the elves on their side, but I don't see how stealing all their artefacts is going to endear them to anyone. Also, what did they mean about 'real elves', as opposed to 'city elves'? What other kind of elves are there?"

Trix's usually confident steps faltered. "It's possible

they might be trying to find an Akrith which contains enough of the power that once resided in our living trees, in order to open a way to the elves' realm."

My heart missed a beat. "To the what?"

He glanced over his shoulder as though worried about being overheard. "The elves' realm was cut off when most of our artefacts were destroyed. None of us know if anyone's even alive over there, but that's where our Elders were last seen."

"I didn't know the elves had their own realm."

"Neither did I," said Miles.

"That's because it'll have been cut off around the time of the last war," said Ryan. "Right, Trix?"

"Right, but there was never conclusive proof the connection was severed permanently," he said. "In fact, a lot of us have wondered if it's possible to open a way back, but most of the Akriths contain little power of their own and no connection to the trees from which they were cut. It's commonly believed that a living elven tree is the only way to open our realm, and I've definitely never seen one of *those* in a long time. The mages burned them all down."

My chest tightened, and the echoing scent of smoke from last night's dream lingered in the back of my throat. "If the Family found a living tree, then would they be able to get through?"

"Can you imagine them seeing a tree without burning it down?" said Miles. "Whatever they're doing, I doubt it's the elves' realm they're after."

"I don't know, Adair did say he was looking for the 'real' elves. Whatever that means." I shook my head. "Are there likely to be any survivors in their realm, Trix?"

"Yes, I think so," he said. "The elves' realm was more

well-equipped for our endurance, so if they *did* survive, they'll still have access to their artefacts and their weapons."

Well, damn. If we were able to make contact with an army of powerful fighters and form an allegiance with them, it would certainly help our cause... but what if the Family got to them first?

"Would the war have caused the same level of damage to their realm as it did to the Parallel?" I asked.

"No more than it did to Earth, the humans' realm," Trix responded. "The mages wouldn't have been able to fight the elves in their own realm, so they did the next best thing."

"They cut it off so nobody else could get in there, either," I concluded. "If the Family finds them, they'll either slaughter them or get them to fight on their side. Like the Houses."

"The elves would never join them," said Trix. "They'd sooner die."

My stomach lurched. "Yeah, that's what I figured. We can't let that happen."

Miles cleared his throat. "Not to minimise the threat to the elves, but we're already unlikely to be able to beat the Family as we are now. Not without a shitload of luck on our side."

"I know," I said. "But the elves are one of the few neutral forces in the Parallel, and if any survive in their realm, they probably won't even know who the Family is, let alone anything else that's happened since the last war. If there's truly been no contact with this realm..."

"Exactly," said Trix. "They won't know the Family is hunting them down."

No. The mages had resorted to simply closing the doors between realms rather than beating the elves outright, though, and if their magic was stronger in their own realm, then for all we knew, they *would* be a match for the Family.

Could we really count on that, though? It was safe to say the elves probably wouldn't happily agree to an alliance with the Family once they learned of the atrocities they'd inflicted on their fellow elves, but that didn't mean they'd join our side either. Especially given the scale of the damage of the last war, and the way the mages had used the aftermath to cover up the elves' own history. The Houses certainly weren't innocent, either, and nor were the other authorities in the Parallel.

"I didn't know the elves built the citadels," I said to Miles. "Did you?"

"No," he said. "I always wondered why they were so resilient, but I assumed the materials they were made from were used up a long time ago or were destroyed in the war."

"Yeah." Discomfort rose within me at the thought that the Family had played a larger role in the previous war than I'd ever known. Did that mean they knew how the elves' realm had come to be cut off from this one? Had they witnessed it?

A scuffling noise came from within the ruins, and Adair surfaced in a shower of glass and stone. He didn't look like he should even be standing, but he staggered towards us, his head lolling and his mouth half-open. Blood smeared his face, and the layer of dust on top made him look like a revenant. How was he still walking?

Adair kept moving. At every step, his feet dragged. Oh,

hell. He was still unconscious… which meant Lex was using his body as a puppet.

"Run!" I shouted to the others.

We ran. Trix and flat-out sprinted using our elven speed, while Ryan kept pace with us by using their air magic to speed up. Miles, of course, could astral project ahead of us with ease, but even moving at our quickest didn't make it any easier to navigate the crumbling piles of stone with a zombie-like Adair trailing behind us.

I leapt over a collapsed wooden beam and into the path of a revenant. Fire blasted from my hands, turning it into ashes, and I kept on running. I could hear crashing from behind us and risked a glance over my shoulder, where Ryan's air magic flung debris into Adair's face to slow him down. Good thinking.

As we rounded the corner, the node came into view. With Trix slightly ahead of me, I picked up the pace towards the current of energy.

As we ran, another bright light detached itself from the ruins. The phantoms were back, several of them, drifting across our path. Not ahead of us, but behind, until they formed a wall between us and Adair. I had no time to stop and wonder what the hell they were playing at, instead sprinting forward until the light of the node surrounded me. A heartbeat later, the others ran into view, and we all vanished at once.

I landed beside the others in an unfamiliar street, breathless. "Who brought us here?"

"I did," said Miles. "We're in Elysium, but nowhere near the Spirit Agents' house. Thought it'd be a wise idea not to give that dude an easy way to follow us."

"Good thinking." I inhaled and exhaled, the taste of

dust and ashes lingering in the back of my throat. "Were those phantoms trying to defend us?"

"I didn't see." Miles stepped into the node again. "Come on, let's leave a false trail in case he comes after us."

"Good thinking." Ryan joined us, Trix at his side, and in a flash, we reappeared on another vaguely familiar street in Elysium. Miles then led the way down the street to another glowing current of light, which deposited us near the Spirit Agents' base.

"I've been doing the same whenever I leave the base," Miles said, the only one of us who wasn't out of breath from our dizzying trip through the nodes. "I know pretty much everyone in the Houses knows where we live anyway, but that doesn't mean we have to make it any easier for them to follow us through the node to our doorstep."

"I never even thought of that." I leaned a hand against the nearest wall to catch my breath. "I just walked straight here last time."

"If you didn't have enemies on your tail, it shouldn't be a problem," he said. "We're just being paranoid over here. It was Shelley's idea."

"You can never be too paranoid," said Ryan. "Am I supposed to tell the Death King that we aggravated Adair and ticked off the rest of the Family, too?"

"You're the one who threw him into a pile of rubble," I said. "Besides, the Family left their mark on the cantrip they used to kill those liches this morning."

"They did?" said Trix. "You never said."

"It was one of those cantrips which can kill the dead," Ryan told him. "Someone used them on a couple of guards and sent some rogue liches to attack the Death King's castle. They didn't get very far."

"But the Family's mark was on the cantrip, suggesting that their real intention was to get to yours truly," I added.

"And now we've really pissed them off," said Miles. "I think we should avoid the ruins for a while."

I grimaced. "I'm starting to think we should have tried to convince Adair to tell us the Akrith's location rather than running away. I know Lex had him under her control, but if we'd dragged him through the node and tied him up or something, we might have managed to get answers from him."

"That wouldn't have helped," said Ryan. "The last time he got locked in the Death King's jail, it ended in disaster for all of us."

"But what if Adair figures out how to get to the elves before we do? If he can use the Akrith to get there—"

"He won't be able to," said Trix. "I have one of my own, remember? So do most of the other elves. If he could get there with the Akrith alone, one of us would have already figured out how to do it. He'd need a living tree to even begin to access its magic, and if the other elves haven't been able to find one, he won't have a chance. Adair has no working knowledge of our kind, mark my words."

"He did help capture some of them," I said. "To work in the warehouses. Also, the Family recruited mages from within the Houses themselves, and Liv said they had spies among the vampires, too. So why not the elves as well?"

"No elf would ever join them," said Trix firmly. "As for the Akrith, I'm fairly sure you're more likely to be able to get one from a mage than anywhere else. Elf artefacts are worth a lot of money, and I see them in the markets all the time. Liv even helped get one of mine back from an earth mage thief back when we first met."

"Which markets?" said Ryan. "Like the ones in Arcadia?"

That figured. I'd already run into trouble in Arcadia's markets once before when I'd been looking into the illegal cantrip trade. I wasn't sure the people running the Collective of Spells in Arcadia's market were entirely innocent of any involvement, for that matter, but the elven artefacts were worth far more than a few cantrips. People wouldn't be foolish enough to sell them out in the open, would they?

"Liv would know," said Trix.

Of course she would. So would Devon, who was more of an expert on cantrips than the rest of us, but I'd have preferred to keep our plan between as few people as possible.

"You think we should ask her if she's seen any recently?" I asked. "Or should I go and talk to the Houses of the Elements while I'm here and see if I can scrape one victory for the day?"

"I'd say we report to the Death King first," Ryan said. "Since the Death King didn't tell either of us to go on a field trip and get ourselves chased through the ruins by Adair."

"You volunteered to come with me," I pointed out. "Don't act like I'm the only one at fault."

The door to the Spirit Agents' house opened and Miles's friend Shelley poked her head out. The Spirit Agents' second-in-command wore her hair in braids and had acquired a new smudgy tattoo on her left cheek which I strongly suspected was due to one of the teenage spirit mages running amok behind the window with a marker pen in hand. "Are you going to stand there chatting all day? Because as fun as it is to watch the kids decorate your face while you're astral projecting, we could use your help in here, Miles."

Miles groaned. "What did they do to my face?"

"Judge for yourself."

On that ominous note, Shelley withdrew into the house, and I grinned at Miles. The handful of teenagers among the Spirit Agents rarely got the chance to just be kids, so it was nice to hear they were enjoying themselves, even if it came at Miles's expense. "I'd like to see the aftermath, but I should probably report back to the Death King."

"Trust me, you don't want to see it." Miles shook his head. "See you later?"

"Sure, I can drop by later if the Death King sends me to speak to the Houses."

He waved and then vanished back to his body. I, meanwhile, headed back to the node with the others, the new discoveries of the last couple of hours running amok in my thoughts.

The citadels had originally been the creations of the elves. That meant the machinery might have been theirs, too. At what point, and why, had the spirit mages taken it as their own? What else had they taken in the process?

How deep did their links to the elves really go?

5

The Death King faced Ryan and me from the dais in the castle's entrance hall. "So you failed to find anything of note on your trip *and* you drew the attention of the enemy?"

"The enemy already had their eye on us, evidenced by what happened this morning," I pointed out.

The Death King wore a furious scowl on his deceptively human face. Perhaps he thought pretending to be alive would make me forget I was talking to the most unreasonable zombie in existence. "Nevertheless, you returned with nothing to speak of."

"My brother tried to bury us under a pile of debris," I said. "And for the record, I know the Family probably has the object we were looking for, so I decided against breaking onto their property and getting myself captured. I doubt you'd have been a fan of that, either."

His eyes narrowed. "Do not test me, Bria. I might have hired you to work for me, but that doesn't mean I have no other resources at my disposal or any other means of finding what I need."

"Do you have an elf's petrified tree carving and a living elven tree?" I asked. "Because Trix told me that's the only way to open a door back to the elves' realm. I might add that the Family already has one elven carving, which suggests they have the same idea."

"Your brother told you that?" he said. "Did he give a reason for their sudden interest in tracking down the elves?"

"Probably to destroy them or exploit them," I said. "Like last time."

The Death King was silent for a moment. "Did Adair mention *how* he intends to open a way to the elves' realm, when it's reportedly been impossible for any of the other elves to do so since before the war?"

"Using a combination of an Akrith and one of their living trees, according to Trix," I said. "Trix said there aren't any living trees anywhere that he knows of, but the Family has resources I don't. They might well start kidnapping and blackmailing elves all over the Parallel until they find one who has the right information."

"Is there another way you can get one of those artefacts, then?" asked the Death King.

"Trix is asking around," I said. "I'm told Liv is an expert on magical objects, too."

"She isn't here at the moment," he said. "I frankly have no idea how much she knows about elven artefacts. You haven't explained what you plan to do if you manage to make contact with the elves, either."

"I can't say I have a plan yet," I admitted. "But I assume if we tell them the spirit mages are starting another war, they'll want to join us for the sake of revenge on the mages."

"I doubt it'll be that simple," he said. "Elves as a whole aren't generally motivated by revenge."

"I didn't know you knew anything about the elves," I said. "Besides, isn't that why you wanted me to contact them? To get their help?"

"I wanted you to try," he corrected. "The part that's not under our control is whether they say yes or not."

"I know." If we did get a face-to-face meeting, I hoped he wouldn't expect *me* to convince them to join our side, given my absolute failure with the Houses. The Death King was the one who'd spent a decade ordering around an army of zombies, besides.

"You're on the next guard duty shift," he added. "You and Ryan."

"You might want to consider hiring more human guards."

"Do you know any humans you'd entrust with that job?"

Well... no. My brother's reappearance was a reminder that he could hypnotise any person he ran into, including any of the Elemental Soldiers... and me. The Spirit Agents were vulnerable, too. There were no easy options when everyone was out to kill us.

"No, but I get the feeling we're running against the clock here," I said. "Adair said he already had an Akrith of his own. Maybe two, if the Family has the one which was supposed to be mine. Without one, I haven't a hope of convincing the elves to help me, let alone finding their realm."

"Then you can think of a solution while you're

guarding the castle," he said. "You can take a five-minute break before your shift, then meet Ryan at the gates."

Ryan gave me a warning look as though daring me to challenge the Death King's word. Biting back a retort, I walked out of the entrance hall and straight through a lich. "Ow, Harper."

"Sorry." Harper's voice came from the shadowy person I'd stepped into. "What're you up to?"

"I'm on guard duty again." I headed down the corridor towards the Elemental Soldiers' area of the castle. "Since I'm one of the four people the Death King trusts to watch out for intruders."

"I'll join you," she said. "You can tell me where you've been all morning."

"All right, but it's not a fun story." As we walked, I told her about our trip to the ruins and Adair's unwelcome appearance.

"Wow," she said. "So you want to find the elves before the Family does?"

"If it's even possible," I said. "Regardless, I'm not letting Adair and the others get there first. You know what they do to people who won't join their team."

"Yeah," she said, her voice going quiet. "I know."

She might not have directly met the Family, but they were the reason for her untimely death. We had that kind of loss in common, since I was an elf who'd lost my history, while she was a lich who'd had her life stripped away. It wasn't much of a consolation for either of us, but at least someone else understood how it felt to be totally adrift.

"I'm not sure it isn't a lost cause already," I admitted. "I couldn't even find a relic of my history in the rubble."

"I wish there was a way I could help," said Harper. "But I don't think that would turn out so well, considering the last time I tried my hand at espionage."

Harper had tried working as a spy for the Death King before she'd almost been caught by the enemy, but she hadn't forgotten her eventual goal to find a way back to her old life. According to Liv, the cantrips which killed the dead were glitchy versions of another similar cantrip which had the power to return a lich to life with no apparent downsides, but she was tight-lipped on the subject of where it might be possible to find one. Since most liches hadn't opted into that lifestyle, courtesy of a curse which affected the majority of spirit mages here in the Parallel, it would be nice if we found Harper a way out of her endless afterlife that didn't involve permanent death.

While Ryan and I took up our positions by the gates outside the castle, Felicity and Cal left on a mission for the Death King. Part of me expected some kind of retaliation from Adair once he woke up to find his mother using his body as a puppet. Assuming it hadn't been him who'd thrown the first punch by bringing those cantrips which had killed the Death King's guards in the first place. In the meantime, we spent a productive couple of hours watching Harper practise conjuring up illusions of her human face until Felicity and Cal returned to the castle.

"How was your mission?" asked Ryan.

"Not too bad, for a wonder," said Felicity. "Cal was recognised by someone who knew him from his days imprisoned in the House of Earth, but they let us be."

"Wait, the Death King sent you to talk to the Houses?"

Had he finally accepted I couldn't be in two places at once?

"Not the House of Earth," said Cal. "That's a lost cause, since they had the most members who allied with the Family and got the worst of the backlash as a consequence. We started with the House of Water."

"Did you have any luck?" I asked.

"A little," Felicity said. "I don't personally know any of their mages, since I grew up on Earth, but we have a starting point."

So Felicity hadn't been imprisoned in the Houses' jail, unlike Cal and me. Ryan hadn't either, but while I knew they'd come from Earth originally, I hadn't known much about Felicity's past. It made sense that the Death King would have struck a balance between recruits from Earth and from the Parallel.

"Unfortunately, they seem to think we want the Houses to join the Death King's side individually, not cooperate with each other," said Cal.

"We can't have one House's help without the others," said Felicity.

"Tell that to them, not me," said Cal. "Besides, we don't know for sure if anyone within the Houses is still working with the enemy. That makes it hard to find a way to compromise without sharing any of our strategies."

That's what I was afraid of, too, but one House as an ally was better than zero. I just hoped the other Elemental Soldiers would have more luck at gaining their trust than I had.

"Your name came up, too, Bria," said Felicity. "Not in a complimentary way."

"That figures," I said. "What did I ever do to the House of Water?"

"You're known to be linked to the Family."

I scowled. I'd bet that dickhead Harris had been involved in spreading rumours to the other Houses. "Well, they'll have to get over themselves if we're going to work together."

Felicity and Cal returned to the castle, while Ryan and I continued watching for potential trespassers. Trix returned near the end of our shift, with a notable spring in his step.

"Good news," he said. "I found out where we can find an Akrith."

"Really?" I cautioned my leaping pulse to simmer down. "Where?"

"There's an auction in Arcadia tonight," he said. "I heard someone's bringing an elven artefact, one which is worth a lot of money. That almost always means it's an Akrith. If we go there and offer the right price, you'll have no trouble getting your hands on it."

"That's placing a lot of faith in chance," I said. "What is the 'right price' anyway? Because I'm not swimming in cash and I don't have any elven artefacts of my own to trade in exchange."

"Doesn't the Death King pay you well?"

"He hasn't paid me yet," I said. "It's kinda complicated. Besides, I'm not planning on walking around Arcadia carrying buckets of gold even if I had them. That's just asking for trouble."

I was supposed to be paid in cash because I didn't have an Earth-based bank account like the others, I'd only ever lived in the Parallel, and I'd always carried everything I owned around with me in case I had to pack up and run. Besides, the Parallel didn't really have safe places to store your cash unless you were rich enough to afford to hire a private bank. While my salary was more money than I'd ever owned in my life, I was pretty sure it wouldn't be enough to bribe someone for a priceless artefact. I'd spent enough time smuggling rare items around back when I'd worked for Striker to know the general value of most black-market goods.

"Oh." Trix's face fell. "Um, you should know... they probably won't let you into the auction if you don't bring proof that you have something to offer and you aren't just there to cause trouble. It wouldn't hurt to disguise yourself as a practitioner either. Mages tend to draw attention, and if they know you're working for the Death King, they might slam the door in your face"

"Bloody perfect." On the plus side, I couldn't imagine the Family showing their faces in that kind of setting. They didn't live anywhere near Arcadia, which made it the perfect place to go artefact-hunting. The downside? What the hell could I bring with me that wouldn't get stolen the second I looked away? It wasn't like I'd kept anything of Striker's...

Ah, shit. I knew *one* thing that would certainly do a decent job of painting me as an eccentric practitioner.

"I think," I said, "I might have to ask Miles for a loan of his vampire chickens."

6

"You want to borrow *what?*" Miles's brow furrowed as he faced me on the doorstep of the Spirit Agents' house. Dark smudges covered his cheeks, remnants of the teenage mages' adventures that morning. He was lucky they hadn't used permanent marker.

"The vampire chickens," I replied. "I know, I know. I don't have anything else valuable I can possibly trade at an auction. Apparently, they're kicking out the riffraff, so I need to look like I belong there, and I'd rather not bring something which can be swiped from my pocket or bag."

"You have the transporter spell," he reminded me.

So I did. "Okay, I don't have anything valuable I'm willing to part ways with. Besides, those chickens are going to draw the wrong kind of attention to your house sooner or later. If nothing else, it'll help us hide what we're really doing at the auction."

"We?" he echoed.

"You wanted to come with me, right?" I said. "Trix

can't. He said elves rarely go to auctions. He usually sends Liv on his behalf, but she draws a fair bit of attention, too. I don't *think* anyone knows my face, but it's better to be on the safe side."

At least I had a way to hide my own elven features, while the Family weren't known for frequenting Arcadian auctions run by the vampiric aristocracy.

"I can come with you," said Miles, "but do you want a repeat of the incident the day we met?"

"Don't remind me." I shuddered at the memory of the runaway chickens escaping through the node to Earth. "We need a decent cage this time. That's one thing Striker didn't provide, as we found out the hard way."

"The cage, I can get," Miles said. "Carrying a vampire chicken through the nodes to Arcadia, though? I can see that going wrong in a dozen possible ways."

"Don't you have those cantrips which make animals obey you?" I said.

"Well… yes," he said. "Do you actually want to sell the chicken, though? Because I wouldn't mind getting it off our hands, but not if it ends up causing more trouble than it's worth."

"If we find a buyer, then I can try to sell it," I said. "If not, then it doesn't matter as long as we get into the auction. The chicken is just a cover, so they don't suspect us of being troublemaking mages."

"All right," he said. "I can use the cantrip on the chicken, but it won't last all night. How long do these events usually go on for?"

"No idea," I said. "Shouldn't be more than a couple of hours, surely. People don't like to stay out too late in Arcadia."

Thanks to the city's network of underground tunnels, all kinds of beasts came out at night, chief of which was the large population of revenants. The vampires' nastier cousins liked to emerge at sunset and feed on the energy of the nodes, yet it wasn't things that went bump in the night that I feared running into at the market.

"Fair point," Miles said. "A couple of hours ought to be okay, I think, but I'm not convinced a chicken would be an acceptable trade for a priceless artefact."

"If the artefact is the genuine article, then there's no way we'd be able to pay for it outright even if we brought a mountain of gold," I said. "Unless we can ask the Death King for a loan, but the vamps wouldn't believe the money was mine unless I admitted I was the Fire Element. Then they'd question why the Death King was so interested in elven artefacts."

"And word would make it back to the Family," Miles concluded. "So you want to wait for someone else to win the auction and then steal it?"

"You read my mind," I said. "The relic is stolen anyway, it's not like I'm doing any more harm than the person who took it to begin with. Anyone who wants to buy that thing for their private collection isn't going to miss it as much as the elves do."

"You're right there," he said. "It's still risky, though. If it's as valuable as you say, the people in the Parallel with the most money are the vampires, and I doubt you'd be able to outbid them *or* pickpocket them without causing a stir."

"Don't you have vampire friends?" I asked. "Like Lord Blackbourne?"

"I wouldn't call him a friend, more of an acquaintance,"

he replied. "*He* won't be seen dead in a place like that. It'll be the less reputable vamps who have money to burn and no morals."

Great. "We'll have to risk it. Can you ask any of your Spirit Agent friends to help?"

"I'm sure Shelley will be thrilled if I asked for her help robbing a vampire," he said, with an eye-roll. "Especially if there's a vampire chicken involved."

"The two of us will probably be able to handle it by ourselves, then." It wasn't my best plan, I'd freely admit it, but it was that or sit back and do nothing while I lost a potential chance at reaching the elves' artefacts before the Family got there first. "Will the others have a problem with it, though?"

"Nah, they'll tell me I'm being ridiculous and then let me do it anyway," he said. "I've been doing this kind of thing for a while. Can't say I've ever taken a bunch of vampire chickens to one of Arcadia's auctions before, but there's a first time for everything."

"That's my motto," I said. "I'll try not to start any fires."

"Unless the vampires deserve it." He kissed me good-bye, wrapping his arms around me. I couldn't quite stifle the surprised reaction that always overtook me in those moments, as though part of me hardly believed that he cared enough to hold me as if he didn't want to let me go.

When we broke apart, he tilted his head on one side with a questioning look on his face which softened as our eyes met. I kissed him again instead of answering his unspoken question. At some point, he'd want to know where our future lay, and I wasn't sure I could give one. I'd never done more than live day to day before. Besides, with the Parallel on the brink of another war, thinking of the future at all seemed a risky prospect.

———

I can't believe we're doing this again.

Late that evening, Miles and I met with Trix near the warehouses in Arcadia, at which point Miles handed me the cage. "Your turn to carry it."

"That's fair." I took the cage from him, holding it carefully. After administering a cantrip to relax the chicken into compliance, he'd managed to coax it into the cage as planned, but the trickier part was carrying said cage to the auction. From the grumbling noises coming from inside it, the vampire chicken was *not* thrilled at being confined, and I couldn't say I blamed it in the slightest.

"Quiet," I hissed at the cage, which emitted a disgruntled squawking noise as we neared the wide, one-storey building where the auction was due to take place. A steady stream of practitioners walked in via the oak doors, and I watched them for a moment, gauging the chances of us running into hostility. The crowd seemed to be mostly practitioners, who wouldn't be much of a threat. They'd be carrying magical items, but the type which were more valuable than useful. Mages were more likely to be a problem, and as for the vampires...

"I'll wait out here," said Trix. "You go ahead."

"All right." I joined the end of the line. "Let's move."

When we reached the front, I entered the room ahead of Miles. Several people hastened to move out of our way when they saw the cage, and it struck me that it might have been a good idea if I'd pretended it was something more dangerous, if just so people would keep their distance. Benches filled the wide room, and we picked a spot near the door, so we'd be able to make a quick getaway if need be.

When the benches were almost full, two smartly dressed individuals entered the room, earning whispers from the crowd as they glided between the rows of benches. They ascended to the stage at the very front of the room and faced all of us, their grins exposing their pointed canines.

Vampires. So that's who was running the show. Made sense, given that the vamps were the richest of all Arcadia's inhabitants, including the mages. They ruled the city and collected valuables to fill their manor houses in the suburbs where nobody else could afford to live. *Now, which one of these rich bastards wants an elven artefact?*

My gaze skimmed the crowd, seeing a handful of other vampires and a few mages were scattered among the practitioners who formed the majority of the attendees. Miles didn't stand out in a major way, but nobody could tell he was a spirit mage on the surface. Except...

As though in response to the thought which had just occurred to me, the vampires at the front of our room glanced in our directions, their eyes drawn past the cage in my hands to Miles's face. Then they looked away, not before I caught sight of the interest in their expressions. They could sniff out a spirit mage, as Ryan had told me, and which I really should have remembered. I fervently hoped they'd be more interested in the auction than in the presence of a spirit mage in the crowd. Miles wasn't that much of a novelty, right? At least the crowd was thick enough to take some of the attention off us, and we weren't the only people who'd brought a living creature into the auction. Someone even had what looked like a miniature wyrm on a leash, which kept nipping at people's ankles. A vampire chicken was nothing by comparison.

The auction kicked off and the vampires began with a few trinkets and ornaments which weren't worth much more than a few coins. The Parallel had adopted a random mishmash of currencies, though a lot of places used barter instead. The result was that auctions were often chaotic and confusing, but my lack of sleep was catching up on me and it wasn't like I intended to bid on anything, so I dozed off for a few minutes, my head resting on the cage on my lap. The vampire chicken seemed to have calmed down, too, since I only woke when Miles nudged me in the side.

I wriggled upright in my seat, my heart swooping when the vampire at the front of the hall held up a gleaming stone, bright enough to dazzle the eyes.

"This is a valuable relic which once belonged to the elves, before their tragic demise," he said. "It's worth a fortune. Who wants it?"

That's the Akrith? It looked more like a shiny rock than a petrified tree carving, but the glowing light painted it as a magical artefact. Hoping it was the genuine article, I leaned forward in my seat.

A raspy voice came from the third row. "One thousand coins."

Another man scoffed. "Five thousand."

"Ten thousand," a stocky practitioner snapped from the row behind me.

"Twenty thousand," someone else cut in.

More haggling ensued. I watched, dizzy at the rapid pace of the back-and-forth shouts, and then a cold voice cut through the others. "A million gold coins."

Silence rang out through the auction hall.

"Nobody going to offer more?" said the auctioneer. "Very well. The item goes to that gentleman over there."

All eyes went to the front row as another vampire stood and approached the stage. He wore a suit fitted to his tall frame, moving with casual grace as he glided to the front of the room to pick up the stone. I watched his every movement as he went back to his seat. Unfortunately, he knew we were watching him, because so was everyone else. That might make things tricky later, if we weren't the only people who tried to take his winnings away from him.

Not many items remained on the vampires' list and most people had stopped paying attention now the excitement had died down. When the vampires called the auction to an end, we rose to our feet along with the rest of the crowd. I kept one eye on the vampire as we waited to leave, adjusting my grip on the chicken's cage. To my consternation, it chose that moment to wake up with an indignant squawk which made everyone in the vicinity jump.

While Miles took the cage from me, I used my elven speed and grace to weave through the crowd after our target. The the vampire had the exact same advantages I did, though, and he was already out the door by the time I got there. As I skirted the line of people leaving, he parted the crowd to glide down a side street.

I followed, speeding up when I saw the current of white light ahead of him. He was walking towards a node.

What the hell is he doing? Most vampires lived here in Arcadia. He ought to be going to his manor house in the suburbs of the city, unless he planned on using a shortcut to get there. *Or he's got something else in mind.*

I walked in behind him, putting on a burst of speed to close the distance between us, and then I snagged his sleeve. "Hey, mate. I think you took something that belongs to us."

He tilted his head. "To whom?"

"The elves."

That's when I hit him. Most people wouldn't expect violence from an elf, and I'd expected him to be surprised enough for me to get an opening. Instead, he spun around and struck me in the ribs.

What the fuck?

I flew back into the nearest stone wall, while the vampire vanished in a flash of white light. Dammit, he'd fled through the node.

"Bria!" Miles hurried up to me, both hands gripping the cage and the cries of its angry occupant echoing in the night.

"Ow." I caught my balance, wincing at the sharp pain in my shoulder blades. "Bastard ran through the node."

"Figures," Miles said. "I can tail him. He won't be expecting a spirit mage."

I walked alongside him, rubbing the back of my head. The node's current surrounded us, and I gripped Miles's arm as he used his spirit mage talent to take us directly to the spot where the vampire had landed.

We stepped out of the node onto a busy high street. Cars roared past, while dazzling lights blared from the buildings on either side and a cacophony of human noise filled the background.

"What the hell is he doing on Earth?" I spotted our quarry running ahead of us and put on a burst of speed. He had a head start, but he wouldn't be able to use the extent of his vampire speed here on Earth, even without human witnesses around. Unfortunately, I had to keep the super-speed to a minimum, too, or else we'd both find ourselves targeted by the Order for breaking their magical secrecy laws.

"Hey!" Miles shot past me with the force of a transparent bullet, firing off a bolt of energy which struck the vampire square in the back. He fell to his knees, while I ran to catch him up.

A solid hand on my shoulder made me whip my head around. One of the two vampires who'd been running the auction appeared at my side, pointed canines showing. "Are you sure you're supposed to be here?"

"Let go of me." I wrenched my hand away, but the other vamp was on his feet again and had taken off. Miles, meanwhile, must have left his body standing by the node in order to follow the vampire via astral projection.

The newcomer caught my arm before I could run after my quarry, his firm grip anchoring me to the spot. "You and your spirit mage friend would be better served if you go back to the Parallel, unless you want to run afoul of the Order."

"What are *you* doing on Earth?" Dammit, the other vamp was getting away again. I gave a firm tug to remove my arm from his grip, and the vampire's fist came up. It would have caught me in the face if I hadn't used my elven speed to dodge.

The vampire's eyes widened a little. "So you truly aren't human…"

"I did warn you." Flames leapt to my hands—smaller than they would have been in the Parallel, but enough to drive the vamp to let go of me. I broke into a run down the street, and swore when the vanishing light of a node told me our vampire friend had given us the slip again.

Miles appeared behind me, in the flesh this time, the squawking cage in his hands making enough of a racket to wake the dead. "Damn, he's fast."

"Watch out—there's another vampire back there." I walked with him towards the node where our target had disappeared, and this time, Miles's tracking skills took us to an unfamiliar street near some office blocks. At first glance, the place looked entirely mundane—until I took in the guards dressed in a familiar black uniform standing outside the automatic doors of one of the office blocks. *Dammit, is he working for the Order?*

The Order didn't hire vampires, right? I crossed the road to look closer, careful to stay out of sight in case the guards spotted me. The last thing I needed was to end the night in a cell, though the guards' attention was occupied. The vampire said something to them, then he glided between the two guards and into the building. I hung back, suppressing the urge to shout in frustration.

Miles caught up to me, gripping the cage in his arms. "Shit. He didn't go in there, did he?"

"He must have contacts in the Order," I whispered. "Question is, did he go there to give someone else the Akrith or is he just hiding until the coast is clear?"

"Either." Miles's eyes narrowed at the building. "Damned vampire. We can wait here to see if he comes out. Pretty sure the Order's headquarters is open twenty-four seven, though, so unless you want to sit out here all night…?"

"I didn't think the Order might be involved with Arcadia's markets."

"In fairness, neither did I," said Miles. "The Order and the vampires… I wouldn't call them enemies, but I didn't think they had close ties either."

"This isn't a normal situation, though, is it?" I said. "The Order is run by a bunch of rogue spirit mages these days."

Spirit mages who wanted elven artefacts? What could an organisation supposedly intended to protect the magical world's secrecy possibly want with items which had no value on Earth? *Please don't tell me the Family is working with* them, *too.*

The sound of soft footfalls warned us of the arrival of our second vampire friend, and I spun around with a growing fireball in my palms. "Last warning."

The vamp struck. Miles's fist came up, punching him square in the chest, and he fell into the path of my flames. Fire ate away at his all-too flammable skin, and I exhaled in a sigh as he evaporated on the breeze.

"Oops," I said. "I think we're off the next auction's attendee list."

"He and the other vamp must have been friends," he said. "I bet you anything that dude in there asked his mate to watch his back in case someone tried swiping his precious elf artefact after he won."

"Then why take it into the Order? They usually send people to return rare artefacts to the Parallel, not bring them to their doorstep." Though their whole system sounded like it was in upheaval after the recent events in London. "I guess I have to go and tell the Death King the bad news. What're the odds that he gives me permission to go into the Order's headquarters and steal the Akrith back?"

"Fairly high, considering how urgent it is," he said. "I can stay here and watch the place while you ask him."

"You sure?"

"Of course I am." He held out the cage. "But please take this with you before the noise draws the Order's attention."

"Watch out for more sneaky vampires," I warned him, taking the cage from his hands. Its feathery occupant squawked at me. "And shut it, you. You weren't even useful."

I heard Miles chuckling behind me as I headed for the node down the street from the Order's building. After checking nobody was following me, I travelled back to the swampland and headed for the gates to the castle, bracing myself for His Deathly Highness to *not* be thrilled with me for failing to get the Akrith. Though the odds had been against us from the start and we'd been lucky not to wind up getting caught, I'd blown any chance of getting into an auction again when I'd torched that vampire. *Serve him right for getting handsy.*

After dropping off the vampire chicken's cage at the foot of the staircase, I entered the castle's entrance hall and found the Death King waiting for me. "Well?"

"They were prepared for us," I said. "The vampire who bought the Akrith expected to be followed and cut a deal with one of the auctioneers. Both of them fled to Earth, then his friend distracted us while he hopped in and out of the nodes until he reached the Order's headquarters and took refuge in there."

"The *Order?*" he echoed.

"Apparently," I said. "I don't know what they're doing with the Akrith. If not handing it to the Family, I mean."

The Order was run by rogue spirit mages who'd worked with the Family before, though, and the Family were no longer hiding in the shadows as they once had. Yet they sure as hell hadn't got involved in anything on *Earth* before. I hadn't thought they'd ever had an interest in the people who had zero clue of the magical world that existed under their feet.

"Is the vampire still in the Order's base?" he asked.

"Yeah, that's why I came here," I said. "Miles is watching to see if the vampire leaves the building, but I figured I'd ask if you wanted me to go after him. I'm not going to be able to go to another auction after I torched one of the auctioneers."

"How inconvenient." The Death King studied me, his expression disconcertingly lifelike for a lich wearing an illusion. "If you decide to break into the Order and get this artefact back, they're unlikely to see you coming. Less so than the Family, at any rate."

He was right on that one, but that didn't make it any less of a bad idea. The Order or the Family's house. What a choice to make.

"Yeah, I know," I said. "Got any advice before I go back?"

"Talk to Olivia," was his response. "She'll help you break into the Order."

7

I left the castle and spotted the fire sprite hovering above the vampire chicken's cage, from which a series of loud screeching noises issued.

"Someone's unhappy," Dex remarked. "What did you bring that thing here for?"

"Nowhere else to put it." What the hell. I opened the cage door and let the vampire chicken hop out, its glowing eyes looking positively demonic in the darkness. "Is Liv around? Or Devon?"

"Not in the castle, no," he said. "Why?"

"I need to talk to them about finding a magical object," I said. "I'm told Liv knows all about them, since she used to be a retriever for the Order."

"Yes, she did," he said. "What kind of object are we talking about?"

"A rare elven artefact," I said. "A vampire stole it and took it into the Order's headquarters. I need her help to get it back."

"You want to break into the Order's headquarters?" He burst into laughter, flitting around my head like a hummingbird.

"What the hell is so funny?" I asked the fire sprite. "Didn't Liv used to work for them?"

"She also broke in a fair few times herself," he said. "Both when she worked for the Order and otherwise. She'll be thrilled to hear that you're doing the same, I'm sure."

"Whether she is or not, this is urgent," I said. "Life and death, potentially. Where is she?"

"She's at home," he said. "If it's *life and death, then I'm sure she'll be willing to listen. I'll come to see her reaction. It's bound to be priceless.*"

"Thanks, Dex."

The fire sprite floated alongside me towards the node outside the castle's fence, past the spot where a sleepy-looking Felicity and Cal stood on security duty.

"Where're you going this time?" Cal yawned.

"Nowhere fun," I said evasively. "I'll be back within the hour."

Without adding any more details. I hurried after Dex and followed him into the path of the node. The light swallowed us up, and a second later, I found myself standing in Liv and Devon's living room, while both occupants gawped at me from the sofa.

I looked up at the sprite. "Dex, you should have mentioned you were taking us into Liv's house."

"I thought it was implied."

"Dammit, Dex." Devon half rose to her feet, scowling at the fire sprite.

Liv sat next to her, a gaming controller in her hands, while the setup from our D&D game covered the table on the left-hand side of the room.

"I forgot the node comes out directly into your house," I admitted. "Sorry. Dex said you'd be willing to help us."

"What do you want, then?" asked Devon.

"There's a magical object I need," I said. "An elven artefact which was sold at an auction in Arcadia. A vampire ran off with it and escaped to Earth."

"You went to one of those auctions?" said Liv.

"Didn't you set an auction hall on fire once?" said Devon.

I turned to Liv. "Seriously?"

"It wasn't me, it was Dex," Liv answered. "I was trying to stop a rogue earth mage from making a quick getaway, and Dex got a bit overexcited."

"Bet the vampires loved that," I said. "Anyway, as I was about to say, the vampire took the object, came to Earth, and then ran into the Order's headquarters of all places."

"The *Order?*" she said. "You're joking, right?"

"Nope," I said. "I couldn't follow him inside, and he never came back out. I don't know if he was going to give it to them to look after, or if he was just waiting for the coast to be clear before running."

"Either way, he must have allies in there," said Devon. "Otherwise the Order would have kicked him out."

"Yeah," said Liv. "They don't take kindly to being fucked around with. They won't be happy with any break-in attempts, either. If you get caught, you won't get any mercy."

"If I do, the best I can hope is that they hand me back to the Houses," I said. "If I wind up back in the Family's home, then I'd be better off being caught by the Order instead."

"Does the Family's home contain a dungeon equipped with anti-magical shielding and hundreds of guards, not to mention cantrips which can destroy even a lich?" asked Liv.

"Not that I recall, but the Family have a vendetta," I said. "The Order... whatever dickheads are running the show in there, they don't know me. There's no personal stake in this for them. The worst they can do is lock me up."

"If you get caught, they'll strip the magic out of you the way they do to other mages who break the law," Liv said seriously. "Trust me, it's worse than death for most people."

"I doubt they *can* strip out my magic," I said. "I'm designed to be more resilient than most humans. The Family saw to that."

Both of them stared at me.

"What in hell did they do to you?" Devon wanted to know.

"Tested experimental cantrips on me, mostly," I replied. "Hard to remember most of it. I was too young."

"They did that to you when you were a kid?" Liv said. "Damn."

"Nobody ever said they were model parents," I said. "To top it off, I'm half-elf, so that alone might grant me immunity to half the spells they might use on me."

"Hell of a risk regardless," said Devon. "The vampire... if he's trading with them, the retrieval unit is down the stairway at the back of the lobby."

"That's where they keep most of the crap they get

people like me to retrieve," Liv added. "As for actual deliveries, they keep those in the yard around the back, but I don't think they'd leave a rare artefact out there unattended. Things like that are delivered by private courier, usually."

"Makes sense, but I don't know who the vamp'll be trading it to." Except for someone who could give him more than a million gold coins or the local equivalent, that is. "I wouldn't say the Family was friends with any vampires, but then again, I didn't think they knew any spirit mages either and now I find out they're supporting another war."

"Some rogue vampires originally started the illegal cantrip trade in Arcadia," said Devon.

"Well, that would explain a lot." I shook my head. "Anyway, I have to get back out there. I left Miles watching the Order, but they might catch him if he stays out there too long. We have to get in there before they realise we're spying on them."

"If that's the case, take Dex with you," said Liv. "Dex? You still here?"

The fire sprite floated into view. "What is it?"

"You know the way around the Order," said Liv. "Bria and Miles are planning on breaking in, so I'm sure you can show them around."

"Another stealth mission?" he said. "Fine, but I expect compensation."

"You'll get some new dice later if you're good." Devon got to her feet. "I have some cantrips which will help you stay unseen, but even they won't be enough if you end up getting caught. They have weapons in their headquarters which can even kill liches. They were developing them for Hawker."

"Great." I watched her leave via the door which led into the shop where she sold cantrips and other magical items to practitioners on Earth. Including Order employees. *What the hell am I doing?*

"You probably won't have to go into the basement, but you should know that's where their prison is," added Liv. "The very top floor is for the upper room, the people who run the show, but I doubt the vampire will go up there. Unless he's really important, he won't be allowed in."

"He's very rich, I'll say that much," I said. "He bought that thing for a million coins like it was nothing."

"Damn," said Liv. "Well, if you're a master of stealth, then you shouldn't have a problem getting around the lower levels of the Order. Just avoid taking the elevator down to the basement. Especially if you have any spirit mages with you."

Spirit mages who broke the laws often paid the price by having the magic stripped from their very bones. That was the fate which might await Miles if we failed. I didn't want him to be the one who suffered for my mistake, but I was in way over my head when it came to the Order. They weren't like the Houses, even if they were working from the same rulebook, and I hadn't had nearly enough time to prepare.

If we let the artefact slip through our fingers, though, we'd lose our shot at getting to the elves before the Family did. Besides, I'd done far more dangerous things than breaking into the Order's headquarters. Regardless of Liv's warnings, there was nothing they could do to me that was worse than what I'd already gone through.

We needed that artefact. And if we had to go through the Order to get it, so be it.

———

After Dex joined me, we hopped through the node once again and found Miles standing in the same spot where I'd left him, watching the doors to the Order's headquarters.

"There you are," he said. "I assumed the Death King was chewing you out, but I was on the brink of coming to find you."

"Don't worry about me," I said. "I topped up our stealth cantrips, if we need them, but it depends if you want to come inside the building with me or not. They're not known for being nice to spirit mages."

"Damn right," Dex said. "I'm here as your lookout. Not my first time breaking into the Order's place, so I know the way around."

"Good, because we don't," said Miles. "I'm coming in, though, Bria."

Two of us going in meant twice the chance of being caught, but if he astral projected, he wouldn't be able to use an invisibility cantrip to hide himself, and the anti-magical defences on the lower levels might well interfere with his magic even if he wasn't there in person. We'd better hope the dungeon wasn't where we ended up having to go to retrieve the Akrith.

Liv had said the retrieval unit lay down a staircase on the ground floor, so that was our first target. I handed Miles one of the invisibility cantrips Devon had given me and turned on my own before approaching the building. Two burly shifter guards stood in front of the doors, dressed in dark clothing. Even invisible, we'd need to cause a distraction to get in.

"Say the word and I'll draw their attention," Dex muttered in my ear. "The best time to sneak in is when someone else is on the way out."

We didn't have to wait long, since people came and went all the time. When two people walked through the automatic doors, I whispered to the fire sprite, "Go on."

Dex flew straight at the guards, and as they parted to look at the sparks showering above their heads, I darted between them, hoping Miles had stuck close behind me.

A wide, clean lobby greeted us, containing few people aside from a receptionist and some Order members wearing durable gear who I guessed had come from the Parallel. People who travelled between realms on a daily basis were less likely to work normal daytime hours than those who lived permanently on Earth and worked in the Order's offices. I didn't see any signs of the spirit mages who'd secretly infiltrated the place, but I doubted they'd be visible on the surface.

A flicker of light drew my eyes to a pillar, behind which Dex hovered, gesturing to the left. *That way.* I followed his directions and found my way to a corridor lined with office doors, which ended in a staircase which I assumed must lead to the retrieval unit in the basement.

I trod downstairs and found myself in a musty room filled with boxes. A sleepy-looking kid sat behind the desk, and he didn't even look up when I tiptoed into the room. I guessed Liv was right when she said the Order viewed the retrieval unit as their lowest priority, and that 'retriever' translated as 'thief of worthless junk'.

Unfortunately, the vampire wasn't around either, evidenced by the fact that the room contained no hiding places to speak of. He wouldn't have dumped the priceless artefact inside one of the boxes along with the rest of the junk, so he must still have it with him.

Dex flitted past, and the flap of one of the boxes lifted a fraction. A moment later, the fire sprite surfaced and landed on my invisible shoulder. "Nope. This isn't the right place."

I backtracked, cursing inwardly, and climbed the stairs again. The kid behind the desk hadn't even noticed the intrusion, but of course the vampire wouldn't have put the artefact in the most obvious place. No, he'd have been sneakier than that.

The fire sprite reached the top of the stairs first, leading the way down a row of wooden doors labelled with names etched into bronze plates.

Where the hell is that vampire? He wouldn't be sitting around in an office holding onto the artefact, surely. He'd either have given it to someone else to look after or locked it in a secure safe. Which depended whether he was going to keep it, hand it to the Family, or to someone else inside the Order itself. Small windows topped each door, and I peered through each of them as I walked along the row of offices.

I halted in front of a door without a bronze plate identifying its owner, seeing the smooth back of the vampire's head through the glass in the window. *There he is.*

"That's old Cobb's office." Dex flew onto my shoulder.

"Holland took over the place before he got promoted to the upper room."

Holland. That name sounded familiar. Wasn't he the guy who'd put himself in charge of this Order branch after the spirit mages' secret coup? I edged closer in the hopes of overhearing who the vampire was speaking to, but with no luck.

"I'm going in," Dex said. "Wait out here. Don't draw attention."

"No shit," I breathed.

The fire sprite inched the door open a fraction and flitted into the room. In the split second the door was open, I heard the vampire say, "He's late."

"What did you expect?" responded another male voice. "He's an elf. They run on their own time schedule."

The door closed, while I stared at the back of the vampire's head. *They're meeting with an elf?*

I couldn't see Miles, but I could only assume he'd invisibly hidden himself nearby. I bloody well hoped Dex knew what he was doing. A long minute passed before the door inched open and the small shape of the fire sprite returned.

"They're waiting for an elf," he muttered in my ear. "Some trader."

"Why would an *elf* come here?" A scheme began to take shape in my mind. "Dex, can you ask Miles to meet me outside the back exit?"

"On it." He flew to a spot opposite the door and poked at thin air. "She wants to talk to you."

A moment later, Miles's hand found my arm and he leaned in and whispered. "You want to intercept the trader?"

"You've got it," I breathed. "I'm not chasing anyone down this time, though. We're going to stage a diversion and swipe the Akrith when the vampire's back is turned."

This time, I wouldn't fail.

8

Miles and I crept towards the back door out of the Order's headquarters, which opened into a yard filled with boxes and the occasional cage. I found myself wondering if any contained vampire chickens. If they did, they'd make a handy diversion if we needed one.

There were two guards outside and nothing more, so Miles and I found a spot behind a stack of boxes and settled in to wait for the elf trader to show up. The guards, both shifters, were more interested in smoking some kind of pipe which emitted puffs of purple smoke—presumably pillaged from one of the boxes—than looking out for trespassers.

"He's got to be coming through the node," Miles whispered. "Pity we don't have one of those neutralising cantrips to turn it off."

"True." I perched on the low wall behind the boxes. "There are other nodes he could use instead, though. Personally, I think our best bet is to ambush him outside the doors and make sure the vampire sees us do it. That ought to lure him out into the open."

"It'll also draw the Order's attention, whether we're visible or not."

At that moment, Dex flew back over the fence to join us. "I saw an elf approaching the Order's place."

"All right." I leapt to my feet, keeping an eye on the guards to make sure they hadn't noticed the sprite's arrival. "Dex, can you tail him? We'll have to make sure the vamp doesn't slip away with the artefact."

"I have a few ideas," said Miles. "I'll cause a diversion out here."

The clicking sound of a cantrip sounded, and a blast of light shot up in the air. The two guards near the building let out exclamations of shock, but I was already entering the back door of the lobby at speed.

At the same time, the elf entered via the front doors. He couldn't be mistaken for human, with his elegantly carved features and his silky dark hair tied into a ponytail. I slid a cantrip into my hand and ran into the elf's path. The cantrip froze him mid-motion, while several people ran for the door at the back, presumably having seen the ruckus Miles had caused outside. Which was precisely the plan.

"We're under attack!" someone shouted.

Still invisible, I grabbed the elf's arm while he was frozen and felt Miles brush past my side as he took the elf's other arm. Together, we yanked him across the lobby and out the back door into the yard.

The two guards startled at the sight of the elf being pulled along by two invisible attackers. I let go for a second and flames leapt from my hands to the pile of boxes in front of me. Several other flashes and bangs echoed throughout the area, suggesting Miles was dipping into his cantrip stash as well. As the guards looked wildly around for the source of the ruckus, I gave the elf a shove in the direction of the cages, which burst open, causing a fresh cacophony of noise to reverberate throughout the back yard.

I spun back to the lobby and spotted the vampire from earlier among the crowd who'd come to see what was going on. He wasn't holding the artefact, so he must have left it in the room he'd vacated. Quick as a flash, I darted back into the lobby and around the corner towards the office I'd seen him in. The door was wide open. *Yes.*

I ran in—and froze. A man wearing a pressed suit, with neatly trimmed grey hair, had remained behind, apparently oblivious to the chaos erupting outside. When he rotated to face my direction, his glasses were balanced on the end of his nose, giving him a deceptively calm appearance. "Going to show your face?"

How the hell did he know I was here? I'd hardly made a sound, and the door had already been ajar.

"It's no use pretending," he added. "I assume you came for this?"

A glow came from his hand when he held up the stone from the auction, which cast a greenish light around the office. The vamp must have told him about being tailed, so he'd known we were coming. But who was he?

The door moved behind me and someone else rushed into the room, forcing me to step to the side. "Mr Holland, there's a fire—"

"Let the guards deal with it," he said. "We expected this. I have it under control."

Holland. This was the guy who the spirit mages had placed in charge of the Order's base, but he wasn't a mage himself, as far as I knew. What the hell did he want with the elven artefact? Nothing good, I assumed.

I gave the room a quick scan, from the leather-backed seat to the metal filing cabinets behind the wooden desk. No obvious traps, nothing magical. Yet Holland didn't seem to be afraid of me despite his own lack of magical advantages.

Nevertheless, this was my shot. Flames leapt to my palms and I directed them at the guy blocking my way out of the room. He stumbled back with a yell as his shoes caught fire, but even that didn't coax Mr Holland to move. Putting on a burst of speed, I zipped behind him and reached for the stone in his hand.

A clicking sounded and an unseen blow hit me like an invisible wall. Reeling, I stumbled back to find myself visible again, while the flames in my palm went out in the same instant.

Holland reached into his pocket and retrieved a gleaming cantrip. "Neutraliser. Very handy. They can even turn off nodes, did you know? The only thing they don't work on is certain artefacts like this one."

Shit. A neutraliser cantrip. I'd seen them before, when my own allies had used them to turn off the transporters in the citadels, and the node linking Elysium to London. I hadn't known it was possible to use one to cut off someone's magic altogether.

"What do you want with the elves?" Trying to squash my panic, I prepared to make another grab for the Akrith the instant his attention slipped. "Who are you giving that artefact to?"

"Someone willing to help us further our goal of uniting all magical beings on both sides of the nodes." He lifted the stone into the air, out of my reach. "I wouldn't try challenging me. You won't get very far."

"Maybe not, but I'll take my chances."

Launching forward, I punched him in the nose with one hand and grabbed for the stone with the other. His brief lapse in attention was all I needed to snatch the Akrith out of his grip, and since the neutraliser hadn't affected my elven speed, I was out of the room a second later, shoving the guard who was still trying to extinguish his flaming shoes into Holland's path.

More guards converged on me when they saw me running, no longer hidden by an invisibility spell, but I streaked past them at top speed. I veered towards the back exit and tucked the stone into my pocket, keeping one hand on it as I ran. Hands grabbed for me, but the guards all seemed to trip over thin air or catch on fire without getting close to me. Sending a silent thanks to Dex and Miles, I leapt over a stack of boxes and ran out the yard— only to find my path barred by more armed guards. All of them held cantrips in their hands, glowing with runes lighting up on their surfaces.

Flashes of light shone as the cantrips flew left and right. I dodged the first few and ran for the fence, but my steps froze mid-motion, my limbs refusing to obey my commands. Someone grabbed my arm, while a fist in my ribs knocked the breath from me. Another grabbed for the stone in my pocket—

That's when the stone exploded.

The next few moments felt like a dream. Light burst out of the stone, piercing the heavens, while the nearest guards flew into the air as though propelled by an invisible force. Even the vampire, who'd crept in behind me, shouted in alarm as he was flung backwards into a stack of boxes. The spell freezing me to the spot wore off in an instant, while I clung onto the blazing stone and staggered to the side, eyes screwed up against the glow.

Then Miles had my arm and we were running, leaping over the low wall out of the yard. Everything slowed to a blur of brightness and noise, and I was hardly aware of reaching the node before we fell through its white torrent. We landed in the swamp, a wave of water crashing over our heads. The cold, filthy water effectively brought me back to alertness.

"Shit." I pushed to my feet, spotting Miles lying sprawled in the mud, fully visible. He must have dropped his cantrip. "Did anyone follow us?"

"No." He sprang upright, breathing hard. "I think we left Dex behind, but he was having too much fun setting boxes on fire for me to get his attention."

"Great." I pushed a handful of sopping wet hair out of my face, feeling unexpectedly energised, as though the stone had given me a boost of energy on top of blasting those guards into the air. "What did that stone *do*? Did it have some kind of defence mechanism on it?"

The stone looked totally harmless now, as though nothing had happened at all. The glow had dimmed to a pale green, the same colour it'd been at the auction. Yet it'd unleashed some kind of power which had knocked everyone back, even the vampire.

"I don't know, you tell me," said Miles. "It's an elven

artefact. Makes sense that it'd have some unusual magic. Which would explain why you carried me halfway around the Order's building to the node in about five seconds."

"Wait, I did?" I hadn't stopped to consider how he'd kept pace with me throughout my wild flight from the Order, but there was no other explanation. "I was too busy trying to get away to pay attention to anything else."

"Who was that elf, though?" said Miles. "I didn't think any of them would be working with the Order, not when the people in charge seem perfectly happy to let the Family capture and kill their fellow elves."

"I know." Some of the buzz of our victorious escape died down. "I have no idea who he was. Maybe Trix knows."

I squelched through the mud towards the grounds of the castle, earning a bewildered stare from Cal and Felicity. Especially when they saw Miles in the same state, trailing behind me.

"What in the Elements' names were you doing, mud-wrestling?" Cal said.

"Nothing so exciting." The sound of squawking drew my attention to a spot near the stairs where the vampire chicken hopped in circles around Trix. "There's a sight you don't see every day."

"Are you going to explain why you brought that thing here?" Felicity asked.

"He's a present for the Death King," Miles shook his head, sending swamp water everywhere. "Did you let Trix in?"

"He said he was waiting for you." Cal rubbed his tired eyes. "You're taking over from us at midnight, by the way."

"I can hardly wait." I walked over to the elf and the

vampire chicken, which hissed at me when it saw me approach.

Trix beamed when I pulled the stone out of my pocket. "You found it?"

"After a fashion," I said. "The vamp who won the auction gave us the slip and hid inside the Order's base back on Earth, but we staged an ambush and stole it back when a trader came to meet him. You should know, though… the trader who wanted to buy the Akrith from the vampire was an elf."

"An *elf?*" said Trix in scandalised tones. "Why would an elf work with the Order?"

"I haven't a clue," I said. "Maybe they offered him a cut of the profits."

He shook his head violently. "No. The elves know the Order is under the influence of the spirit mages."

"Or blackmail was involved," I suggested. "We didn't get the chance to ask who the elf was working for, but if the Order let him in, he must be one of their allies."

"I'm going to the Order's headquarters, then," he said. "Liv won't like it, but I want to know who he's working for."

"I wouldn't go near them," I warned. "They'll be on high alert for a while. Our priority was getting the stone by any means possible. We barely made it out without getting locked up, and it's thanks to the stone itself that we did."

"What do you mean?" asked Trix.

"It… well, the stone kind of exploded," I said. "It gave off a flash of light which pushed away all the guards who were trying to grab us, so we ran for it while we had the chance."

The elf's eyes widened. "The Akrith… exploded?"

"Looked that way," I said. "I was kind of hoping you might be able to explain why, because I'm lost. Holland shut off my magic with a neutraliser cantrip, so I can't have been the one who turned it on."

"The Akrith must have a significant amount of the elves' power still inside it." His mouth pulled down at the corners. "No elf would willingly hand it over to the enemy. There must be a misunderstanding."

"Didn't look that way to me," said Miles. "Sorry, mate."

Without another word, Trix marched off, looking more annoyed than I'd ever seen him. I hoped he was going to speak to his elf allies in Arcadia and not on his way to the Order, considering the chaos we'd left behind us.

"Poor guy," I said. "I have a feeling we might have to go back to his ally in Arcadia again. Maybe she knows who the elf we saw at the Order is working with. I'm not going back there anytime soon."

"Nor me," said Miles. "I was already on the Order's shit list by virtue of being born a spirit mage. That's why I didn't use my spirit magic during our escape, only cantrips."

"You didn't want them to guess your identity?" I said. "Or… you wanted to make sure none of the other Spirit Agents took the blame? I did say you didn't have to take the risk for me."

"I know you did," he said. "Bria, we should talk."

My throat went dry. "Those words usually don't mean anything good."

"Ah, shit," he said. "That's not what I meant, Bria."

I did my best to ignore the swooping sensation in my chest. "Then what did you want to talk about?"

His mouth parted. "Do you see us having a future after all this?"

"Honestly?" I struggled to put my whirling thoughts into words. "I never thought about the future. I try not to look beyond the present. It's better for my sanity that way."

"Oh." He gave a tight nod. "Understandable."

The disappointment in his voice prompted me to add, "But I do like you. A lot. If there's a future after all this, I'm all for it."

"Of course." He stepped forward and kissed me good-bye. "I'd better go update the others before Shelley sends a patrol after me."

He left for the node, while I couldn't help feeling I'd messed up in a major way. Even if I'd only spoken the truth, and I hadn't wanted to lie. With the Family still alive, I didn't dare plan for a future they might snatch from my grasp.

9

"Well done," said Liv. "You're officially ahead of me on the Order's most wanted list. And trust me, that's saying a lot."

"I'm honoured," I said.

After Miles had left, I'd returned to let Liv and Devon know we were alive after our flight to the swamp and to check the Order hadn't shown up at their house. I'd wondered if they might have assumed we were working together, given Liv's tenuous history with the Order, but luckily, it seemed they'd left her alone.

Dex zipped overhead as Liv and Devon hammered at their gaming controllers, blowing up something onscreen. "Hey, you should take it as a challenge."

"I'm sure I'll piss them off again soon," Liv commented. "It's pretty much a hobby of mine. Anyway, you had a legitimate reason to break into their headquarters."

"I hoped we'd just find the stone in the retrieval unit,

but that would be expecting too much," I said. "Instead, this dude called Holland had it."

"That would explain a lot." Liv's knuckles whitened as she clenched her fists around the controller. "Holland is the guy calling the shots—in that Order branch, at least. He used to be chief interrogator before he started working with the very spirit mages he used to lock up and torture."

"Fucker," said Devon. "He's part of the upper room now. What does he want with the elves?"

"I wish I knew," I said. "The elf he was selling to… he was still at the Order, last I saw. We'd need to ambush him if we wanted to find out what his motive is."

And why he'd effectively sold out his entire species. What in the world had the Order offered him in exchange? Or had he intended to smuggle the Akrith back to its original owners?

"Might have to put one of those neutralising cantrips on the node, just in case," Devon suggested.

"I didn't know you had many of those going spare," I said.

"We don't," said Devon. "We have to keep putting them in the citadel to keep Hawker and his mates from reactivating the transporters linking up the citadels again."

"Holland used one against me," I said. "How long will it last?"

"A few hours at most," said Devon. "They belonged to the Order to begin with, before I stole one to learn how to make my own. I've been making more, but I can only craft one at a time."

Liv wore a thoughtful look on her face as she pounded

the buttons on the controller. "Did the Death King approve of your plan?"

"Of course he did."

"At least then he'll have your back if they march over to the castle to find you."

"Do they normally send people to the swamp?" I doubted it. The Order might talk a big game, but their defences left much to be desired.

"Depends how badly they want that artefact."

"Not like they can even use it," I said. "I'm heading back to the castle. Dex, are you coming?"

"I think I'll stay here for a bit," said the fire sprite.

"All right." I waved at Liv and Devon. "Be seeing you."

By now, I'd got the hang of pinpointing the node running through the middle of their house, and I hopped through to land in the swamp again. Cal and Felicity stood by the gates dressed in their armour, both of them looking exhausted.

"You have five minutes before your shift," Felicity told me.

"Great." I heard a squawking noise from nearby. "Didn't Miles take the vampire chicken back?"

"Apparently not," said Cal. "Better hope the Death King doesn't mind."

It wasn't my problem if he did, and he'd have bigger problems if the Order opted to come after me for swiping the artefact from under their noses. Or maybe they'd send the elf trader instead. I wouldn't deny I'd be interested to speak to the guy, if just to know who he was... and what had made him turn against the others.

I looked dubiously at the vampire chicken. "You think this will work?"

Trix, as promised, had offered to give me lessons in magic. Since I was also playing security guard in every moment of spare time I possessed, that meant I had to take said lessons while standing outside the gates, trying to ignore Ryan's comments from the sidelines. Since neither the Order nor their elf trader had elected to show their faces, I could do worse than learn how to enact a mind-control spell on a vampire chicken. A wyrm was a bit much for a newbie, so I'd need to start with a smaller target.

I crouched beside the fowl as it pecked at the ground as if in the hopes of finding sustenance in the swampy earth. "Come here."

The chicken didn't so much as lift its head. So much for that idea. I even had my cantrip turned off, so my ears were on full display, but my elfin appearance didn't seem to encourage the bird to obey my commands. Probably it'd got used to the freedom after spending the night roaming around the Death King's grounds. Even the liches seemed to avoid it for some reason. Maybe it'd tried to bite one of them at some point. I'd crashed out as soon as I'd gone back to my room after my midnight shift and Ryan had practically had to break my door down to wake me for my second shift at noon, so I couldn't say I'd paid close attention.

"Try again," Trix said. "Get closer."

I reached out a hand, and the chicken bit me on the wrist. I bit back a yelp and stifled the impulse to conjure a warning flame to tell it not to screw with me. Mercifully, the neutraliser cantrip had also stopped working at some point in the night so at least I had my fire magic back.

Ryan laughed, and I shot them a glare. "Very funny. I'd like to see you try taming a vampire chicken."

"Most of us have more sense," they remarked. "I appreciate the free entertainment."

"I'm only here because I'm not allowed to move from this spot." I scowled at the chicken. "Do as I say."

"Ask nicely," said Trix. "Like this."

He approached the vampire chicken and dropped to one knee, whispering words I couldn't make out. The chicken waddled over to him, happy as anything, and let him stroke its feathered head. The elf made it look so easy.

"Now you try," he said.

I remained in a crouch and lowered my voice to a non-threatening whisper. "Come here."

The chicken didn't move. I suppressed my frustration and tried again. On the third try, the vampire chicken turned its head. *Yes. That's more like it.*

"Come over here," I said coaxingly.

The chicken approached at a waddle. I moved my hand in case it tried to bite me, but it halted placidly at my feet.

"Good job," said Trix. "You'll be riding that wyrm in no time."

"Maybe I should start with the zombie horse first." I looked around for Neddie. "If he bites me, I can test out my healing abilities, too."

All elves had some level of resilience, but I wouldn't mind knowing how much of mine came from my elf side and how much from the Family's meddling.

"Pretty sure you got in enough practise when you were blown up by the fire mages' inferno cantrips," said Harper, floating over to join us. "In case you've forgotten."

I pushed to my feet. "Wish I could use my healing skills on other people."

If I could, Tay wouldn't have died, but bringing another person back from the brink of death might be out of reach even for the elves. Besides, while I'd left the Akrith securely stored in the castle, I hadn't the faintest idea how to use it. After its spontaneous explosion on my flight from the Order, it'd remained dormant.

I turned back to Trix. "Have you spoken to Drina since last time?"

"I haven't," he said. "I went to look for the elf trader you mentioned, but I couldn't get near the Order. I don't know how Drina will react when I tell her one of the elves betrayed us."

"You're lucky you weren't caught," I said. "Would Drina know why the Akrith reacted to me the way it did? You said there was a chance it had more power inside it than the others?"

"I think it does," he said. "That's why it's a good thing that we got it away from the enemy. If the Family was able to find a living elven tree, then that Akrith would doubtless possess enough magic to allow them passage into our realm."

"Seriously?" My heart sank. "Why would an elf work against their own people?"

Trix's mouth pressed together, his unhappiness returning. "It shouldn't be conceivable."

"Maybe it's a one-off," said Ryan. "Most of the vampires probably don't understand why another vamp would work with the Order, either, but if the vamp in question is power-hungry like the dude who invented those lich-killing cantrips, then they might not give a toss what happens to the other elves."

"Not the elves," Trix said firmly. "We don't care about power. Not in the way humans or vampires do."

I had the impression it wouldn't be much use arguing with him on that point. "I can't say I know what his motives are, but he must be selling the artefacts to someone in particular, whether it's the actual Family or an intermediary. If we track him down, we might be able to thwart their attempts to get more of those Akriths. As a bonus, we'd find out what the Family said to convince him to join them."

It was a safe bet that we wouldn't be able to get away with another stealth mission to the Order, but the elf didn't work for them directly. He most likely lived here in the Parallel. Too bad we couldn't ask the vampires who'd run the auction, because I'd turned one of them to ashes and probably got myself blacklisted from Arcadia's auctions for life.

"He can't be local," said Trix. "I'd know if he lived in Arcadia, but I'll ask Drina if she can put word out among her contacts to track him down, unless you want to come with me to speak to her again."

"I'll have to wait for the Death King to let me off duty." At least we'd had no more incidents with lich-killing cantrips in the past day. Maybe the Family had been watching the situation at the Order instead.

Ryan shot me a frown. "Stop looking at me like that."

"Looking at you like what?"

"Like if you smile nicely enough, I'll agree to cover the

rest of your shift so you and Trix can go and pester the elves."

"This is my normal face." I folded my arms. "Just because you insist on glaring at everyone—"

"I'll take over your shift," said Harper.

"No chance," I said. "You know what those cantrips can do to liches."

"You think I'd let that happen to her?" Ryan said.

"I didn't imply you would." Damn, I was tired. I'd barely snatched a few hours of sleep in the past two days. We *really* needed to sort out the security situation at the castle. "All right, if you want to take solo guard duty while we go and visit Drina, then by all means, go ahead."

"I'd prefer you to wait until our shift's over so I can come with you," Ryan said, "but I'd rather not go near those plants again."

"Drina will be more likely to talk to Trix and me alone," I said. "Actually, I'm not sure she'll want to talk to anyone except Trix, but if we need some brute force, we know who to call."

"Fine," Ryan said. "Go on, before I change my mind."

"We'll be back later," Trix said to the Air Element. "Within the hour. Promise."

I waved goodbye to Harper, and then I followed the elf to the node. It wasn't like I didn't trust Ryan's skills, but the recent events had made me twitchy, and it was hard to guess where the next attack would come from. The Order, the vamps who ran the auction, their elven allies… but as usual, all the roads led back to the Family.

Once we were in Arcadia, Trix led the way to Drina's house again. I was prepared for her wild collection of plants this time around, but I had to walk sideways through the door to avoid getting speared by a particularly spiky one.

"Back again?" She stepped back to allow us to enter the room. "Good, you left your grumpy friend behind. Did you find what you were looking for?"

"Yes, but there's a slight issue," I said. "We had to chase down the vampire who won the Akrith at the auction, and he took sanctuary in the Order of the Elements' base while they waited for a trader to show up. I managed to cause a diversion—"

"I didn't ask for your life story," she said.

"The trader buying from the vampire was an elf," Trix said.

Drina stared at him for a heartbeat. "Impossible."

"It's true," I said. "I saw him myself."

"Why should I believe you?"

"Because *I* believe her," Trix said. "He was one of us, Drina."

She looked at me with surprise that mirrored my own. I couldn't deny I was startled at Trix's support, since we didn't know one another that well, but it said volumes for the elves' general loyalty towards one another. Maybe that was why Trix simply couldn't see an elf betraying the others, and Drina held the same viewpoint.

"If there's an elf trader aiding the enemy, they're bound to be easy to track," Trix continued. "Nobody else will want to be associated with them. As soon as we ask for their name, someone will tell us."

I doubted it would be that simple. "He might be based in Elysium. That's where the Family has the most allies."

Drina blew out a breath. "That's quite the trek. I can't

say I have any close friends over there either, but I can ask my contacts and see if they have anything to share."

"That would be appreciated," said Trix. "Bria, do you want to go look for the trader in Elysium?"

"I'm not entirely sure he's there, but it's worth having a look around." The Family hadn't been seen in Elysium since the battle with the Houses, but I wouldn't put it past them to get one of their illegal cantrip schemes off the ground again while my back was turned. With elven artefacts as an added bonus.

Besides, even if the elves weren't typically fond of power, the Houses definitely were. Maybe even enough to risk allying with the Family again.

10

In the end, I opted to go to Elysium alone. Perhaps it wasn't a wise idea, but it was about time I got over my reservations and spoke to the Houses again. Finding our elusive elf trader would be a bonus, but I'd wait for Drina to ask her contacts before I jumped to any conclusions. Despite the elves' obvious loyalty to one another, I couldn't discount the possibility that more of them might be working with the enemy.

The House of Fire's plain brick facade looked the same as it always did, not at all like it'd recently had its doors blasted or had been bombarded by so many lethal cantrips that the House had lost a huge chunk of their numbers. The door opened after I knocked, and I found myself looking up into a familiar face. Harris had survived, apparently, and was as flat-faced and greasy-haired as ever.

"You again?" he said. "Does the Death King want to ask another favour, by any chance? If he wants to volunteer to come and help us rebuild our headquarters, then he's welcome to."

"You wouldn't dare say that to his face," I said. "Besides, the fact that you locked up his Fire Element hasn't endeared you to him. Also, your headquarters look perfectly fine to me."

"Thousands of mages are dead," he snarled. "Thousands. How many did the Death King lose?"

I leaned back out of range of his stale breath. "Most of the Death King's people are *already* dead, in case you've forgotten. Anyway, have you seen any elves in the city lately?"

"Any *what?*"

"Elves. You heard me." This was probably unwise, but from the way my temper was rising, the odds of getting a second chance to talk to the Houses were plummeting by the second. "There's an elf suspected of being involved in trading with the Family. You know those illegal cantrips? That and worse."

"What does that have to do with us?"

"Zade worked with the family." I named the former jailor who Tay had killed to prevent him from bringing the enemy's forces into the Houses. Her plan had succeeded in the short term, but in the end, the enemy had wormed its way into the Houses' ranks anyway.

"And your friend killed him," he said. "I remember the sort of people you associate with."

"Look, you know perfectly well she was trying to save the city from a massacre that you could have prevented yourselves if your head wasn't jammed so far up your own arse that you haven't seen the sunrise in years," I snapped. "Get over yourselves and consider the bigger picture here. It wasn't just you who was under attack, it was the whole city, and it'd have been worse without the Death King's involvement."

"The Death King did nothing for us," he retaliated. "He let us get slaughtered."

"He was trying to keep his own people safe at the time," I said. "Besides, you turned down his offer of help. I tried to get through to you, countless times. Maybe if you'd accepted the offer instead of locking me in jail and treating me like a criminal, we wouldn't be in this mess."

His face flushed with anger. "You expected me to take you seriously after that speech?"

No, but it felt good. "I don't know why I bothered coming to talk to you."

In answer, he closed the door in my face. *That went well.* Shaking my head, I rounded the corner and debated checking in with one of the other Houses instead. Felicity had spoken to the House of Water already… and then there was the House of Earth, who'd dealt with the worst level of corruption in their ranks and were justifiably most likely to have links with the elf who'd betrayed the others. Then again, so were the illegal cantrip traders. Come to think of it, they might still be in the city. Miles would know.

Mind made up, I headed in the direction of the Spirit Agents' house. As I neared the street's end, the sound of shouting rang out from near the house. Then a blurred figure jumped down from the rooftops and another ran atop the fence circling the Spirit Agents' garden, both of them clad in dark clothing and carrying knives.

Assassins. It seemed the Family had already launched a

direct attack on the Spirit Agents. I sprinted around the corner towards them, fire igniting in my hands.

"Hey!" I yelled, taking aim with a bolt of flame, which knocked the nearest assassin off the fence before he could leap into the garden. He tumbled back and landed in a crouch, and I ran up and kicked his knife out of reach before he could grab it again. I caught up and slammed my foot into the back of his kneecap, prompting a shout of pain.

Then I went for the second guy, only for a blurred light to shoot out of the garden and slam into him. Several transparent spirit mages floated out of the house and shot spirit magic from their hands, knocking two startled assassins off the rooftops.

"Get away from our house!" Miles's voice sounded from nearby. I assumed he'd been one of the spirit mages who'd astral projected outside of the house to fight off the intruders. A wise idea, because it both kept him out of the line of fire and helped with his advantage over the attackers, who didn't have magic of their own.

A knife whipped past, missing me by inches. For an instant, my body froze as a thought sprang to mind, unbidden. *This is how Tay died.*

Anger sparked. I would not let the same happen to Miles or the other Spirit Agents. I spun in the direction the knife had flown from. A fireball grew in my hand, and I positioned myself in front of the fence around the property. If anyone tried to get close, they'd get caught in the inferno.

"They're running!" Shelley yelled from somewhere nearby.

Brightness shone as several bolts of spirit magic

knocked two of the assassins into the road. I shot a fireball at them from the inferno coalescing in my hands, and they fell back, writhing in pain. Tate, Shelley and Miles ran out of the house, chasing down the remaining interlopers, but it was obvious they'd got away.

"They'll be back," said Miles. "Dammit. We can't stay in the house now the Family has made an open attack on us."

"Come to the Death King's castle," I said. "Pretty sure there's room for all of you in there, and it's safer."

"No," said Shelley. "We've fought for this place for years. It's ours."

"I know we have," Miles said, "but they targeted us at home for a reason. Besides, everyone in the Houses already knows where we live, and it's not exactly a secret that we're opposed to the Family's bullshit."

"Exactly," I pressed. "I wouldn't want to give this place up either, but the Family only sends out those assassins when they mean to keep striking until you're dead. They'll send a new batch soon. They won't do anything to the house if you aren't there."

"I agree with her." Tate nodded to his sister. "We can come back when it's safe, right, Shelley?"

"All right," Shelley relented. "We'll stay in the castle, but only if the Death King agrees to pay our expenses."

"Will he go for that?" I asked Miles.

"Maybe, with conditions," Miles commented. "If there's something he needs from us... like more security guards, for instance."

"You think the Death King's going to ask us to take over guarding the castle?" said Shelley.

"I was going to volunteer anyway," said Miles. "Come on, look at the state of Bria. She needs some sleep."

"Do I really look that bad?" I pretended to sound insulted.

"Yes," said Shelley. "I know he only has the four of you on guard duty at the moment."

"In fairness, he didn't expect to be targeted by people who can kill what's already dead," added Miles. "We can help him out. We're all stronger when we're in the same place."

"Not to mention safer." They'd had a damn close call. If they hadn't been spirit mages, they might not have been able to drive off the assassins the way they had.

"Right." Shelley picked up one of the assassin's knives. "I'll keep this. Hard to get decent weapons these days."

"That's fair." Tate approached the house. "C'mon, everyone. We've gotta pack up and move. Only bring what you need, that clear?"

While Shelley went into the house to wrangle the spirit mages into packing up for their impromptu holiday to the Death King's castle, Miles walked over to join me. "You okay? I didn't know you were coming here."

"I went to see the Houses today, but it didn't turn out well."

He arched a brow. "You asked them to join the Death King?"

"Not exactly," I said. "Harris didn't let me get that far. In fairness, I may have yelled at him a bit."

"I imagine he deserved it," he said.

"I wanted to find out if the elf trader was here in Elysium or not, too," I explained. "He's likely to be working with the Family directly, and this is the closest city to their base. Harris didn't seem to know what I was talking about when I asked, though."

"I don't know that the Houses will have seen him," he said. "They wouldn't have any use for elf artefacts. Cantrips, they can always use."

"Speaking of cantrips, I thought Dawson might be able to give us a clue about the situation here," I said. "Or his assistant, if he's around."

"You mean if he's still alive," said Miles. "Given that he was here when those cantrips were infecting everyone and he's the reason they spread so far to begin with, I have my doubts."

"Whether he is or not, he was the one supplying the mages working with the Family with their illegal cantrips," I said. "Maybe it's worth finding out if he knows about their most recent plans. If not the elves, then the cantrip which showed up on the Death King's doorstep marked with the Family's signature."

"You aren't wrong," said Miles. "I doubt Dawson's still around, but we can see if anyone's moved into his place."

"Miles, are you coming?" Shelley walked out of the house with a backpack slung over her shoulder, two of the assassins' knives strapped to her waist. "If you two are gonna stand there nattering all day, we'll leave you behind."

"You go on ahead," Miles said. "Bria and I need to have a word with our former cantrip trader before we leave."

"All right," said Shelley. "You can come and grab your own stuff later when you come back. Also, you'll probably get the shittiest room at the castle by the time you catch up."

"That's fair." Miles began to walk away from the house. "Pretty sure there's only dorms for visitors at the castle anyway, not individual rooms. I doubt the Death King will be willing to donate his suite to us."

"You can always sleep in my room," I said, before realising what I'd implied. Not that I was averse to the idea, but Shelley's raised eyebrows told me I'd inadvertently opened myself up to questions I didn't want to answer at the moment.

Luckily, some of the others interrupted by coming out of the house carrying an array of bags and weaponry, talking loudly among themselves. Miles and I let them pass by, and I stole a glance at his face, which displayed no obvious reaction towards my comment. Deciding to come back to that later, I watched the others walk towards the node and then turned back to Miles.

"Are you absolutely certain none of Shawn's allies are hiding among the Spirit Agents?" I lowered my voice in case any stragglers overheard. "Because if they are, we're rendering the Death King's security measures useless by sending everyone into the castle."

"I know," he said. "It's a risk we'll have to take, if we want everyone to survive. We've lost too many people already."

I had to agree. "Do you think Dawson survived?"

"If he did, he hasn't tried to get in touch, not since we ambushed his assistant helping those earth mages."

"Either he's dead or he's lying low."

Considering Dawson had likely also known the Spirit Agents' address, it was a miracle they'd managed to stay in the city for so long after the battle without an open attack. While I couldn't quite dispel the lingering feeling that I'd been partly responsible for the assassins' arrival, the Spirit Agents had long been the Death King's allies and had even been betrayed by some of their own people as a consequence.

The last I'd seen of Shawn, Miles's former second-in-command, he'd been ditched by the Family amid a warehouse full of the corpses of the people they'd murdered after forcing them to carve illegal cantrips for their own use. I sometimes wished I'd killed him right there and then, but the guy was below average on the danger scale compared to our other enemies.

The last Spirit Agents vanished into the node in a flash, at which point Miles gave one last glance at the house and then turned away. "There won't be anything there the two of us can't handle, don't worry."

"I'm not." I fell into step with him as we walked. "Those cantrips, though? I hoped we'd seen the last of them."

"I think we have," said Miles. "If Dawson's alive, I guarantee he'll think twice about picking up dodgy cantrips again."

Admittedly, it'd been Dawson's apprentice who'd helped spread the cursed cantrips which had claimed hundreds of lives across the city, but I didn't believe Dawson himself was entirely innocent either.

Miles knew the way to the supplier's shop, which was a good thing, because I'd forgotten. The streets to the south of the Houses all looked the same, while the debris from the battle hadn't all been cleared away yet. While the Houses had cleaned up the streets around their own headquarters, Dawson's shop was in a sorry state and so was the surrounding area. Broken glass crunched underfoot, the windows were boarded up, and the door hung from its hinges. Not a good sign.

When Miles pushed the door inwards, we found an empty room waiting for us on the other side. "The cowardly knobhead ran off."

Nothing more than a few empty boxes on bare floorboards remained inside the shop. Even most of the furniture had gone, aside from a wooden table with burn marks from old cantrips etched deep into its surface.

Miles stepped inside. "Let's poke around and see if he left anything behind."

I didn't hold out much hope, but I circled the whole room and came to a halt behind the wooden table. A glint underneath caught my eye. Had he left a cantrip behind? I crouched down to look, and the ground stirred below my feet as though a tremor had passed under the surface. *Something's underground.*

Miles's alarmed gaze met mine. "Is that an earth mage?"

I rose to my feet, but not fast enough. The ground heaved, and a crack zigzagged through the wooden floorboards from one side of the room to the other. Another heave shook the walls, and something sharp and pointy appeared in the crack between the floorboards.

"Yeah, that's not a mage." Miles backed up to the door, but he'd been left on one side of the rapidly expanding crack in the floor while I was on the other. The crack expanded, revealing more and more sharp points until the distinct shape of a mouth full of teeth became visible.

"Wyrm." I shuffled back, trying to find an obvious escape route. Ah, damn. I'd have to jump over the crack in the floor to get to the exit.

Miles's eyes widened. "Bria..."

"Don't look down," I told myself. "Don't look..."

I jumped over the gap. Teeth snapped inches from my feet, and as I slammed down on the other side as its tail whipped up in a shower of dirt and splintered wooden boards. Miles snagged my arm, and we ran out of the door into the street.

The sounds of the beast thrashing about reverberated behind us. How it'd had the patience to lie in wait all this time, I had no idea. Either it'd been sleeping, or someone with unusually high influence over magical beings had ordered it to be quiet up until someone came into the shop.

Inspiration struck. Before I lost my nerve, I sprinted back to the open door and yelled at the beast. "Hey, you!"

The beast's head swung in my direction, its teeth closing on thin air as I sprang back to avoid its bite. Miles ran behind me. "Bria, what are you doing?"

"Testing a theory." I faced the wyrm, certain it must be the same one I'd previously encountered. I'd know if the Family had kept more than one of them on their estate. "Do you remember me? I'm Bria. You liked my friend, Trix, when you met."

Without taking my eyes off its sharp teeth, I reached for my pendant and turned off the cantrip hiding my pointed ears. The beast's head shook from side to side, displaying more confusion than anger.

"You don't have to attack us," I said. "You don't have to do anything they told you to. If you leave the city, you can be free. Fly far away from here..."

Miles's nails dug into my arm. "Bria..."

The wyrm let out a screeching cry and reared back, and I finally let Miles pull me out of range. A shower of dirt and wooden fragments erupted from the house as the beast slammed back into the ground. The resulting tremors echoed throughout the air, rocked the earth beneath our feet... but before we'd reached the street's end, I glanced back and saw that despite the growing cloud of dust, the wyrm hadn't come out to attack anyone in the city.

It'd gone back underground.

"I think it listened to me."

Miles's eyes were wide. "Since when could you mind-control a wyrm?"

"Trix taught me, but it's the first time I've tried it on a creature that size." I took a few hesitant steps towards the gutted shop. "I think it recognised me from before."

"Lucky it did." Miles overtook me, and then quickened his pace. "Look at that."

I caught him up outside the shop, where the wyrm's departure had exposed a large hole in the ground. Or rather... "That's a tunnel. It dug its way in."

Miles eyed the upturned soil. "Are you sure? That looks more like an earth mage's work."

So it did. If I looked past the mess the beast had made of the floorboards, the tunnel's edges were far too neat to have been made by a subterranean monster. I knew an earth mage's handiwork when I saw it.

I grinned. "Whoever did this, they've left us a direct route to their hideout."

11

Needless to say, Miles wasn't keen on taking a trip into the tunnel we'd found. "That beast is still underground, Bria. What if your spell wears off?"

"I'll cast another one." For now, I turned my cantrip back on, hiding my ears from sight. "Besides, it'll have headed for the nearest exit, which might take us directly to the person who dug the tunnel. I don't know about you, but I'd like to know if there are more of those rogue earth mages lurking underground."

Miles swore under his breath. "I don't like this, but you're right. Let me go in first."

I crouched beside the upturned earth and watched him lower himself into the hole in the ground before helping me climb down to join him. The wyrm had left a clear way into the tunnel open and we had to crawl at first, but we soon reached a wider tunnel with a high enough ceiling for us to stand in. Several earth mages could comfortably walk side by side, and while it looked like a couple of alternative routes had been closed off by barriers of earth, the main route led in the opposite direction from the cantrip store. We headed that way, relying on the dim light of a flame in my hands to illuminate our path.

"This is weird," I remarked. "I don't think this is one of the routes the earth mages used when they were spreading those cantrips around. It's too far south."

"We aren't underneath the Houses," Miles agreed. "I think we're going *away* from the main part of the city."

He was right. The tunnel was circuitous, but it headed in the opposite direction to the citadel and the Houses. "Then we'll see where it ends."

We walked in silence for a few minutes. The tunnel mostly took us in a straight line without any detours, but it showed no signs of coming to an end.

"Maybe I should have warned the Death King I'd be gone all day," I said after a while.

"At this rate, we'll end up in Arcadia," Miles said. "We've come too far to turn back, though. We'll have to follow the tunnel to the end, unless you have a shovel somewhere on you."

"I forgot to pack one," I said wryly. "This took some planning, though. They must have been digging these tunnels for days. Even earth mages can only go so fast."

"True," he said. "On the plus side, it confirms the people who dug this really didn't want to be followed out of Elysium. Which means whatever we find on the other side ought to be worth the time and effort."

All the same, the lack of any openings to the surface made me uneasy. Even with my elf speed, I'd tire out eventually, and Miles didn't have the same advantage. Just when I was about to suggest turning back and finding another way to track the tunnel to its end, a glint near my foot caught my eye.

"Hello, cantrip." I crouched down to examine the cantrip without touching it in case it turned out to be a cursed one left over from the battle... and spotted a familiar signature on the back.

"The Family," Miles said.

"I think we're close." I glanced at the packed earth ceiling. "Must be."

We walked for a few more minutes until natural light began to filter in from somewhere ahead, allowing me to extinguish the flame in my hand. Before long, an opening led aboveground, via a ladder. I checked for traps before climbing up to the surface.

Miles followed, shielding his eyes against the bright daylight. "Doesn't look like there's much out here."

"Doubt they'd leave their hideout in the open." I scanned the barren ground and spotted the shimmering lights of a concealment spell. Upon closer inspection, the spell covered a large area... a warehouse-sized area.

So this was where the illegal cantrips were being manufactured.

"This is the second warehouse." Miles whistled, the truth dawning on him. "That caved-in tunnel way back in Elysium... I bet that one led to the other warehouse near the citadel. The one the Family already abandoned."

"Then this one is probably still active." *But not for long.* I trod closer to the huge concealed shape of the warehouse. Glass and debris crunched beneath my feet, while the carcasses of smaller buildings lay in ruins all around us and an overall air of abandonment filled the surrounding area.

"This used to be a town," Miles said. "Or village."

"We aren't near the Death King's territory, I don't think."

I'd lived in the Parallel my whole life, but the sheer scale of the damage the last war had caused had always been a distant, abstract concept to me. Elysium, for all its flaws, had weathered the storm better than most towns and villages without any magical protections. While I'd spend years running from one abandoned house to another, dodging phantoms and other beasts which made their homes in the abandoned corners of the city... none of that compared to the expanse of devastated landscape stretching in all directions, without the towering shape of the Death King's castle as a landmark. Anyone who'd lived out here had fled to the cities, or they'd been trampled flat.

This is what the spirit mages did. What some of them are still trying to do, and the Family would be happy to help them do it.

"We don't have to go and confront whoever's in the warehouse yet," said Miles.

I dragged my gaze away from our dismal surroundings. "Huh?"

"If we find a node, then we'll be able to come back here at any time," he said. "Besides, I think we should plan an escape route before we walk inside that illusion spell."

"Good point." If the warehouse turned out to be booby-trapped, the only way out was to run back into the tunnels or out into the wilderness, and there might be hordes of monsters out there for all we knew. Besides, if the people inside had been imprisoned against their will like the ones at the other warehouse, I doubted we'd be able to herd everyone underground. Better to find a node instead. If the Family had picked out this area for a reason, there must be one nearby.

Miles and I trod around the flickering illusion surrounding the warehouse, and sure enough, I made out the shape of a current of bright energy within walking distance.

"Good," said Miles. "That's our way out."

With one eye on the node, I circled the illusion hiding the warehouse. Miles did likewise, and his foot scuffed against a cantrip hidden in a pile of rocks.

"That's our illusion." I gave a nod. "Okay. I'm ready."

Miles turned off the cantrip. An instant later, the large shape of the warehouse appeared out of thin air, occupying the entire area in front of us. Its smooth walls displayed no doors or windows, but I tilted my head, spotting another camouflage cantrip near the front wall. When Miles turned that one off, a door popped into existence.

Approaching, I tried an unlocking charm, and the door clicked open. Taking in a deep breath, I pushed the door inward.

Part of me was braced to find another massacre inside. Instead, rows and rows of people filled the space within the warehouse, standing at long wooden tables and carving cantrips with delicate tools. People with pointed ears, lank dark hair, and weary, elegant features.

"Elves," I murmured.

Miles swore under his breath. "This shouldn't be legal. But it's the Parallel, so…"

I stepped into the warehouse and took in each piece of the scene before us. At the very back of the warehouse, a large chunk of gold took up a sizeable amount of space, surrounded by a group of elves. The elves wielded tools which must have been brought straight from the Family's mines, chipping pieces of the golden substance away and throwing them into wheelbarrows. When each wheelbarrow was full, someone would wheel it over to a row of tables nearby where more elves were expertly chiselling the pieces of gold into perfect circular cantrip shapes. At the front of the warehouse, piles of newly chiselled cantrips lay on tables where the nearest group of elves etched runes onto the surface of each coin to turn them into spells.

The elf closest to me was doing the latter, and he didn't even seem to see or hear us as the carving tool twirled in his hand and he added the finishing touches to a sinister mark which I knew all too well. The elves were marking the cantrips with the Family's signature.

If ever I'd believed they were here voluntarily, that notion disappeared in a heartbeat.

"Hey." I addressed the elf. "Excuse me?"

The elf didn't look up. His face remained intently focused, his shoulders hunched in concentration. Dammit. The Family's brainwashing was in evidence, but how deep it ran, I wasn't entirely sure yet.

"Excuse me." I raised my voice a little. "Who hired you? Who brought you here?"

The elf continued to carve the cantrip's smooth golden surface, his movements graceful yet somehow robotic. A glance at his neighbour brought a similar impression. *The*

Family. They had their claws in everyone inside the warehouse.

"They aren't here," I went on. "You can talk to me. Who gave you orders?"

"I'm not supposed to answer questions," he said. "I can't."

Ah. Compulsion. Adair had been the one responsible, then. I glimpsed Miles standing by the door, watching with a horrified expression on his face.

The elf picked up another blank cantrip. His hands were trembling with fear, or exhaustion, and I knew I couldn't turn my back until I got through to him.

"We've come to get you out of here," I said.

"No!" His voice rose higher, yet the others still didn't look up. "You can't."

"Hey." I put on a soothing tone. "It's okay. Nobody is going to hurt you. I'll get you out."

"You can't." He shook his head violently. "We're under a spell. We can't leave."

"Was it a woman who told you not to leave?" I said.

"No."

Not Lex this time, then. As I'd thought. "Adair mind-controlled you, right? Did you know his orders have a time limit on them?"

His grip on the cantrip faltered. "What do you mean?"

"I can't give an exact time frame, but his mind-controlling ability only works for an hour, or so, and then resets when you next make eye contact with him," I said. "How often does he come here to give you instructions?"

"I don't know," he said. "Maybe once or twice a day. We're not allowed outside, so I'm not sure."

"That's not often enough to keep you under his spell

while he's not here," I said. "Trust me. I've worked around those limits before."

If I had to guess, Adair kept the elves captive by fear more than compulsion, which made more sense than the Family constantly keeping a close watch on them. Scumbags.

Miles stepped forward and addressed the elf. "What's your name?"

"Belgi," he said.

"I'm Miles," he said. "And this is Bria."

"We're here to help you in any way we can," I added. "Try to step away from the table. Put the cantrip down. You'll be fine."

"We can't leave," he insisted. "Not as long as his words bind us."

"What exactly did he tell you do?" I asked.

"To stay here until he came back," he said. "We're given specific times when we're allowed to eat, sleep or use the bathroom, but otherwise we're here around the clock."

"There aren't even clocks out here," I muttered under my breath. "Okay. I'm trying to think of a way to get around his orders. What would happen if someone took away your tools?"

"We'd get them back. Or find new ones. If none were available, we'd have to carve the cantrips with our bare hands."

Damn. Adair wasn't that smart, but he was following Lex and Roth's lead, and they thought of everything. Or so it seemed, anyway.

"When did he last come in?" asked Miles.

"I don't know," he said. "This morning."

That meant the odds were high that he'd be back

tonight, but not yet. If we wanted to get everyone out, we'd need to act fast, but not without somewhere to take everyone.

"Where did you come from?" I asked. "Arcadia?"

"No," said another male elf, who'd evidently begun to listen in on our conversation. "Our town is at the top of the hill across from here. He fetched everyone who could work and brought us all here."

My heart missed a beat. "You're all elves?"

"Yes," said Belgi. "Why?"

"Did…" I paused. "Did he mention he was looking for elven artefacts?"

"How did you know?" Belgi looked up from his carving at last, his piercing green eyes shining with desperation.

"Because that's what led us here," I said. "I know the Family are collecting the Akriths, and I think that's why they're targeting elves. Did he find anything in your town?"

"No. We lost all of our artefacts a long time ago."

He didn't seem surprised to hear such a question from me, but he averted his gaze and turned back to his carving. Was he telling the truth? I wouldn't blame him if he wasn't, considering he had no reason whatsoever to trust me with the knowledge of his people's artefacts… but if the Family had coaxed any information out of him, they were one step closer to their goal.

I reached for my pendant. "Look at me."

Then I turned off the cantrip, exposing my face. A dozen gasps rang out, while the elf in front of me stared openly. "You're… you're one of *them*?"

He sounded more fearful than surprised. Not the reaction I'd hoped for. "The Family? They'd like to think so, but no, I'm not. I'm working against them, and I'm here to set you free."

"And… him?" He indicated Miles, his gaze fearful.

"Miles is a Spirit Agent," I said. "He's also working against the Family. We aren't here to trick you, we're here to make sure the Family doesn't get hold of any more Akriths. If we can set everyone here free in the process, we'll gladly do so."

His mouth parted. "You know of their hunt for the Akriths?"

"I do," I said. "They've been sending people to Arcadia's markets to hunt them down. They even have another elf helping them, if you can believe it."

"Him." He gave a shudder. "He betrayed us. He gave away our location to *them* in order to save his own life."

Murmurs rose among the others, while Miles and I exchanged stunned glances. This was the last place I'd expected to learn anything of the elven trader who'd worked for the Family, but it made sense. It also explained how Trix hadn't known the elf's identity, if he belonged to a community which existed out here in the middle of nowhere.

"Do you… do you think there's a chance the Family might actually be able to pull off their plan?" I asked. "To get into the elves' realm, I mean?"

"No," Belgi said firmly. "Not a chance."

"They won't make it," Belgi said.

"How do you know?" Wariness hit me when I saw the sheer number of others listening in, but all semblance of keeping our plan quiet had vanished when we'd burst in here. "Are you sure?"

"Yes," he said. "Most of the Akriths currently circulating in the Parallel are fakes."

"Seriously?" I said. "I... I've only seen one of them, but it didn't look like a fake to me."

More whispers rose up among the elves, several of whom had stepped away from the table and abandoned their tools to listen to us instead.

Belgi's eyes widened. "You have one with you?"

"Not with me," I said. "But I can show it to you, if you agree to come with me."

He shook his head. "The others... I can't leave them here."

I moved closer to Miles and whispered, "We've got to get them all out. If Adair comes back, who knows what he'll do when he finds out we've been here?"

"Yeah, slight problem," said Miles. "We're in the middle of nowhere, and I don't think we're gonna be able to hide an entire warehouse of elves on the Death King's territory."

"What about their town?" It didn't sound like the Family had razed the place to the ground, but given their usual methods, I couldn't count on it being in one piece. Addressing Belgi again, I asked, "Do you have somewhere in the area you can hide? How close are we to your home?"

"Close," he said. "Our families... our children are still there. If we leave, they might suffer for our transgression."

My throat went dry. "I don't want to risk anyone getting hurt, but if managed to get my hands on a real Akrith, then the odds are high that the Family will have, too. That means they won't need the warehouse any longer. Did you hear what they did to the people who worked in the last one?"

Fearful murmurs came from among the other elves, hushing almost at once when a voice came from outside. A distinct shout. "Hey! Who the fuck turned off my spell?"

Crap. It looked like a certain someone had discovered his camouflage spell had been turned off. Sure enough, a moment later, the warehouse door opened a fraction and Adair's face appeared in the gap.

12

I didn't stop to think. Flinging myself underneath the nearest table, I saw Miles vanish in the same instant, presumably due to an invisibility cantrip. If Adair spoke a single word of command to the elves, everyone in here would end up under his thrall again, but he hadn't taken more than a step into the room before the clicking sound of a cantrip sounded and the whole warehouse was plunged into darkness.

Assuming Miles was responsible—Adair needed eye contact to use his power and Miles had been quicker on the uptake than I had—I wriggled out from underneath the table in time for an invisible Miles to catch my arm. "Was that you?"

"Darkness cantrip," he breathed in my ear. "Won't last."

"Can you get everyone out the back door if I distract him?" I whispered.

"Sure."

"Who the hell is trespassing in here?" Adair bellowed.

Silently thanking him for leading me to his location, I

ran alongside the table and put on a burst of speed before tackling Adair head-on. The element of surprise was on my side, and his legs gave way, carrying both of us through the open door. Cold air battered at our faces, while the darkness of the warehouse was replaced by an overcast sky.

"You again?" He shoved me off him. "How the hell did you find this place?"

I rolled to my feet. "If you put a giant wyrm inside a tunnel beneath a dodgy cantrip seller's store, I'm gonna assume it leads somewhere important."

Adair scowled. "You're too late. We won't need the warehouses for much longer anyway."

"And why's that?" If he planned to demolish the place, I'd see to it that he wouldn't get the chance to hurt anyone inside.

A smile curled his lip. "Because we have the means of getting to the elves, of course."

Shit. I did my best to keep my expression blank, but I couldn't confidently say that I believed every word Belgi had said. What if one of the Family's Akriths didn't turn out to be a fake? If I'd found a real Akrith, then perhaps they had, too. Whatever the case, I was out of ideas as to how to divert his attention from the warehouse while Miles helped the elves escape.

I faced Adair. "What are you waiting for, then?"

"Huh?" he said. "What's that supposed to mean?"

"You heard me," I went on. "If you're ready to ask the elves to join your cause, then why delay? Or are you scared they won't listen to you after all?"

A scowl appeared on his face. "I'm not scared of the elves."

"Then why are you avoiding them?" My wildly improvised plan might backfire in my face, but Adair seemed to have entirely forgotten the warehouse in favour of glowering at me. If I kept pushing, he might snap, but the more time I gave Miles to help the elves sneak out of the warehouse, the better. "You won't get very far if you spend all your time terrorising people in a warehouse instead."

His jaw tightened. "You dare to accuse me of being a coward, when you've spent the last few weeks hiding in the Death King's castle?"

"You wouldn't turn down the opportunity to live in a fancy castle if you were in my place, trust me." I supressed the impulse to check to see if any of the elves had made it out of the warehouse. They were far more vulnerable to Adair's magic than I was, and I wouldn't be able to protect all of them at the same time. If they didn't get away as fast as possible, they'd end up far worse off than they'd been in that warehouse. "I think you're bluffing. You don't have a way to reach the elves at all. Our adoptive parents helped see to that."

"That's where you're wrong," he said. "If you don't believe me, I can show you."

"Really?" He couldn't be telling the truth. Even if he did have a genuine Akrith with real power in it, I couldn't see how he could have possibly figured out how to use it. Besides, didn't he need a living tree in order to access its potential? I'd thought they all died.

"Yes, really." He snagged my arm and yanked me forward.

"Hey!" I squirmed, but his grip was hard as iron. He kept tugging, pulling me uphill, around the warehouse and up the cliffside at the back. Or rather, what had once been a cliffside. The illusion covering the warehouse had also masked a giant hole which had been blasted into the side of the cliff, revealing a large monolith within. The tower-like shape's snow-white colour stood out against its bleak surroundings, while I couldn't figure out what it resembled. Tall and thick, its arms stretched out in all directions, like...

Not arms. *Branches.* Bleached-white branches from a trunk made of stone. I never would have taken it for a tree from a distance, but up close, the shape was unmistakeable.

Adair's mouth curled in a smirk. "Turns out the elves were hiding one of their trees after all. It's dormant, but I know how to wake it up. Had to ask one of the elves first, but one of them was pretty talkative once I got him to tell me why he'd failed to bring us the Akrith from the market."

Nausea rose. "I knew the elf trader was working for you. What did you do to force him to betray his people?"

I doubted Adair had given him much of a choice. Sure enough, his smirk deepened. "His people owe him their lives. I'd have killed them much quicker if he hadn't agreed to help me. Anyway, I'm guessing you weren't foolish enough to bring the Akrith with you. Were you?"

When I didn't respond, he reached into his pocket and pulled out a gleaming stone. The same bleached-white colour as the tree, its surface glittered, and I didn't need to touch it to know it was as real as the one I'd held myself. *Shit.*

"Would Lex and Roth be happy if you ran off alone?" Damn, I'd thought he'd been bluffing.

"They don't have to know." He stepped towards the

tree, the stone lighting up in his hand. "I can't wait to see what the elves' all-powerful Elders think when they meet their new masters."

"You're deluded." I made a wild lunge for the stone, but he used one hand to restrain me, while the other pressed the glowing stone against the tree.

Brightness split the sky like a lightning bolt—or rather, a node. The blinding light made me screw up my eyes, and when I opened them a fraction, I found myself floating, my arm still firmly in Adair's grip. I'd have pulled away from him, except the ground was no longer beneath my feet and nothing seemed to be around us except for the tree, and the blazing light.

Then the light dimmed, revealing a path the colour of chalk or snow. It felt solid enough for me to step away from Adair, yanking my arm out of his, and I found myself looking uphill into a forest of bone-white trees.

This wasn't the Parallel. Certainly not a part of it I'd ever set foot in before, anyway. I'd never seen so many trees in one place, but they weren't anything like the ones on Earth. Every one of them was the same bone-white colour as the tree which had brought us here, while their sheer size indicated they were ancient, as though we'd stepped back in time to a world which had existed since long before our own.

Adair strode up to my side, staring at the path ahead as though unsure about what he was supposed to do next. "Anyone out there?"

"I thought you had a plan." I gave him a hard stare. "Go on. Prove you aren't a coward and lead the way into the creepy forest."

For the first time since we were kids, he looked uncertain, almost confused. But he wasn't about to let his sister bully him into submission, so he walked uphill, his hunched figure looking surprisingly small beneath the towering trees.

Silence shrouded us as I walked close behind him until the path opened up into a clearing edged with yet more of those strange, white-branched trees. I looked around, realising for the first time what unnerved me so much. Silence smothered the whole forest, while the trees' branches didn't sway in the breeze. Not a single leaf adorned them, as though they were frozen in time, and the silence…

"Is anyone out there?" Adair said.

A faint rustling sounded, raising the small hairs on my arms. Then three tall slender figures appeared, walking through the trees into the clearing. *Elves.* They couldn't be mistaken for anything else. With their pointed features, dark hair and light brown skin, they might have been related to one another… or to me. Their graceful movements reminded me of Trix, but they wore clothing made of something tough that resembled leather, their weapons hewn from branches rather than metal.

They spoke. For the first few seconds, their voices blurred to a dull hum, and then the words began to filter through the part of my brain not frozen with shock.

The first elf, a male wearing dark green armour who looked no older than me, stepped forward and said, "Have you come to claim sanctuary?"

The words were clear to my hearing, but not English. They were speaking the language of the elves: a language that Adair and I had both been taught as children, but I'd never expected to have to use in reality. Even the elves rarely spoke it these days—or rather, in the Parallel they didn't. Here, though, it seemed to have survived.

Not that I had the faintest idea how to respond to his question. Alarm flickered inside me when Adair recovered first and swaggered towards the other elves, speaking fluently in their language. "No. I'm here on behalf of the Family. I want to talk to your Elders. You're going to take me to them."

"Don't—" I broke off as the elves closed in around him. Doing, in fact, the opposite of what he'd commanded. Had his abilities somehow not worked on them? The language barrier couldn't be responsible. Adair's powers worked no matter what language he spoke.

"Get out of the way," said Adair, his voice wavering a little.

Instead of moving an inch, the elves spoke to one another, too fast for me to make out the words. Then one of them grabbed Adair by the arms and dragged him out of sight in a blur of movement, vanishing down a nearby path.

Holy shit.

I stared at the remaining elves for a moment, too shocked to move, until they turned to me next. "Ah... I'm not with him. He's not my ally."

I hoped I'd remembered the right words, and my chest tightened when the male elf in the green armour stepped towards me. "You're *Vetren?*"

"I'm what?" I echoed.

"You speak our language," he said. "But you're not..."

He and the other remaining elf exchanged glances and more words which I didn't understand.

"I'm not with him." I pointed in the direction Adair

had been taken in. "He's here to make trouble, but I'm not. I can leave. Or I would, if I knew how to get out."

"You're *Vetren?*" said another elf, this one female. She spat out the word as if it meant something unpleasant.

"Sorry, I don't know what that means," I said. "I'm half-elf, if that's what you mean."

"No," she said. "*Vetren* means you belong to *them.*"

"The Family?"

The male elf lunged at me without warning, and his fingers clenched around my arm. I bit back a startled yell of pain, but I couldn't break out of his grip. He was too damn strong, pulling me across the clearing and down a path between the trees, the same way the other elves had removed Adair from sight.

"What are you doing?" I couldn't break his grip no matter how hard I tried, but he didn't deign to answer my question.

The female elf from earlier walked alongside us, while I struggled to force down my panic. If I could get him to understand why I was here, I might have a chance of making sense of this situation. I'd explain that Adair had come here on an ill-advised mission to prove his superiority and got himself captured for it, but that I hadn't condoned his plan. I might have to skip over the part where I'd goaded him on, but how was I to know he'd had a genuine way of getting into the elves' realm, much less that he intended to use it?

Damn that trader. He was the one who'd given Adair the information he needed, yet the elves had got the upper hand on him anyway. If they were ready to pay him back brutally for his intrusion, I only hoped I didn't end up suffering the same punishment as he did.

The elves quickened their pace, then slowed as we reached another clearing surrounded by short trees. Between each tree, interlocking branches formed cages.

"Hey," I said, as the female elf seized my other arm, too. "Listen to me. I'm not your enemy."

Ignoring my words, they pushed me towards the nearest cage of interlocking tree branches, all of which were the same bone-white colour as the surrounding trees. When they stepped away, the branches closed over the entrance to the cage, leaving no way for me to climb out. Somewhere nearby, I heard Adair yelling, presumably from a separate cage to mine.

I'm gonna go out on a limb and say that wasn't how he wanted things to turn out.

The two elves departed without a word, while I paced on the spot, estimating that the cage was bigger than the cell I'd had when I'd been locked up in the House of Fire… but that didn't make it less of a cage.

I sat down on the forest floor, unable to believe I'd got myself imprisoned in the elves' realm of all places. What was Miles doing right now? Had he managed to help the elves in the warehouse get to safety? He'd been gone for so long that the Spirit Agents might have been worried enough to follow him, but they'd never find their way here. Even the Death King and the Elemental Soldiers wouldn't know how to reach us.

As much as I wanted to talk to the elves and find out how they'd survived this long without anyone being able to reach them, I needed to get back home. Did the elves even know who the Family was, much less the horrors that threatened the Parallel at the moment?

They called me Vetren, whatever that means. They said it

meant I'm with them... the Family... but they can't have met them before. Can they?

Several minutes passed before my captors returned. This time, they brought a third elf with them. He looked surprisingly old for an elf, with shoulder-length dark grey hair and deep green eyes the crisp colour of the kind of forest I'd only seen in pictures.

"So this is the one." He looked at me with an odd curiosity in his gaze. "The *Vetren.*"

"I'm Bria," I said. "I'm half elf, and I came here by accident. What is a *Vetren,* anyway?"

"Do you have any idea what you are?" said the older elf. "I don't think you do."

"I get that it means something to do with the Family, but I've never heard the word before," I said. "What does it mean?"

"It means *abomination,*" he said. "It means they gifted you with our skills using something they stole from us."

"What?" My blood iced over. "I don't know what you're talking about. What did they steal?"

The elf's gaze flickered to my pointed ears. "They stole our artefacts and corrupted our magic to make themselves immortal. And they used the very same magic on their children."

I shrank away, numb with disbelief. "No..."

"Yes."

Then... then Lex and Roth *had* already been here to the elves' realm. They must have found the elves a long time ago, taken away their artefacts, and used them to give themselves the unique powers they'd always pretended to have come by naturally. I'd known for years that they'd experimented on Adair and me, but I'd assumed they'd used cantrips. Not that they'd stolen from the elves and used their magic to turn us into *abominations* that even the elves would never accept.

"I didn't know," I whispered. "I—it's not like they *told* me. I thought I was half elf, and that's where my magic came from."

I *was* half elf, but that wasn't where all my magic came from. With the obvious exception of my fire magic, which I'd inherited naturally, my magic had been pushed upon me at the expense of others. A fuzzy sensation settled in my chest as though a scream rattled inside my lungs, demanding to escape—but what would be the point? While I was stuck in this cage, I couldn't do a damn thing.

The group of elves turned around and walked away without another word, leaving me with no company but the sound of Adair's shouting. I ought to be grateful that they'd imprisoned us separately, or else it wouldn't have been pretty. Neither of us could kill the other, not permanently. Another quirk that came from the elves' stolen artefacts.

No wonder the elves thought we were both abominations.

I sank into a sitting position and buried my head in my hands. I couldn't stay here and accept my fate, but the elves' anger towards my family was justified. Even towards Adair, though he hadn't been responsible for what Lex and Roth had done, because he'd come here looking for a fight. It was safe to say he hadn't foreseen being bested by the elves himself, but what if Lex and Roth followed him, searching for their son? They'd come here before, and I was willing to bet they hadn't left without blood on their hands. If Adair knew how to get into this realm, then it was a safe bet that they did, too. If they had another working Akrith, it was only a matter of time before they figured out where he'd gone.

Adair's shouting dimmed and I heard the three elves' voices in the background again. Adair's indignant grumbling followed. So they'd gone to speak to him, perhaps to confirm his reasons for being here. I rose to my feet and paced in circles around the cage, fighting the urge to shout and draw their attention.

When they stopped talking to Adair, I heard their footfalls coming towards my cage again. As the three elves came into view, I faced them through the interlocking branches.

"I'm sorry." I didn't know what else to say. "I didn't know the Family stole your artefacts, but I'm not working with them. I never have been."

"What makes you think we're willing to believe a word you say?" said the younger male elf. "The other man in the cage over there meant to dominate us. He admitted it."

"Can't I speak for myself?" My voice cracked. "I know what you think of Lex and Roth, but I'm not their biggest fan either. They raised me to be their soldier and they used me to further their ambitions to gain power over the entire Parallel. When I found out, I ran away from them and tried to kill them, but they can't die."

"Yes, they can."

My mouth went dry. "They what?"

"They can die," he repeated.

No way. The elves knew how to kill Lex and Roth?

"If they can die, then why hasn't anyone killed them yet?" I asked. "I thought they used the artefacts they stole to make themselves immortal."

The older male elf gave me an appraising look. "You really don't know."

"Of course I don't," I said. "Lex and Roth killed my birth parents, burned my home, and raised me to believe they were the only family I had. They lied to me for years, but the moment I realised what they were doing, I incapacitated them and had them imprisoned by the mages. I've done nothing but try to avoid them since then, but they're cunning. They broke out of jail and came after me, and now they're after you, too."

"If you're telling the truth, then why did you come here with *him?*" queried the female elf.

"He was threatening my friends and boasting about how he knew how to get here," I said. "I didn't know he'd found one of your trees. I thought he was lying. He proved me wrong."

"Really." The older male elf's voice was flat, disbelieving, but the other two exchanged whispers behind my back which sounded more curious than angry.

Despite myself, a flicker of hope stirred within me. They know how to kill the Family. Too bad they hated Adair and me so much they'd sooner leave us both to rot in these cages than offer us any help. How could I possibly prove I was on their side? I didn't even know how to get back to the world I knew from here, much less contact Trix or someone else who might speak up for me. Besides, I didn't know what they thought of the elves in the Parallel who'd been left behind. Maybe they hated the lot of them. I'd have to try another route instead.

"I need to get back," I said to them. "My friend Miles and I—we freed a group of elves the Family had imprisoned in a warehouse, and if we don't go back and make sure they get away safely, the Family will kill all of them. They're the reason I was trying to divert Adair's attention."

"You freed a group of elves?" said the older male elf.

"Yes, I did," I said. "That guy in the cage over there used his mind-control abilities to force the inhabitants of an elven town to carve magical cantrips for the rest of the Family to use. My friend and I set them free, but I had to distract Adair and I didn't expect him to open a way into your realm."

I'd smudged the facts a bit, but it wasn't like Adair could challenge my accusations without making himself look even worse than he already did. Besides, all I'd done was attempt to fix the damage he'd done.

The female elf looked at me for a moment. "I'll be back. Don't move."

As if I could go anywhere. Still, I forced myself to stay calm, waiting for her return. When she strode back into view, she addressed the other two elves. "The other man seems to back up her story. It seems she was trying to free a number of other elves from that man's control when he opened the way into this realm. He used the magic of the *Vetran* on the elves to force them to do his bidding."

"Is that true?" asked the older male elf.

"It is," I said. "My friend and I were trying to help the elves get out of the warehouse before Adair showed up, but I'm worried that the rest of the Family might have caught them while we were gone. They killed the last people to defy them. I don't know what they did to you, to your realm, but I promise, I'm not on their side."

The older male elf gave a slow nod and gestured,

causing the branches to part in front of me. "Come with us."

Relief spread through me. They believed me, at least partly. As I stepped out of the cage, the younger male elf jabbed me in the spine with his weapon, urging me to walk in front of him. Okay, maybe they didn't all trust me, but I was willing to work with that.

13

The elves led me deeper into the forest of bone-white trees. It hit me that if I got away, I'd have a hell of a time finding my way back to the path I'd originally come from, but that was assuming the elves would ever let me go. Firstly, I had to convince them of my innocence.

Our group came to a halt inside another clearing, where the older elf took a seat on a carved tree stump, joining a second elf, this one female, who sat on an identical stump. A waterfall of silver hair fell to her waist, and her pointed features were similar to the man beside her, suggesting they were the same age. Then it hit me that the twin carved tree stumps they sat on looked awfully like… thrones.

"You're the elves' leaders." Was I supposed to bow or curtsey or something? It wasn't like I'd been prepared for this moment, especially after my capture.

"We are the Elders," said the female elf. "I am Elder Datra, and this is Elder Veksis."

Elder Veksis studied me from his throne. "I have confirmed she is entirely ignorant of our kind, which puts us in a difficult position."

"Really?" said Elder Datra, addressing me more than the man at her side. "Explain to me why you are here."

"I was raised as human," I began. "By two people who wanted me to forget I was anything other than theirs."

"My guards told me of your enmity with that man who accompanied you here." Elder Veksis said, indicating the other two elves who'd accompanied us here. "Yet you have the same magic he does, and I recognise its source."

"I didn't know," I said. "Until you told me, I had no idea where my magic came from. I assumed it came from being half elf and half human, but I didn't know the Family stole anything from you. They told me nothing about the elves at all, nor that they'd ever been to your realm."

"Yet you found your way here anyway," said Elder Datra. "Why did you come here, if not to finish the work those two despicable individuals started many years ago?"

"I came here to stop Adair—he's the other man who was with me—from attacking you," I explained. "*He* came here for the purpose of either killing you or recruiting you to help him and the rest of the Family take over the Parallel."

"From what I've heard from that man, she's right," added the female elf who'd accompanied me here. "He came here to threaten us. She followed in an attempt to stop him. But she's still his kin."

"She claims to have reneged the *Vetren's* claim on her and attempted to take their lives," said the younger male elf from behind me. "I have yet to see any evidence to back up her word."

"I apologise for what the Family did to you," I said. "I want to stop them in their quest for domination over the Parallel if I can."

"What is it you want from us, then?" said Elder Datra.

I hadn't said I wanted anything, but perhaps she'd read the desperation in my face anyway. Present dilemma aside, they'd hinted at knowing how to kill Lex and Roth … permanently. I wasn't likely to find a means of ridding the Parallel of their depravity anywhere except for here.

On the other hand, I had a more pressing matter at hand. "The Family captured an entire town of elves in the Parallel and forced them to make weapons for them to use. I was in the middle of helping my friend to free them before Adair caught up to me, but I'd be grateful if you could let me go home."

"They captured other elves?" Anger rang through Elder Datra's voice.

"They did," I said. "My friend and I tracked down their hiding place and set them free. Adair forced them to work for the Family, since he has the ability to mind-control anyone…"

But not the elves in this realm. His powers hadn't worked on them. Why? Because they were stronger than he was? Trix had mentioned the elves' magic was stronger in their own realm, which made it a logical conclusion to draw, but I didn't quite dare hope they might be able to fend off Lex and Roth's magic in the same manner.

"He will stay caged until we devise an appropriate punishment," said Elder Veksis. "And you…"

"I need to go home." I fought to keep the panic from

my voice. "I didn't lie. I need to help those elves, and afterwards, I want to take a stand against the Family. As for whatever they stole from you, I might be able to figure out how to get it back if you tell me what it is."

"That's not possible," said Elder Veksis. "The *Vetren* would have seen to it that nobody could steal it back."

"Elder Veksis." Elder Datra turned to him. "Our Akrith must be intact. They wouldn't be able to retain their immortality otherwise."

My heart began to beat faster. "If they do still have it, then I know the way around their hideout. I've been there before. Is the Akrith they stole the same as the others of its kind?"

Elder Veksis gave me an appraising look. "The Akrith they took belonged to the Elders—that is, to Elder Datra and myself—and is to my knowledge the strongest of its kind. When it was removed from this realm, the consequences were vast. Our other artefacts began to lose their power. Our trees were reduced to a dormant state. I imagine the impact was even worse for the elves who lived outside of our realm, but since our Akrith was taken… we have been unable to return to the Parallel."

My throat went dry. *That's what they used on Adair and me… and to make themselves immortal.* They'd had the nerve to steal the Akrith belonging to the Elders themselves? Was *that* what had cut off their realm from the Parallel, preventing anyone from leaving this realm to take back what had been stolen from them?

The depth of what the Family had done to them rendered me speechless for a moment. I sought a path through the tangled array of thoughts in my mind to form a coherent sentence. "I've never seen it. I don't think. But I know their house, and I meant it when I said I can help you get it back."

"Why should we believe her?" insisted the male elf who'd brought me here. "If we follow her into the ruins those abominations made of our former home, we'll be without our protections against any foul traps they concoct against us. They'll slaughter our people just like they did in the past."

Damn. I hadn't known leaving their realm would deprive them of their magical advantages. While I'd confirmed how they'd got the upper hand over Adair, it lowered the odds of them being able to join us in the battle. Yet I couldn't see any scenario where I walked into the Family's home alone and retrieved the Akrith without ending up behind bars once again.

"I'm not working alone," I told them. "I'm working for the Death King, and he's willing to help you, too."

Elder Veksis rose to his feet. "You're working for *whom?*"

"The traitor to the House of Spirit?" said Elder Datra.

Shocked whispers passed between the two messengers behind me amid a ripple of hostility which spread among the elves. With his weapon in hand, the younger male elf took a step closer to me. "You dare admit to working with the mages who drove us out of our homes?"

Huh? "The Death King hasn't been in power that long. Who was in charge of the Court of the Dead the last time you saw them?"

I wasn't sure how long they'd been cut off from the Parallel, but the Death King had only been in charge for ten years or so. I was pretty sure it wasn't possible for him to have done anything to the elves, considering their realm had been out of reach for the entire time in which he'd been their leader.

"What is the name of current Death King?" demanded Elder Veksis, ignoring my question.

"He—uh," I stammered. *Shit. What was his name again?* Miles had told me... "Grey... Greyson something."

"That's not him," said Elder Datra. "The traitor must have been ousted from his position. More's the pity."

"The new Death King stands in opposition to the Family and is seeking an alliance with any elves who are willing to help us fight against them," I said. "That doesn't have to include you, but he's no enemy of yours and neither am I."

"The Death King is opposing the *Vetren?*" said the female guard behind me.

"Yes—along with their allies," I said. "There's a group of vigilante spirit mages who formed an alliance with the Family and are trying to start another war, and they'd be more than happy to wipe out anyone who opposes them. That's why they captured elves to make weapons for them. It's also why they planned to come here. Now you have Adair held prisoner, it wouldn't surprise me if they came looking for him."

This time, the elves' hostile whispers weren't directed at me. The two messengers exchanged urgent mutters, while the Elders rose to their feet.

"We will need to discuss our options among ourselves," said Elder Veksis. "But you will not be punished."

"I—thank you," I said. "What should I tell him? The Death King?"

Elder Datra looked me over. "Go to the Death King and tell him that if he offers us a guarantee of his protection, we will consider accepting his offer of aid. If the *Vetren* come here in search of their son, they will not find themselves unchallenged."

"I'll tell him." Gratitude swept over me. "Thanks again."

Now I just needed to find the way out. The Akrith Adair had used to open the way to this place had disappeared, but I assumed they'd confiscated it from him when they'd taken him captive.

The male messenger elf exchanged a few words with the Elders, then beckoned to me. "This way."

I followed him, keeping a wary eye on his carved bone-white sword. I'd never seen an elf carrying a weapon made of wood before, but it made sense that the elves here would have made their own weapons from their available resources after so long of being isolated from the Parallel's resources. Besides, it looked as strong as a metal sword. Given the magical properties of their trees, it was probably stronger.

The elf pulled out the gleaming Akrith as he halted in the middle of the path. "This will take you home."

"Will I be able to return to your realm?" I asked. "Would I have to find another Akrith and bring it back to the tree I found?"

"Yes," he said tersely.

I hope the Akrith is still where I left it, then. I'd locked the elven stone inside the securest part of the Death King's castle, but knew what might have happened while I'd been gone? I'd better hope the tree was still standing, if nothing else, but if it was the only one of its kind, the Family needed it to follow Adair.

If they'd already found the warehouse abandoned and

Adair missing... then I might find myself in a world of trouble when I returned.

Miles. I need to get back to Miles and the other elves. Figure out the rest later.

I drew in a breath. "I'm ready.

The elf held up the stone. Light flooded the area, and then the ground vanished below my feet. A moment later, I touched down on barren ground at the foot of the towering elven tree. Its branches extended to either side, touching the walls of the newly created cave which had been unearthed in the cliffside behind the warehouse. Nobody had turned the illusion spell back on, so the large blocky building remained in front of me. I trod around the side, heart thudding against my ribcage, and peered through the slightly open front door into the gloomy interior.

Nobody was inside. That was a good sign, right? Miles's plan must have worked, while the Family had yet to come here in search of their son. *Yet.*

After a quick search of the surrounding area, I found my way to the node and stepped into the current, picturing the swampland in my mind's eye.

A moment later, I landed in front of the fence circling the Death King's castle, spotting a skeletal horse padding along the swampy ground.

"Neddie?" I walked towards him. "Hey. Good to see a familiar face."

When I got too close, the horse snorted and tried to headbutt me in the ankle. I gave him a stern look. "Stop that."

He stopped in an instant, letting out a huff of surprise. He'd actually done what I told him? I grinned, more delighted than I had the right to be, but I couldn't help feeling a sudden rush of euphoria. Adair was imprisoned, the elves had set me free, and I'd successfully met the Elders face to face without ending up being punished for the Family's crimes. Even better, they might be willing to agree to work with the Death King and help me finish off the Family for good. Part of me—the part which had devised my three rules for survival in the Parallel—knew it wouldn't be as simple as all that, but it was hard not to feel a rush of dizzy joy when I approached the gates and saw who was on guard duty.

Miles stared at me as though I'd risen from the grave before his eyes. Then he ran over and hugged me so tightly I couldn't breathe.

"I thought you were dead," he said, his voice muffled. "Thank the Elements... I thought you were *dead*."

"You know I'm hard to kill, right?" I hugged him back, then relaxed my grip, aware of the mud caking my clothes and Shelley staring at both of us from the other side of the gates. "You saw me go into the elves' realm, right?"

"I didn't," he said. "I was too busy trying to help the elves get out of that warehouse and hide from that scumbag Adair. Once I got them out, I ran back to where I last saw you, but you and Adair were gone. Nothing was left behind except for that tree. I figured it'd played a role in your disappearance, but there were no signs of either of you left."

"What happened to the other elves?" I asked. "Did you manage to get them to safety?"

"Yeah, their old town was more or less intact, but I didn't dare stick around in case the Family followed me," he said. "I thought Adair was preparing to follow them, but when I didn't find him, I wondered if he'd taken you hostage instead. I was sure you must be alive, but I've been going mad with worry the last few days."

"Few days?" I asked. "It's only been a couple of hours, if that."

"Not for me." Wonder entered his expression. "It's been three days since you vanished, Bria."

I gaped at him. "How is that even possible?"

"I was hoping you could tell *me* that," he said. "Is the elves' realm on a different time zone or something? Shit, I can't believe you were really there."

"The elves' realm isn't linked to Earth the same way the Parallel is, so maybe it doesn't follow the same clock," I said. "I didn't know time was that far out of sync, though."

No wonder the elves didn't seem to know what was going on in the Parallel, if they'd been unhinged even from the regular passage of time. They didn't know we were on the brink of another war, or that so long had passed since the last one… and it was all the fault of the people who'd taken their artefacts and severed the links between our realms.

Shelley cleared her throat. "Why don't you ask someone else to take over guard duty if you two want to catch up? Because a horde of revenants might have lumbered in behind you right then and you wouldn't have noticed."

"I will," said Miles. "Come on, Shelley, she went to the *elves'* realm. This is big news."

"Tell me everything once you've caught up," she said.

"Of course." Miles didn't let go of my hand as we

walked through the gates, at which point he called over Tate, Shelley's brother, to take over his shift.

"Hey, is Bria alive?" Tate goggled at me.

"Looks that way," I said. "I'm fine. I just need to—"

"Come on." Miles dragged me into an alcove near the castle. "I know the other Spirit Agents and the Elemental Soldiers want to hear from you—not to mention your boss—but I want you all to myself for a bit."

"That's fair." I grinned, happy beyond measure to be back at his side again. "I didn't get hurt or anything. I'm fine. The elves were a bit more hostile than I expected at first, but I managed to convince them I wasn't on Adair's side."

"I'm surprised there's anything left of their realm," he said. "Considering everything I heard from Belgi and the other elves when I helped them move back to their town. They made it sound like their realm was permanently cut off."

"It was, but I'm assuming they were responsible for taking care of that tree the Family unearthed behind the warehouse," I said. "If you use a genuine Akrith—one that contains a lot of power—then it can react to the tree and cause it to open a way back into their realm. I know that guy at the warehouse said there were a lot of fakes, but Adair's worked. He dragged us both into the elves' realm, and once we were there, I couldn't get back until they let me go."

Miles nodded slowly. "Makes sense that it would take a hell of a lot of power to reopen a path which has been closed for years. Question is, why haven't the elves been able to come back to this realm? They must have plenty of their own artefacts, right?"

"They do, but..." I paused for a moment, then ploughed on. "The Family took the Elders' Akrith. The most powerful of its kind. When they removed it from the elves' realm, it had side effects, including draining the power from their other artefacts, and I'm pretty sure that's the reason they've never been able to return to the Parallel. The guy who brought me back had to use Adair's Akrith to open a way through."

His brows shot up. "The Family stole from the Elders? *They're* the reason the elves' realm was cut off from this one?"

"It gets worse." The words jammed in my throat, but I forced them out. "Turns out the Elders' Akrith is what they used to make themselves immortal and to give Adair and me our own abilities. I assumed they used cantrips to do it, but no... they stole from the elves instead. The elves call them *Vetren*—abominations—and they deserve it, because everything they did was a result of the magic they stole. Including me."

"They *what?*" His eyes widened. "What the hell did they do to you?"

"They stole the Elders' Akrith," I repeared. "Lex and Roth used its power on themselves, *and* they forced it on Adair and me when we too young to remember. That's what gave us our resilience and probably some of our other skills, too. It's why we're so hard to kill... but I found out it's not impossible. The Family *can* be killed."

He blinked, a slightly dazed expression on his face. "Holy shit, Bria. Are you sure you haven't been gone that long? Wait, where's Adair? Is he dead?"

"He's locked up in a cage in the elves' realm," I said. "Let's just say his plan backfired on him. I can't get back without another Akrith, but I think the one I took from that dude at the Order was real. It wouldn't have defended me if it wasn't."

Miles gave a low whistle. "Damn. Lex and Roth won't be pleased when they find out."

"Haven't they come back to the warehouse yet?" I asked. "If it's been three days, you'd think they'd be a little concerned about Adair's absence."

His mouth parted. "Not that I'm aware of. I've been back to check on the elves a couple of times and I haven't seen them yet. Granted, I've been spending most of my time on guard duty. The Death King has us trading shifts in exchange for letting us stay in the castle. Shelley volunteered me for back to back guard duty while you and I were at the warehouse."

Oops. In fairness, I hadn't planned on us spending hours traipsing through an underground tunnel, nor had I intended to rescue a warehouse of elves and then get myself transported to another realm.

"Did I miss anything else?"

"Hawker went after the Order." Miles grimaced. "Not sure what's going on over there, but the Death King and Liv have been run off their feet."

"But the Family… they haven't attacked the Death King?" I frowned. "They haven't even gone looking for Adair when he's been missing for days?"

They wouldn't have let their beloved son get kidnapped, would they? Admittedly, it wasn't the first time they'd left him in jail as punishment for the mistakes he'd made. When he'd got himself caught by the House of Fire and then transferred to the Death King's jail, they hadn't intervened, and he'd had to free himself without any input from them. On the other hand, they couldn't possibly have known their quick-tempered son had opened a path into the elves' realm in a fit of hubris unless they'd gone back to the warehouse. Which they hadn't. Right?

"I have no idea what they're up to," he said. "I think Adair might have been telling the truth when he said they didn't need the warehouse any longer. It's Hawker who holds all the lich-killing cantrips now. He's the one with the vendetta against the Death King."

"I just hope the elves have got over theirs," I said. "From what I heard, the previous Death King was a bit of a prick to them."

"The elves said that?" he said. "Yeah... I can't say I knew the guy, but it fits with what I heard from Grey."

"It was lucky I remembered his name," I added. "Otherwise I might have ended up speared to death."

"Damn." He whistled. "The elves aren't as mild-mannered as that elf friend of yours, are they?"

"We're in need of powerful allies," I said. "But the elves want a guarantee of protection from the Death King before they make their decision of whether to help in the war or not. I need to get that first, but it shouldn't be a problem for him, right?"

"Well..."

His slight pause made my heart miss a beat. "Shit. He's not mad at me for disappearing, is he?"

"Not yet," he said. "Like me, he assumes you're dead or unavailable."

Ah. "Then I'll have to tell him otherwise."

14

I walked into the castle's entrance hall, not expecting the Death King to show up right away. It wasn't like he knew I was coming, after all. But when I passed the entrance to the hall of souls, he walked into view with his human face on and his usual armoured clothing covering him from head to toe. I found myself glad I'd remembered his real name, Greyson, because I might have ended up in serious trouble with the elves if I hadn't.

"Bria." The Death King studied me. "So you *are* alive. I was beginning to wonder."

"I am," I said. "Sorry I disappeared. I went to the elves' realm, and it turns out time doesn't work in the usual way over there. For me, it's only been a couple of hours since I left."

"Tell me everything," said the Death King.

Once again, I ran through my experiences in the elves' realm, including Adair's ill-fated attempt to challenge them and his subsequent imprisonment, along with my conversations with the Elders and the Family's role in cutting off their realm from the Parallel. I didn't share the details of what the Family had used the Akrith they'd stolen to do to me, figuring he could read between the lines if he needed to. Our priority was getting him to agree to meet with the Elders before the Family realised I'd returned from the elves' realm and Adair had been left behind.

"The elves agreed to speak to you and potentially form an alliance," I told him. "But they want a guarantee that you'll do your best to protect them from the Family. They also want my help to retrieve the Akrith they stole from the Elders, but their magic isn't as strong outside their own realm, while the Family is periodically using the Akrith to top up their own power."

"So that's how the Family obtained their unique skills?" he said. "I did wonder why they seemed to have talents far out of reach of what can be achieved with a cantrip. Given their previous ties to the elves, I ought to have guessed sooner."

So should I, given that I'd *lived* with them. Yet I hadn't set eyes on an Akrith until I'd held one in my own hands and felt its power humming beneath the surface, while they'd taken care to restrict my magical education to human methods only.

"Luckily, the elves believed me in the end, and they let me go," I said. "Have the Family really not tried to make any trouble since I left?"

"Miles told you that?" he guessed. "I can't say I've been watching them closely, but I don't expect their silence to last much longer."

"Yeah, I expect they'll reappear as soon as they figure out where I've been," I said. "Adair didn't consult them before opening the door to the elves' realm. He did it in a fit of bravado because I taunted him as a distraction so that he wouldn't notice the elves sneaking out of the warehouse. I didn't expect his plan to actually work. Not sure he did either, come to that."

"That doesn't surprise me," he said. "Adair doesn't strike me as a sophisticated planner. Even when he was in jail here, he didn't have a strategy."

"Yeah, the Family left him to rot when he was jailed here in the castle, but they might feel differently about the *elves* holding him captive," I said. "Especially when they might mean him bodily harm. In fact, they hinted that they might know how to kill the Family permanently. I didn't think it was even possible."

"I thought they might," he said. "That's why I wanted you to contact them."

I suppressed an eye-roll. "Is there anything you *didn't* predict?"

"I'm sure you'll find something if you think hard enough."

Honestly. "I nearly got speared to death when I mentioned you, because it sounds like your predecessor was a bit of a dick. Did you see that one coming?"

The Death King arched a brow. "That's certainly consistent with what I know of the former Death King, but I can't say we were close to one another."

Guess not. I was pretty sure he'd killed the last Death King in order to take his place, in fact. Miles had mentioned he and the Death King had grown up in the Spirit Agents' house together, which meant neither of them would have been alive when his predecessor had taken power and the elves' realm had been cut off. As a result, he could hardly be blamed for the last Death King's crimes, so the elves should have no problem forming an agreement with him. I hoped.

"Did you know the elves built the citadels, not the spirit mages?" he asked. "I didn't, until Miles told me."

I raised a brow at the change of subject. "I know. Trix told me. Why did the spirit mages want to take credit, do you know?"

"The spirit mages wanted everyone to believe they were the destined rulers of the Parallel," he said. "Before the war, they ruled alongside the rest of the Council of the Elements, but some among their number believed they were entitled to more than their fair share of the power. Perhaps some of the punishment the survivors inflicted on them was justified."

"You mean the people who cursed the House of Spirit and turned the other Houses into prisons?" I asked. "I know they were murdering maniacs, but it's not like we're responsible for their crimes."

"Perhaps not, but it's on us to fix the damage," he said. "I hope you're ready."

"You mean to fix what the Family did to the elves?" The Family had cut off their realm from this one and stolen the very heart of their magic. Was it even possible to undo the damage, let alone make up for what they'd done? Regardless, before anyone could even consider how to rebuild the links between the elves in their realm and this one, I needed to find a way to bring the Family to justice for their crimes. Preferably before Lex and Roth reached the elves first... though I did have *some* leverage at the moment. Namely, I knew where their son was held captive. If I could figure out how to use that information to my advantage without drawing the elves into an open conflict with the Family before they were ready, it would be a starting point.

"To start off with, go and rest," said the Death King. "I'll have another update for you tomorrow."

"Sure," I said. "Thanks."

As I left the hall, a lich passed right through me, prompting a grimace at the cold sensation. The lich spun around, revealing Harper's face, which split into a delighted grin. "Bria, you're alive!"

"I am," I said. "Did Miles tell you?"

"He also said you found the elves."

"Yeah, I did." I walked with her down the corridor leading to the area of the castle which belonged to the Elemental Soldiers. "Guess everyone wants to know where I've been."

"You've got it," said Harper. "Liv and Devon aren't in, but the others are here, and we're all *very* interested to hear your version of the story."

I let out a fake groan. "Can't Miles tell you?"

"Sure, but we also have food. Since I can't eat, you'll have to take my portion instead. Does that convince you?"

Come to think of it, I was starving. "Yes, it does."

As I'd expected, the other three Elemental Soldiers waited expectantly for me in the break room. I launched into an explanation of where I'd disappeared to for the last few days while devouring a large pizza someone had presumably ordered from Earth. Trix entered the room halfway through my explanation.

"Is it true?" asked the elf. "You made it to the elves' realm?"

"Yeah, thanks to Adair." I bit into a slice of pizza, while

Miles reached for another from his spot next to me on the sofa. "Long story short, he got in way over his head and is currently locked in a cage."

Trix listened in awed silence as Miles explained what I'd already told the others. I interjected when he reached the part about the meeting with the Elders.

"I'm lucky they agreed to speak to me, considering their history with the Family." I put down my half-eaten pizza slice. "Turns out the Family stole some artefacts when they had access to their realm, in order to make themselves immortal."

I didn't say they'd done the same to Adair and me, but from the way Trix's eyes rounded, he'd read between the lines. "The elves still let you leave?"

"Yeah, eventually," I said. "Once I convinced them I wasn't working with Adair, they let me explain myself to the Elders. I asked if they'd be willing to meet with the Death King, though I did have to clarify that the Death King isn't the same guy who was in charge back when their realm was cut off from this one. His predecessor was apparently a complete dick."

"Yeah, he was," said Miles. "Can confirm."

"Anyway, it sounds like the Elders are willing to meet with him if he agrees to help protect them against the Family," I added. "Which he will. The slight issue is that they also want to get back what the Family stole from them before the first war. Namely, the Elders' Akrith."

Trix swivelled to face me. "They stole the *Elders'* Akrith? No wonder they've never been able to open a way back through to this realm."

"They must still have it, too," I said. "The Elders said it must be the source of their immortality, but I don't remember seeing a pretty tree carving in their house at any point. I assume they stashed it in a safe somewhere."

"I don't doubt they'll have hidden it well," said Trix, "but I'm willing to help you retrieve it."

Ryan shot him a disapproving look. "We're not breaking into the Family's house. Even with Adair locked up, the others are just as dangerous, if not more."

"They are," I admitted. "But we have the elves as potential allies. As a bonus, Adair's power didn't work on the other elves. Trix, do you know why that might have been?"

"Probably because the elves' power is stronger in their own realm," said Trix, confirming my guess. "In this realm, it would be trickier to subdue him... and the others."

An idea occurred to me. "Should we lure Lex and Roth to their realm instead? If they came with us into the elves' realm and walked right into a trap, then they'd be at the elves' mercy."

Especially if I told them Adair was imprisoned and the only way to get him back was to talk to the elves directly. I'd have to discuss the idea with the Death King first, but what better way to corner them and leave the path to retrieving the Elders' Akrith wide open.

"Not a bad shout," Miles commented. "In fact, it might just work."

"Are you sure they'd go for it?" said Ryan.

"It's worth trying," I said. "What I'd like to know is why the Family hasn't checked up on the elves who were working in that warehouse. You'd think they'd have sent someone after Adair by now."

"The warehouse was probably too far away for them

to bother with," said Miles. "Not like they can be in four places at once. I reckon it was Adair's responsibility, and he was supposed to shut it down when it no longer became necessary."

That made sense. The Family might be occupied with other matters, but one of them would go to check up on Adair eventually. We had to corner them beforehand, but only with the elves' permission. The Family had already inflicted enough pain and destruction upon them.

Like the Death King had said… it was on us, or on me, to fix the damage they'd done.

———

I intended to take a shower when I got back to my room, but instead I passed out fully clothed on the bed. Nobody woke me for guard duty, for a wonder, so I slept straight through the night. The following morning, I took my time showering and changing into clean clothes while I thought about how to explain my plan to the Death King.

The universe had other ideas. When I reached the break room, it was to find no signs of Miles or the other Elemental Soldiers. Instead, Trix sat alone in the room, and he gave me a smile when I headed to the kitchen to scrounge some leftovers from the previous evening. "Is Ryan not around?"

"Not at the moment," he said. "Assassins attacked my house yesterday, so Ryan insisted on letting me stay at the castle for the foreseeable future."

"You might have mentioned that earlier." I retrieved a slice of cold pizza. "What about Drina?"

"I haven't seen her since our last visit," said Trix. "She'll want to know the Elders survived, I'm sure."

"You want to drop by her house today?" It wouldn't be a bad idea to put word out among the local elves that their realm wasn't completely cut off after all. "We could take her to see the Elders, too, but I'd need to use the Akrith. Is it still in the hall of souls?"

"Why'd you put it in there?" asked the elf.

"It's the safest place I could think of," I said. "I need to ask the Death King to loan me the key."

"He isn't in," said Trix. "He went out earlier, and I don't think you can get into the hall without him."

"Seriously?" I said. "He picked a fine time to go walkabout."

I needed the Death King with me when I spoke to the Elders, too, or else they might not take my word for it that he'd hold up his end of the bargain. Admittedly, I'd also need to run my plan past him first, but I'd slept for the better part of twelve hours and was acutely conscious of the ticking clock.

"I'll come with you to see Drina first," Trix said decisively. "She'll want me to let her know I'm safe."

"If she knows someone tried to blow up your house, then I imagine she'd appreciate an update." I spotted Dex flitting around the ceiling, chasing one of the other sprites. "Hey, Dex. If you see the Death King around, can you tell him I need to speak to him? Whenever he gets back from where he ran off to."

"Where are you going, then?" he asked.

"To speak to a friend." Cramming the rest of the pizza slice into my mouth, I walked out of the break room with Trix and left the castle via the back doors.

I didn't see any signs of Miles near the gates, instead finding two unfamiliar Spirit Agents on guard duty. He'd mentioned being on the rota with the other Spirit Agents, but I hadn't seen him since before I'd crashed out the previous night and if he'd been on security duty, his shift must have finished. Admittedly, I'd been in such a deep sleep that I wouldn't have heard him knock on my door anyway. Maybe he'd gone with the Death King on whatever urgent quest had taken him outside the castle.

Trix and I made our way to the node before transporting ourselves into Arcadia. From there, we retraced our steps to Drina's house. Trix reached the door first, but when he knocked, the door moved inwards as though she'd left the house without properly locking the place up.

Trix's expression was tight with worry as he pushed the door fully inward, revealing an empty room on the other side. The same spiky plants covered the interior, and when we entered, they waved their thorny vines threateningly in our direction. I backed into the doorway and my heart sank when I saw several dark bloodstains on the floor.

"It's not Drina's blood," said Trix immediately. "Look at the plants."

I grimaced at the sight of more spots of crimson gleaming on the spiky plants. "Guess we're not the first trespassers they've attacked."

Who did the blood belong to, then? The thorns circled me as though keen to add mine to the décor, so I backed out of the room before they speared me. *Who took Drina? Not the Family? They* weren't active in Arcadia, but that didn't mean they hadn't sent assassins after her if they'd somehow found out about my visit to her.

"She might have gone into hiding, like me," said Trix. "But she wouldn't have left her plants behind."

"Why would anyone capture her? She said she was no fighter." Her plants were a different story, but unless someone had been watching when Trix and I had visited her house, it made no sense for them to take her.

"I don't know." Trix's expression clouded. "Maybe her neighbours saw who took her."

Guilt and worry churning within me, I approached the door of the house next to Drina's and knocked. A young male practitioner answered, his face nervous and stained with soot. I recognised the acrid smell within the house as similar to the stench that hung around Arcadia's warehouses and wondered if he made a living carving cantrips for the Collective of Spells to sell at the market.

"Hey," I said. "Sorry to disturb you, but I came to visit your neighbour and she's not in. Did she go out?"

His moth pressed together. "I don't know my neighbours."

"It's okay, I'm not with the authorities or anything," I reassured him. "I just wondered when you last saw her. I'd be really grateful if you let me know, because I think she might be in trouble."

"I saw a group of people break the door down," he mumbled. "They… they took her away with them."

"Were they human?" I asked.

"I didn't see their faces. They wore masks."

Assassins. Of course the Family had been up to their usual tricks. Had they targeted her alone, or had other elves been taken, too? They couldn't possibly know what we'd discussed in our meeting, but now I had an extra incentive to get our plan underway.

Once the elves and the Death King came to an agreement, we'd spring our trap on Lex and Roth, find the Elders' Akrith and give it back to its rightful owners, and then the Family's long-lived immortality would come to an end.

15

The Death King, thankfully, had returned to the castle by the time Trix and I got back to the swampland. He listened with surprising patience as I laid out my plan to ensnare the Family by using Adair as bait. "And you're sure they'll come to Adair's rescue?"

"If they find out the Elders have him?" I said. "I guarantee they won't be able to resist. But we need to hurry. I just found out the Family's assassins have been kidnapping elves from Arcadia and they might have attacked Trix, too. They've been entirely too quiet while I've been gone, and I'd rather get them into our trap before they realise Miles and I freed those elves from the warehouse."

"So you'll use the Akrith to open the realm of the elves so I can meet with their Elders," he said. "Then after we make sure they're on board with our plan, you'll go to the Family yourself and tell them their son is their prisoner?"

"I think I'm the only one they'll listen to, to be honest,"

I said. "Do you still have the Spirit Agents guarding your territory?"

"Most of the time," he responded. "Why?"

"Where's Miles?" I asked. "I haven't seen him all day."

"I believe he went to check on the elves who he freed from the warehouse."

Uneasiness skittered down my spine. I'd been out for the count and he probably hadn't been able to wake me before I left, but his absence bothered me. Still, the first and most urgent stage of our plan was to bring the Death King to meet with the Elders, and we didn't have any time to waste.

"We'll need to go to the tree near the warehouse," I told the Death King. "Then I'll use the stone to get us into the elves' realm. Unless you want me to bring an ambassador from the elves to meet you here? I'm not sure what effect their realm has on liches."

When liches roamed too far from the nodes on Earth, they turned to dust and expired. I didn't know if the same was true of the elves' realm, but now did not seem a good time to experiment, especially with the Death King being one of the few who had the ability to resist the Family's powers.

The Death King studied me. "A fair assessment. I would also prefer not to disappear for several days while my Court is in a crisis."

"That too." Time was of the essence. "I'll bring an ambassador to speak to you, then. I need my Akrith first, though. I left it in the hall of souls."

"You mean this?" He held up the stone, which dazzled me with its light, and then tossed it to me so I had to catch it one-handed.

"Have you been carrying it on you all along?" I frowned at him. "Death King, you do realise this is a prized artefact of which there are only a few in existence, don't you?"

"Yes, I do," he said. "I thought it'd be safer with me than anywhere else. Don't be long."

Shaking my head, I pocketed the Akrith before leaving the castle and using the node to transport myself back to the warehouse. From there, I retraced my steps to the sprawling shape of the elven tree underneath the cliff, tensing when footsteps sounded behind me.

I spun on my heel as the Death King walked into view. "I thought you were staying behind."

"I'd like to see how this elf stone works," he said. "Go on."

"Right." I held up the stone to the tree, mimicking what Adair had done and hoping it would obey me in the same way. Light shot from its surface, and I screwed up my eyes against the vibrant glare.

A discordant shouting noise came from behind me and my eyes flew open as a spear flew past, grazing my cheek. I stumbled back, my feet on the forest path, staring into the furious eyes of two elves bearing down on me.

"Whoa!" I said. "Hey, it's me. I'm here with the Death King—"

"You're with the *Vetran*," snarled the elf on the right, who I recognised as the male who'd escorted me to the Elders when I'd last been here. "Aren't you?"

My heart dived. "They already came here?"

Dammit. We're too late. They must have come looking for Adair and used their own Akrith to travel into the elves' realm as soon as they'd figured out where he'd gone.

"She's not responsible," insisted his female companion. "She didn't do this."

I looked past her, my heart sinking in my chest. Several elves lay on the path, bearing grisly wounds, some of which appeared to have been inflicted by their own wooden spears and swords.

"And him?" said the male elf, his gaze fixed at a point over my shoulder.

Belatedly, I remembered my companion. The Death King came into view, still wearing the appearance of a human, though I frankly had no idea of the rules governing whether or not he could use his lich abilities in this realm. He must have been confident that he wouldn't fall to pieces without access to a node, at least, or else he wouldn't have followed me here.

"Who are you?" asked the female elf.

I didn't expect the Death King to understand the elves' language, but to my bafflement, he replied fluently. "I am Greyson Beaumont, more commonly known as the King of the Dead. I wish to meet with your Elders."

The male elf gawped at him. "You are the King of Liches?"

"At present, yes," he said.

"The Elders requested to speak to him," I told them, deciding to save my questions about how in the world the Death King had learned to speak the elven language until later. "The Family isn't still in this realm?"

"No," responded the female elf. "The prisoner broke out of his cage as soon as the other *Vetran* showed up, and then they ran. Not before inflicting a great deal of damage to our forest in the process, of course."

Shit. "That means we need a new plan. I hoped we

might be able to use Adair's capture to convince the Family to surrender, but I didn't count on the Family making it here first."

I'd naively assumed the Family had only had the one genuine Akrith between them, but not only had they been prepared to come back to the elves' realm, they'd been prepared to take them on in battle as well. Now we'd lost our advantage, and to add insult to injury, they were probably kidnapping more elves back in the Parallel as we spoke. Including—

My heart sank into my shoes. "Death King… if the Family knew Adair was here, they must also know the warehouse is empty. They'll have figured out Miles and I helped the elves escape captivity."

And Miles had been missing since his own visit to the elves. Dread clenched tight jaws around my lungs, constricting my breath.

"You want to go back?" The Death King switched back to English. "You think they might have targeted the other elves?"

"Unfortunately, I think they have." I turned to the two elves and switched back to speaking their language. "The elves who we saved from the Family's warehouse might be in danger. I need to go and help them, but I'll come back as soon as I can."

"You mean to abandon us again?" said the male elf.

"Not at all," said the Death King. "I am willing to assist you in taking on the Family, as I'm sure Bria told you. If you choose to come to the Parallel, then the forces of the Court of the Dead will have your back."

"Too late." The male elf spoke in bitter tones. "We need to rebuild our army before we can amass a defensive force. They were more than prepared to meet us in battle."

"I'll come back," I promised the elves. "As soon as I possibly can."

Urgency blared inside me. Lex and Roth must have come for Adair and found the warehouse empty, and the elves' former domain was the logical place for them to search for him. If Miles had been there at the time… I shut off the thought. In a trembling hand, I held up the Akrith again, and a flash of brightness filled my vision.

A moment later, the elves' forest vanished, leaving the Death King and me alone beside the tree near the warehouse.

I drew in a breath. "The bastards. I should have known they wouldn't take Adair's capture lying down."

The Death King eyed the warehouse. "I can't sense anyone in there."

"No…" I walked away from the tree, scanning the area at the top of the cliffside. No sign of Miles… or any of the elves either. "The elves' town isn't far from here, but only Miles knows where it is. I never saw it for myself."

"Ryan knows," said the Death King. "Miles told them. We'll go back to the castle and ask them to show you the way."

"All right." I returned the stone to my pocket and followed him back to the node, hopping over into the swampland.

The Death King and I entered the grounds, where Trix strode over to join us. "You're back already?"

"The Family got to the elves' realm first," I explained. "There's a good chance they might have found the elves Miles and I saved from the warehouse, too."

Trix's eyes widened. "The Family attacked the elves in their own realm?"

"They also rescued Adair, so we need a new plan." I waited for the Elemental Soldiers to catch up to us, then addressed the Air Element. "Ryan, the Death King said you know the way to the elves' town. The elves from the warehouse, I mean. The Family found out we rescued them—and Miles is missing."

"I know the way," said Ryan. "If the Family's there, though, we might well be going to our deaths."

"We have to help them," Trix insisted. "We can't leave them to die."

"The Family might not be there at the moment," I added. "They just rescued Adair from the elves' realm, and the elves in the Parallel aren't their priorities at the moment. I think they've mostly been delegating."

I hope. Worry over Miles's disappearance writhed inside my chest like a serpent, and each second made the constricting sensation tighter. Especially when I recalled Adair's warning that he had no need of the warehouse any longer.

"We'll go," said Trix. "I'll be right behind you, Bria."

Ryan's gaze slid to Trix. If not for the elf, I had little doubt they'd have refused point-blank to walk into a potential trap, but they said, "Fine, but if we're outnumbered, we have to run."

The Air Element strode out of the gates, while Trix and I followed them towards the node.

I'll find you, Miles.

We reappeared back by the warehouse, where Ryan strode into the lead uphill. Before long, we came to several dilapidated buildings. As Belgi had said, the elves' town hadn't been far from the warehouse, but the downside was that the Family would have had no trouble tracking them down again.

The houses grew more numerous the further we walked, and though nobody came to the doors or windows to look at us, they remained intact enough for me to suspect the Family hadn't unleashed any inferno cantrips. *Please say they were more concerned with finding Adair than with punishing the people here. Please...*

A surprising number of trees overshadowed the rooftops, while greenery sprouted between the stone walls and their gardens looked even better tended than the lawns around the Spirit Agents' house. No wonder the Family had found this the natural place to search for a living elven tree—and found one, too.

Our group came to an abrupt halt when two figures appeared among the houses, dressed in dark clothing and carrying gleaming knives in their hands. *Assassins.*

"There they are," I muttered. "Ready?"

"Ready," said Ryan, raising their hands.

The assassins broke into a run towards us, and the Air Element's magic sent both of them flying back several feet. Both men landed sprawling on the path, but they were back on their feet by the time we caught up to them. One had even managed to keep hold of his knife, and dread trickled through me at the memory of Tay's death. Miles had been here. If the assassins had caught him first...

No. I won't let that be true.

Two more assassins ran out of the shadows as my fist came up into the nearest man's jaw, a torrent of flames setting him ablaze. Ryan did battle with the second assassin, while Trix intercepted the newcomers with an uncharacteristic expression of fury on his face. The assassins might have a speed advantage over regular people, but Trix and I were more than a match for them, while Ryan's magic flung the assassins into the air like rag dolls.

Seeing the others had the situation in hand, I moved towards the nearest house, where movement stirred behind the window. The elves must have sheltered in their only available hiding places, though I wouldn't have been keen to give up a nice town like this either. The Family had no right to barge in and terrorise everyone.

I spotted several figures crouched behind the window, and recognised one of them as Belgi, the elf I'd spoken to at the warehouse. He lifted his head, relief flitting across his face for a brief instant. "You have to leave before they come back."

"I'm here to help you," I said quickly.

"Are you, now?" A familiar soft voice spoke from behind me, and my body tensed. *They're already here.*

I rotated on my heel as Lex walked into view. As per usual, she was dressed entirely inappropriately for the wasteland backdrop, and wore a lilac dress and a flowery hat as though she was on her way to a summer carnival. Her face was artfully made up, while her elfin features made her look scarcely a day older than me. *Of course she's still using the Akrith's power to restore her youthfulness.*

"Where the hell is Adair?" At a guess, they'd sent their assassins here instead of coming in person once they'd realised Adair had crossed into the elves' realm, but I should have guessed that either Lex or Roth would be back to see to it that the elves were punished for escaping captivity. Question was, where did that leave Miles?

A grin twisted her mouth. "He's at home, thinking about what he did. The foolish boy was always too impatient for his own good."

"I don't think his master plan of invading the elves' realm played out the way he hoped it would," I said. "Care to tell me what you're doing here?"

"I thought I'd come and check up on Adair's pet project," she said. "I have to admit I've been guilty of underestimating your commitment to making a nuisance of yourself."

"You're guilty of far worse and you know it." I raised my fists. "Get out of here. These people have done nothing to you, and Adair *told* me he had no use for the warehouse any longer."

"Adair needs to learn when to keep his mouth shut, too," she said. "But if you won't obey me of your own free will…"

She gestured, and I found my arms contorting painfully as my body turned against itself. Pain screamed through my limbs. I bit the inside of my cheek in order to avoid crying out, determined not to break.

Behind me, the elves in the house didn't move an inch, but none of them were immune to her powers, either. A scream built in my chest, and I heard another strident noise from somewhere further down the path. Not a scream. A whistle, and one I'd heard before. *Trix?*

An answering cry sounded from somewhere nearby, and a dark shape appeared in the sky, soaring overhead. A long spiky worm-shaped creature with pointed wings. I hadn't even known the wyrm was still in the area, and while Trix had said that they weren't usually inclined to attack people, the wyrm would surely remember its years held under the Family's spell.

I tilted my head to the sky and gasped out, "Get her."

Triumph washed over me as the beast obeyed my command, diving at her from above. Lex gave a startled shout when the wyrm's body slammed into her, crushing her into the dirt.

At once, the pain vanished from my arms. I straightened upright, breathing hard, and when the wyrm lifted its head, Lex lay in a crushed tangle of limbs and blood. Silently thanking Trix for his quick intervention, I pushed open the door to the elves' house. They all flinched away from me when I walked in.

"Relax, I'm not here to hurt you," I said. "You have to leave before she recovers."

"There's nowhere we can go where we'd be safe from them," Belgi insisted. "We have people to take care of here. Injured elves. Besides, we will not abandon our home."

"The Family are willing to hurt everyone who stands in their way." I grimaced when another twinge of pain went through my abused arms. "Have you seen my friend Miles? The spirit mage who helped you get out of the warehouse?"

"He was here earlier, but I thought he left," said the elf. "Before *they* came."

Wait. Had the Family *not* taken him captive. A brief spark of hope appeared within me, while the wyrm gave Lex a prod with its claw, growling.

I walked out of the elves' house and faced the creature, looking into its pitted eyes. "Can you pick her up and toss her somewhere far away from here? Preferably not a place with humans living in it, but not near Elysium or

Arcadia, either. She might look dead, but she'll get over it."

I wasn't certain the wyrm would understand every word I spoke, but it growled and picked up Lex's limp body in a claw before taking to the sky.

As for me, I had the inkling I was fighting a losing battle when it came to convincing the elves to move out of their town to somewhere safer. It wasn't like there was room for all of them in the Death King's castle, especially with all the Spirit Agents currently sheltering in there.

"I haven't seen your friend since this morning," Belgi said from behind me. "I think he mentioned going back to Elysium."

"Did he?" Then he might have just missed them. Or else he'd run into trouble in the city. "Thanks for telling me. It's appreciated."

Ryan jogged over to me with Trix on their heels. "Are we getting them out of here?"

"They don't want to leave," I explained. "I ordered the wyrm to drop Lex as far away from here as possible, but that won't stop Roth or Adair from coming back to finish what she started."

"I doubt we're their priority," said Belgi. "Don't waste your resources on us."

"I have an alternative," said Trix, reaching into his pocket and pulling out an Akrith.

I looked at the glowing stone. "Are you going to open the elves' realm again? I mean, they were just attacked by the Family as well. Not sure they want visitors."

"They did agree to help the Death King, didn't they?" said Ryan.

You're only saying that because it's Trix's idea. Maybe they had a point, though. The elves sheltering here would be more inclined to listen to their Elders than to anyone else, right? Not to mention, the Elders would have more avenues to catch up on everything they'd missed while their realm had been cut off.

Belgi eyed the stone, his eyes wide. "You mean to take us back to our kin?"

"If you want to," I said. "You know the Family will come back to punish you for escaping the warehouse. There's nowhere safer for you than in your own realm."

The elf closed his eyes. "We've never found a genuine Akrith with enough power to reopen our realm in all our years of tending our town. We've guarded our tree for decades, regardless, but to know that the first visitors to our realm since before the war inflicted such grievous harm on them..."

"I know," I said softly. "I'm sorry. I really am. They deserved so much better, and so do you. I believe the Elders would be willing to help you. I did tell them we rescued you from the Family's warehouse."

The elf lifted his head high. "Then I will talk with them."

"Trix will lead the way," I said. "I have to run. If Miles isn't here, then the Family might have ambushed him in Elysium."

"Are you sure?" asked Ryan.

"He's been gone for hours," I said. "Besides, Roth's still unaccounted for. I don't know where else to look."

"You can't go alone," said Trix.

I shook my head. "The elves don't have long before the Family comes back. Help Belgi and the others get to safety."

"Go on," said Ryan. "We'll be right behind you once we help the elves get out of here."

I doubted it'd be quick or simple, but it was the only way I could think of to keep the elves safe without giving the Family any more openings to get at them. I wished I could be there, too, but Miles needed me more.

I needed to find him before he suffered the same fate as the last person I'd trusted with my life.

16

I ran towards the warehouse and returned to the node, thinking hard. The only reason I could think of for Miles returning to Elysium was to get supplies from the Spirit Agents' old house on his way back to the castle, so that would be my first stop. I transported myself to the node nearest to the Spirit Agents' base, and a blazing light caught my vision, shining over the rooftops from the direction of the citadel in the city's centre.

The transporter must be active again. *Shit. I think I know where Miles is.* If I were him, I'd have run straight for the citadel the instant I saw the light. Question was, who'd turned it on?

I pelted down the streets, not stopping until I reached the citadel. I glimpsed a few people as I tore by, but none wore the uniforms of the Houses. In fact, when I passed the door to the House of Fire, it looked as though it'd been bolted from the inside. Maybe they feared the light in the tower signalled a repeat of the incident with the cursed cantrips, because it wasn't like they could see inside the tower to find out whoever had turned it on. Didn't make them any less cowardly, though.

Leaving the Houses, I sprinted up to the citadel and tried to open the door, but it wouldn't give. "Dammit!"

The only way in was via the transporter on the inside or to ask a lich to let me in, but before I could take more than a step backwards, a hand grabbed my shoulder from behind and the cold kiss of a knife pressed to my throat.

I twisted free, turning on the masked figure behind me, but the assassin snagged my arm in an iron grip and pushed me towards the citadel door. An instant later, the door flew open to reveal a second assassin, who caught my arm and hauled me into the downstairs room. Dazzling lights gleamed from the runes on the walls, while a humming noise permeated the room. One brief glance told me Miles wasn't downstairs, so he must be on the upper level.

I let the assassin steer me towards the stairs, and then I pivoted and kicked his legs out from underneath him. Breaking out of his grip, I punched him in the throat and rammed an elbow into his solar plexus. He flopped over backwards like a dying fish, gasping for breath.

Leaping onto the staircase, I shot a fireball that sent the assassins scrambling for cover before running up the spiralling stairs so quickly it made me dizzy. Reaching the top, I shoved the metal door open. The machinery inside the room gleamed with multicoloured lights, including the raised platform in the room's centre, while a cage was hooked up to the machine at the side of the room.

Inside the cage, Miles lay in a limp heap on the floor, unmoving. *No. Elements, no.*

"I thought you'd show up to rescue him." Shawn the former Spirit Agent stepped into view, the lights making his pale face look ghostly. "But you're already too late, Bria. He's gone."

I launched myself at the spirit mage with a strangled cry, tackling him to the ground. My fist hammered into his face before he pushed me off him with more strength than he should have possessed. I caught my balance against the wall, launching myself at him again, but a burst of energy slammed me in the chest, pinning me to the metallic surface. *Bloody spirit magic.*

Worse, Miles still wasn't moving. *No. He can't be dead. I won't accept it.*

"Fuck—you," I wheezed. "Are you alone? Because I don't think Hawker would be impressed with you for stealing his transporter."

"Why shouldn't I?" he said. "I'm the one who rebuilt this place, not him. I did more for the good of the spirit mages than anyone else, and *this* dickhead and his friends decided to reward me by turning on one of their own."

"You opened the portal and risked kicking off a war just for the sake of revenge on Miles?" Damn. Shawn. Why had I forgotten he was out there, alive and angry? Why had I forgotten he wanted to kill Miles?

"Why not?" he said. "He ruined my life."

"You're the one who turned against your allies!" Anger pulsed through my blood. "You betrayed the Spirit Agents and you conspired with the worst of what the Parallel has to offer. Miles fought back, but you're the one who threw the first punch. You can't deny it."

Shawn's jaw clenched. Out of the corner of my eye, I

spotted movement in the cage. Miles's hand lifted a fraction. He was alive. *Alive.*

I looked away, but not before Shawn caught the direction of my gaze. "I think I'll let you watch me torture him for a bit before I kill you."

"You're only hurting yourself," I warned him. "Your own allies will be pissed off with you for hijacking their transporter. They've willingly slaughtered people they've worked with before, and don't think they won't do the same to you."

"I don't give a shit what they think." His hands glowed, and he reached for a button on the machine.

I leapt at him first, tackling him to the ground. We crashed to earth in a tangle of wires, and I kicked Shawn in the head, half-crawling towards the cage. Pain exploded across the back of my head as something hard struck me from behind, but I ignored it and grabbed the cage door with my fingertips.

Miles lifted his head and mouthed my name. I tugged harder, and the cage door came open. I leapt upright, positioning myself between the cage and Shawn's oncoming attack.

"Why did you give up everything I offered you for *her*?" Shawn spat at Miles. "She's not even human. She's a freak show."

"Wow, I'm wounded." I could feel warm blood trickling down my face, but that didn't matter. Miles was alive, and I refused to let Shawn lay a finger on him again. "Word of advice? Get in that transporter and take yourself somewhere nobody can follow you, or else I'll kill you here and now."

Energy blasted from his palms. I dodged and returned

fire, literally, and Shawn leapt behind the bank of machinery to avoid my attack.

"Ow." Miles pushed his way out of the cage. "Fucking coward."

"Are you okay?" I walked over to him, keeping one eye on Shawn. When the other spirit mage emerged from behind the machinery, Miles raised his hand and shot a vibrant bolt of spirit magic into his chest. Shawn flew head over heels, landing on his back on top of the transporter's controls.

Miles climbed upright, unsteady on his feet, and approached Shawn's sprawling body. "I should have killed you the first time you betrayed us."

Shawn rolled off the machinery and tackled him to the ground, but Miles's fist slammed into the other spirit mage, and a glowing light ignited in his hand as he drew a bright stream of energy out of Shawn's body.

"You're—no match for me," Shawn gasped.

"I beg to differ." Miles's face showed the strain, but he held onto the stream of energy tightly while Shawn's struggles grew weaker. "You burned yourself out when you turned that machine back on, didn't you?"

Shawn choked on a breath, and then he fell back as a final bolt of white-blue energy surged into Miles's hands. I stepped in and caught his arm to help him keep his balance, the torrent of magic making my teeth rattle in my skull.

The vibrant glow dimmed, and Miles reeled back on his feet. A faint glow outlined his body and shone in his eyes, while my fingers tingled with static when I took his hand. "You okay?"

"Better than he is."

"He's dead?"

He grunted yes, and I wrapped him into my embrace. His head pressed to my shoulder, his arm around my back. "You're bleeding."

I rubbed my face, blood caking my skin along with the mud from the swamp. "I thought you were dead. I thought…"

"Came pretty close," he said. "I have a soul amulet with me, but I hoped not to have to use it."

"Don't joke about that." I hugged him fiercely. "Seriously. You were lying there in that cage, and—I thought I got here too late." *Like Tay,* a voice in the back of my head whispered.

He released me, but that static tingle still hung in the air between us. "No. He zapped me pretty hard when he threw me in that cage, but I'm good. Better than good, now I have Shawn's life energy rattling around inside me."

"You spirit mages really know how to throw a party." I turned to the glowing transporter. "Got one of those neutraliser cantrips handy?"

"The one which was already there might still have some power left inside it." He crouched down and picked up a discarded cantrip from the floor. "I'll put it back in and ask the Spirit Agents if any of them wants to volunteer to guard the place for a bit to make sure nobody else shows up here. I think Shawn was acting alone, but you never know."

"Wise idea." I slumped to the floor, more out of relief than exhaustion. Miles was alive. Alive…

Miles decisively shoved the neutralising cantrip into a slot in the machine. At once, the lights died down, the transporter's humming noise fading to silence. "I think we need to tell the Houses the coast is clear in case they think Hawker's taken over the place again."

"The cowards are hiding," I said. "Let them think what they want. Anyway, the Spirit Agents at the castle are probably worried about you."

He grimaced. "Yeah, I know. I shouldn't have taken a detour. I came here to grab supplies, but I didn't count on running into an old friend."

"I thought it was the Family," I said. "While you were gone, they got to the elves' realm and set Adair free. Then Lex threatened the elves from the warehouse. Trix and Ryan were helping them evacuate their town the last time I saw them, but I had to make sure you were okay."

"Oh, damn," he said. "I actually tried to convince them to move elsewhere when I visited their town this morning, but they refused point-blank."

"Trix and I talked them into following him into the elves' realm so they can meet the Elders," I said. "I hope it goes smoothly, though it doesn't help that the Family left a real mess behind them when they broke Adair out of jail."

"I bet they did," said Miles. "Guess taking them to the elves' realm is probably the only option, short of bringing yet more people to the Death King's castle. Is Roth around?"

"I've no idea where Roth is, but Adair's at home in disgrace," I said. "I also had the wyrm take Lex for a ride, so that'll keep her busy for a bit."

"You did what?" he said. "Seriously, where do you come up with these ideas?"

"Improvising, mostly," I admitted. "And compensating for bringing disaster on everyone I care about."

"You didn't bring disaster on me," Miles insisted. "I walked into Shawn's bait intentionally."

"Still." The clenching sensation in my chest intensified. "They don't care who they hurt. Hell, they specifically target the people I care for the most. They think that because they—they *made* me, they turned me into this—they have the right to control my life. It's like Shawn said, I'm a freak of nature. I can dress it up how I like, but that's what I'll always be."

Like them. They want me to watch everyone I care about die while I endure alongside them. Forever.

Miles met my eyes. "I'm not bothered by them. Besides, I just ripped out a man's soul. I'm pretty sure I can handle you."

My heart leapt into my throat to see the intensity in his gaze. "You know nothing will ever be simple for us."

"Doesn't matter to me." He took my hand in his. "You know, when I was stuck in that cage, all I could think about was that I'd never told you how I felt."

The clenching sensation in my chest withdrew like the bars of a cage had lifted, and an inexplicable grin came to my mouth. "You did tell me. When you rescued those vampire chickens."

"Guess I did." He released my hand, casting another glance at Shawn's fallen body. "Come on, let's get out of here."

We headed for the stairs and climbed down into the main room of the citadel, stepping over the burned bodies of the assassins who'd dragged me into their trap. On the other side of the front door, a deserted town square greeted us.

"I think the mages in the Houses were scared someone

had started throwing infected cantrips around again," I said to Miles. "They barricaded themselves inside their headquarters."

"Yeah, they all ran off as soon as the citadel lit up," he said. "You know what, you're right. We'll let them hide for a while before we send someone to tell them there's no threat."

One trip through the node later and we landed in the swampland, where Miles approached the Spirit Agents on guard duty to explain where he'd been. I, meanwhile, found Trix and Ryan nearby, without any signs of the besieged elves. Did that mean their mission had been successful?

Spotting me, Trix glided over to my side. "Good, you found him. He wasn't with the Family?"

"One of the ex-Spirit Agents who used to work with the enemy decided now was the time for revenge, but it backfired on him," I said. "Did you manage to help all the elves escape their town?"

"We did," said Ryan. "Had a few hitches, but Trix managed to convince the elves in the other realm to help the refugees from the town. It helps that he speaks their language, because I didn't understand a word they said."

"You met the Elders?"

"No," said Trix. "The guards said the Elders were too busy to speak to anyone, considering the Family attacked them so recently, but they were glad to help their kinsmen."

"Good." A wave of relief crashed over me. The elves had made it to safety, Miles had survived, and we had one enemy crossed off our list now Shawn was taken care of. "I worried you might run into Roth."

"You didn't see him when you went to find Miles?" asked Ryan.

"No, Shawn was acting alone," I said. "I'm sure Lex will be back to berate me when she scrapes herself off the ground wherever she ended up, but I haven't seen any signs of Roth. As for Adair, he's back at the Family's house in disgrace for his major fuck-up in the elves' realm."

"So we can't use him as bait anymore," Trix said.

"Yeah, our plan blew up." Which left me at a loose end. "It wasn't a perfect strategy, but the elves' magic is stronger in their own realm and I hoped they might be able to collectively overpower Lex and Roth. I didn't count on them striking that fast or doing so much damage."

I'd been a fool to underestimate them, given that it hadn't even been the first time the Family had attacked the elves' realm and left chaos in their wake. It was unsurprising that the elves had instantly suspected foul play when I'd shown up again, and I was grateful beyond measure that they'd been willing to help their fellow elves escape the Family's siege despite their own troubles.

Trix's eyes clouded. "What about the Akrith they stole? How will we get it back without anything to trade in return?"

"You think they might have accepted Adair in trade?" I said. "Not sure they would have, but I hoped we might have been able to distract them in the elves' realm so we'd be able to sneak into their house and steal back the Elders' Akrith."

"I'm lost on what this Akrith is," Ryan commented. "Isn't it the same as yours?"

"No, it used to belong to the Elders and is far more

powerful than any other," I said. "The upside is that if we take it awa from the Family, the elves implied it ought to be possible to take them out permanently."

"The Akrith enables their bodies to keep regenerating," Trix explained. "Without it, they'll age as normal humans would. I expect they've been using the Akrith's energy for decades."

Nausea flooded me. "The same can't be true of regular Akriths, can it? I know elves are long-lived, but not invincible."

"The Elders' Akrith is stronger than any other," Trix said. "It's not meant to be used on a single individual."

"Aren't most elves more or less immortal, though?" asked Ryan.

"No," said Trix. "We can heal from most injuries and we're resilient, but we don't live forever the way vampires do. Even the Elders don't. Our trees are everlasting, however, which is likely what gave the Family the idea of stealing pieces of them in order to extend their own lifespans."

My mouth parted. That probably meant *I* would live a normal lifespan, as I hadn't had contact with the stolen Akrith at all. At least I didn't think I had.

"Why don't you try to steal the Akrith back from the Family, then?" said Ryan. "You can get into their house if you need to, can't you? Once you have the Akrith in hand, I can't imagine they'd want to risk declaring war on anyone in case you used it against them."

"That'd be an option if I had the slightest clue where they hid it," I said. "I could pretend to surrender to them and try to get them to give up its location, but I doubt they'd fall for the act. I'd be more likely to end up stuck under their roof and at their mercy again."

Miles walked up to us, hearing the end of our conversation. "Could you fake being under Adair's control?"

"Theoretically, but I'd have to be really careful," I said. "I definitely couldn't fake being under Roth or Lex's control, because their powers are controlled by their intentions and it's not like I can read their thoughts to know when they're giving me commands. With Adair, it's just words. Or rather, the words he speaks aloud."

"So Adair's the only one you have a chance at fooling," he concluded.

"A low one," I said. "Also, if he thinks he has me at his command, he might tell me to hurt people or to do things which I wouldn't normally do. If I refused, it would give me away."

"Bastard," said Ryan. "Let's face it, I doubt the rest of us could convince the Family we wanted to surrender. You're the only one they won't kill outright."

"Not permanently, but they'd try." I was less than thrilled at the notion of placing myself at their mercy in any capacity again, but neither could I think of any better options at the moment. "Did I ever mention the first time they killed me was for breaking a priceless ornament? Lex 'accidentally' used her powers to snap my neck. I was twelve."

Miles's jaw tightened. "She's fucked in the head."

"No kidding." I blew out a breath. "Can we scheme later? I'm too tired to think, and we have a brief reprieve from Lex's scheming for as long as she's incapacitated."

"Wish I could see the wyrm drop her in the middle of nowhere," said Miles. "Ah... they're back."

A loud cheer rose from elsewhere in the grounds, prompting me to look for the source. "Who's back?"

"I sent a couple of Spirit Agents to tell the others Shawn is dead," he explained. "Honestly, I'm all in favour of ignoring the Family for tonight and celebrating our victory."

"The elves are safe," said Ryan, when Trix's expression turned anxious. "We've done all we can for them. And Bria made it back from her solo rescue mission in one piece, which is another minor miracle."

More cheering ensued as a pack of Spirit Agents walked in our direction, and I found my heart lifting despite my lingering worries. With Shawn dead, his plan to take over the Spirit Agents had come to a decisive end. The others seemed thrilled at this development, running around high fiving one another and generally not being sad in the slightest about the loss of their former second-in-command. A group of them dive-bombed Miles and dragged him over to demand he tell the story again, while Ryan and Trix retreated away from the noise. I, meanwhile, spotted Liv standing nearby, along with Harper. The latter wore a perplexed expression on her illusory human face.

"What is going on?" she asked me. "I heard there was an attack in Elysium… but everyone's celebrating?"

"Turned out to be a false alarm," I said. "An ex-Spirit Agent turned on the transporter, not the Family. Miles killed him."

"Good," said Liv. "We have enough crap going on here already. What've you been doing? I haven't seen you since you got back."

Was Liv… trying to make friendly conversation with

me? "What have I been doing? Visiting elves, avoiding my evil relatives, and taking down an ex-Spirit Agent who wouldn't quit."

"So just like a regular day." Miles walked over, having shaken off his questioners, and casually slid his hand into mine. A thrill jolted through me at his open display of affection, and Liv's brows lifted a fraction. "The others are ordering takeout and planning a low-key celebration in the castle, but I figured you'd want to change out of those muddy clothes first."

"Speak for yourself." He had a point, though. Mud covered me from head to toe and blood smeared one side of my face, though my bruises had faded without my paying any attention. "All right. I'll go clean up. See you later, Liv. And you too, Harper."

As Harper waved me off, I walked back into the castle via the back door. Miles followed close behind me, and when we were alone, he said, "Bria... I wanted to ask whether you're okay with what I did to Shawn."

"You're joking, right?" I halted in front of the door to my suite, digging in my pocket for my keys. "Why wouldn't I be?"

"I figured you'd seen enough trauma," he said. "You know, the reason I started the Spirit Agents was because of him."

"Oh?" I glanced at him, the keys dangling from my fingers.

"Yeah, it was his idea," he said. "Before that, we were a group of mismatched orphans or disowned teenage spirit mages. Even when Greyson joined up."

"You mean the Death King."

He dipped his head. "Yeah. He was way better

connected than the rest of us… he even went to school at the Order's academy on the other side of the nodes, before he fell under the House of Spirit's curse. Anyway, Shawn was the one who suggested forming the Spirit Agents as our own equivalent to the Houses. I think he was always jealous that I got voted in as the leader instead of him, even though I won the position fair and square."

"I can see why the others picked you as their leader." I turned the key in the lock and pushed open the door to my suite. "They trust you."

"Hmm." He caught my hand, and a frisson of warmth sparked inside me. "You always know the right thing to say to me."

"If you're being serious, it was by total accident." Heat rushed to my face. "I'm not good at complimenting people."

"You're not good at *accepting* compliments," he corrected, drawing me closer to him and kissing me on the mouth. "Not that I'm giving up that easily."

I kissed him back, the warmth within my chest intensifying, along with the desire to strip off my filthy clothes for a very different reason. Ah, screw it. "Want to come try out the fancy shower in my room?"

He grinned. "I'll grab a change of clothes. Be right back."

"I'll hold you to that." I walked into my room and discarded my coat. As I kicked off my equally muddy boots, a knock came from the door.

"Who're you?" I opened it. "I don't remember ordering a spirit mage."

"Sure you didn't." Miles stepped into the room and

tossed a pile of clean clothes onto an armchair. "Damn, this place really *is* fancy."

"Only the best for the Death King's Elemental Soldiers." I closed the door firmly and put the latch on from the inside so nobody could barge in. "Though I've really not spent as much time in here as I'd have liked."

"We can explore." He shrugged off his coat. "In fact, we can get up close and personal with every inch of the place."

"Let's start with the shower." I walked to bathroom and turned on the water, the sound hiding my thudding heartbeat as Miles strode up behind me and spun me around to face him.

His lips met mine, his hands caressing my neck with faint touches which made me shiver with anticipation. His fingers found the pendant, his touch questioning. In answer, I pulled the pendant off and placed it beside the sink, catching sight of my pointed ear in the mirror. I wasn't wearing the illusion spell. I'd forgotten to turn it back on after the last time, and self-consciousness urged me to pick it up again. "You might have to get used to me looking like this."

Miles caught my face in his hand. "You're perfect to me."

I leaned in for another kiss. "Maybe I can get the hang of the compliments thing."

"I'll be persistent." He stripped off his shirt, grabbing the door handle and pulling it shut. I hesitated for a heartbeat before fumbling my own shirt over my head. As I shook my hair loose, Miles's fingers cupped my chin again, his other hand undoing my bra strap. Our mouths crashed together, bare skin slick with water, and the need built between my thighs as he eased off my jeans and underwear at the same time.

Divested of my clothes, I felt more vulnerable than I'd anticipated, but the heat in his eyes ignited my own desire, and he was more than ready for me with quick fingers and a sinful tongue, while the pounding of water swallowed my cries of ecstasy. By the time he'd removed the rest of his clothes, I was too far gone to care for the water flooding the bathroom floor and the fogging reflection of my pointed ears in the mirror.

———

I didn't expect our victory to last, and sure enough, the sound of someone pounding on the door of my room woke me several hours too early.

"What?" I called, from where I lay tangled in Miles's arms on the bed. Admittedly, it was our own fault that we hadn't got much actual rest the night before, but the sleepy smile he flashed in my direction made it worth the indignity of being yanked out of bed.

"We need you at the gates," Ryan called back. "We have a situation the Death King needs you to help with."

I groaned. "Is it the sort of situation that literally anyone else in the castle can handle instead?"

"Trust me, you need to be there."

That didn't sound promising. I scrambled around the room looking for my clothes and weapons, having the distinct feeling our brief reprieve had come to an end. Miles seemed to think so, too, and while the kiss he placed on my lips before we left the room brought back memories of the previous night, all my old worries returned upon leaving the castle.

A large crowd gathered near the gates, a mixture of Spirit Agents and liches and Elemental Soldiers, forming a barrier which prevented me from seeing what awaited on the other side. Another dead lich or two, perhaps a threatening note from the Family--or worse. When they saw me, the crowd quietened, and then parted on either side at a command from the other Elemental Soldiers.

Through the gap, Adair entered the castle grounds with his hands raised above his head in surrender.

17

I stared openly at Adair, unable to believe he had the audacity to set foot anywhere near the Death King's territory. Not only had he attempted to make us believe he'd surrendered, he even wore a blindfold over his eyes as though to imply he wasn't going to mind-control anyone. All my 'bullshit' instincts flared up in warning.

"What the hell are you doing?" I demanded. "Do you think we're dense enough to believe a scrap of fabric means you mean us no harm?"

"No," he said. "I'm wearing this so I can't look you in the eyes. I'm not manipulating you. I want to surrender."

"Right." It was as if he'd overheard my plans from yesterday to infiltrate the Family's house by tricking him into thinking he had me under his spell, though of course he couldn't have. Then again, we'd been raised by the same people and it shouldn't have surprised me that the same duplicity lived in both of us even as we stood on opposite sides of the conflict. "The gate is that way. I'd advise you to take off the blindfold when you walk through the swamp, though it'll be entertaining for the rest of us if you don't."

"I'm not screwing with you," he insisted. "I want to help."

"Stop that bullshit," I said. "Everyone here remembers how you sat there in the Death King's jail and laughed at me as you forced my best friend to put a cursed cantrip in my hand and manipulated me into setting you free. Just because being stuck in the elves' prison hurt your ego—"

"I didn't know," he interjected. "I didn't know what Lex and Roth did. How they created us. I didn't know they stole the Akrith from the elves either."

"Nice try," I said. "That's exactly what you'd say if you were trying to emotionally manipulate me into giving you a second chance."

"I'm not manipulating you!" he protested. "If Lex and Roth find me here, they'll kill me. I only managed to sneak out the house because Lex isn't around, and Roth went out looking for her."

"She's rotting in a field somewhere," I told him, with a twinge of satisfaction. "I ordered a wyrm to crush her into paste and then dump her body as far away as possible, and I'd gladly do the same for you."

Adair grimaced underneath the blindfold. "I know you have a good reason not to trust me."

"More than one good reason," Miles said. "In fact, I'm pretty sure you've betrayed every single person in this castle, and none more than Bria."

"Are we letting him go, then?" said Shelley. "I wouldn't put it past him to have brought his allies ready to attack us when our backs are turned."

"Good point." I turned to address Miles and the Spirit Agents, as well as the Elemental Soldiers. "I'd say we should leave him with the liches for now, while we vote on what to do with him. Oh, and we should tie his hands behind his back so he can't remove that blindfold."

It'd be nice to believe he'd had a change of heart, but this whole situation stank of foul play. His claims that Lex *and* Roth had left the house weren't necessarily accurate, either. Which was a shame, because getting the Elders' Akrith back would be a damn sight easier if I didn't have to fight my way past the Family in order to do so.

When the liches had Adair surrounded, the rest of us gathered far enough away for him not to overhear us debating his fate. The Spirit Agents and the Elemental Soldiers all looked equally distrustful of our new visitor.

"This isn't happening," I said to the others. "There's no way we can trust him in any capacity."

"Agreed," said Ryan.

Trix stepped in. "But what if he's being truthful? You didn't know what your family did before you went to the elves' realm either, Bria."

"I didn't, but I'm not a manipulative sociopath like he is," I said. "This is the guy who tricked me into letting him out of jail. He kept my best friend under mind control for weeks. He's the reason she *died*." My voice cracked on the last word. "I can't trust him."

"I understand," said Trix. "I don't think we should let him walk free, though. Why not keep him under close watch in the castle? It's better than sending him back to the Family."

"You want to lock him in jail?" asked Shelley.

"No," I said. "Last time he threw temper tantrums and

then manipulated me and Tay into letting him out before stealing my cantrips to escape the grounds."

"He's too dangerous to leave anywhere in the Death King's territory without someone watching him," said Tate. "Even the jail."

"Agreed," added Ryan. "With liches guarding him and not humans, he can't use his mind-control talent, but that doesn't mean he hasn't got more surprises up his sleeve. Are you positive the rest of the Family aren't in the area?"

"No," I said. "But I had that wyrm take Lex as far away as possible, and I'm not certain Roth would leave their base unattended, whatever Adair claims. I think he did come here alone."

Didn't mean he'd told the truth about anything else, though. Especially the part where he'd claimed the elves' revelations about Lex and Roth had changed his views on them. He'd never objected to any of the depraved things they'd done in the past. Why should stealing the Elders' Akrith have been any different?

No. I couldn't afford to believe a single word he said. For all I knew, he'd come here to divert my attention while the Family went after the elves again, and while it might be tempting to believe his stories about the Family's house being empty, over my dead body was I getting myself locked up in their prison again.

The others began to argue among themselves, so I approached the steps leading to the castle. "I'm going to ask His Deathly Highness if he objects to us taking a new prisoner. Back in a second."

Ryan tailed me through the doors to the castle's entrance hall, which was empty. Even Dex wasn't guarding the door to the hall of souls as he usually was.

"Bria, the Death King isn't in the castle and neither is Liv," Ryan said in a low voice. "They're dealing with something urgent at the Order's headquarters."

"Damn." That would explain why neither of them had come outside to see Adair's arrival. "So they don't know Adair's here."

"Unfortunately not," said Ryan. "We'll either have to wait for them to come back, or deal with him ourselves. Did you say the elves managed to imprison him in their realm?"

"Before Lex got him out," I said. "I'd hoped to use him as bait to lure them into a trap, but that plan imploded when they attacked the elves and helped him escape. Do you have any more ideas?"

"Me?" they said. "I'm not in charge here."

"You're basically the Death King's favourite Elemental Soldier, the one he sends on all his important missions," I said. "Aren't you?"

"That," said Ryan, "is because Felicity is too nice, while Cal is too unfriendly. And you…"

"I'm an untrustworthy ex-criminal who also happens to be a half elf with a weird and twisted family."

"You're new here," Ryan corrected. "Also, I don't think you're an untrustworthy ex-criminal."

"Seriously?" I arched a brow. "That's as good as a declaration of loyalty for life coming from you, isn't it?"

"If you like." A smile played on their mouth. "Anyway, I think the elves have more cause to inflict punishment on him than anyone else, considering he brought a war to their doorstep. I doubt he'll expect us to hand him back over to them… and I doubt the Family will, either."

"Fair point." It'd go a long way towards rebuilding

trust with the Elders if I gave them their prisoner back. It wasn't like the Family had any intention of leaving them alone either way. "Okay, I need the Akrith… oh, damn. I can't get into the hall of souls."

"Yes, you can." They reached out and pressed a key into my hand. "This is from the Death King."

I stared at the small metal key. "You want me to take the key to the hall of souls?"

"The Death King said we can all use it, yes."

I turned the key in the lock, unable to hold back a grin. Thankfully, the Akrith was easy to spot on a shelf near the door, while the other shelves in the room were covered with carved soul amulets. Once, I might have found them creepy, but the Death King's hard-won trust in me was like a flame burning inside my chest. I'd never thought the sense of belonging I'd always craved would come in a castle decorated with pillars of skulls and full of the souls of the damned, but I wasn't complaining in the slightest.

Ryan's voice drifted from outside. "I'll get some of the Death King's super-strength restraining spells to use on Adair."

"Good idea." I pocketed the Akrith and then locked the door to the hall of souls before leaving the castle and joining Miles at the foot of the stairs.

"You're going to speak to the elves now?" asked Miles, eyeing the stone-shaped lump in my pocket.

"Once we have our hostage secured," I said. "Ryan will be back in a second to restrain our guest."

"You've decided to take him to the elves, then?" said Miles.

"Recapturing their prisoner might put them in a better mood," I said. "I don't want him near the castle."

Especially with the Death King absent. Not that I wanted Adair to know he wasn't here, but something about his apparent surrender struck me as ominous. So did his claims that the Family had vacated the house. If I didn't need the Elders' Akrith so badly, I wouldn't consider going near the place… yet the temptation remained in the back of my mind. How many opportunities would I have to retrieve what they'd stolen?

Ryan descended the stairs, carrying a pair of magic-suppressing handcuffs, and approached the group of liches guarding Adair.

"Hey!" Adair shouted, as Ryan secured his hands behind his back. "What are you doing? Where are you taking me?"

"Somewhere you're familiar with." Squashing my misgivings, I walked ahead, leading the way through the gates and out into the swampland.

Adair's complaints filled the background as I walked to the node, while Ryan and Miles dragged Adair along with them. Then we all entered the node at the same time and transported ourselves to the area outside the now-abandoned warehouse.

"You can't take me back there," said Adair, the truth dawning on him as he recognised where we'd brought him. "Look, I can help you beat the Family. You can't do it without me. Even the elves can't."

"You expect me to listen to you now?" I reached into my pocket for the Akrith. "If you're telling the truth, then I'll see if the elves can back up your claims."

I led the way around the warehouse to the elves' tree, carrying the Akrith in my hand. Light spread outward from my palm as it came into contact with the tree, and at once, the path of the elves' realm extended in front of us.

The coppery tang of blood hit me first, along with the sound of sobbing. I reeled back, knowing that something was horribly wrong, even more so than last time. Blood streaked the pale ground, while several bodies lay sprawled among the trees. Other elves crouched over their dead kin, wearing expressions of shock and grief.

There could only be one person responsible for this carnage. It seemed the Family hadn't left the elves' realm after all. Or one of them hadn't. The question was… *which* one?

Miles swore under his breath, while Adair strained against the cuffs on his wrists. The skin on my arms prickled as Roth walked into view, striding down the path as though he belonged here.

Like Lex, he maintained a youthful appearance out of step with his actual age. Tall and slim with curly dark hair and pale skin, he looked more elfin than human, though his clothes were firmly modern rather than the hand-crafted gear the elves wore. To my horror, the nearest elves fell to their knees on either side of him, and I recognised the pained expressions of those who'd fallen under the insidious power of his emotionally manipulative magic.

Roth's gaze fell on me before I could even think of making an escape.

"Bria," he said. "I have to admit, what you did to Lex was crueller than I'd expect of you. It seems I underestimated your capacity for violence."

"What the hell are you doing?" I demanded. "Haven't you taken enough from the elves already?"

"Ah, but some of their number broke an agreement we made," he said. "I had to show them the consequences of turning their backs on us."

My throat went dry. At a closer look, I recognised several faces among the fallen elves. He'd come here to get back at the elves who'd escaped captivity in the warehouse and had gone as far as to slaughter them in their own realm in order to convince them nowhere was safe. Scumbag.

My hands clenched on the stone in my hand. "Your low-life son *forced* them to work for you. It wasn't a fair agreement. Besides, you stole from every single elf in the Parallel when you cut off their access to their home."

"What lies have they been feeding you?" he said. "We merely took what was ours by rights, not unlike the spirit mages you admire so much."

"Fuck that." Miles stepped up beside me. "I don't support what the spirit mages who started the war did, and no spirit mage with any sense of integrity does either. I sure as hell don't support *you*."

"There are always outliers," said Roth. "Frankly, I think I've done more for the elves' employment in our warehouses than any other authority, including the Houses of the Elements and the vampires."

"You're wrong." Adair ran behind us, hands still cuffed but having shaken off his blindfold, and shot a furious stare at his father. "Leave them alone."

Was he putting on an act? If he was, Roth wasn't in on the plan, because he merely scowled at Adair. "What are you doing here? I told you to stay at home."

Adair shook his head. "I couldn't let you get away with harming anyone else. You lied to us—lied to Bria and me

—when you stole from the elves and used their magic on us, taking away our choice and making us complicit in your crimes."

Damn. Either his plan to deceive me went beyond letting even his father in on it… or he was being genuine. Not that I could bet on the latter, but at least he'd taken the attention off the elves and enabled the surviving few to shake off the effects of Roth's magic and back out of the line of fire. Anger clenched inside me at the sight of Belgi among them, along with Trix's friend Drina, whose expression was dull, her eyes glittering with grief. *They even took her, too?*

Roth gave a short laugh. "So the elves poisoned your mind during your capture, too, I see. Or Bria did. I have to admit, I always wondered who would end up corrupting the other. It's been fascinating to watch the two of you struggle against one another."

Adair looked his father in the eyes and spoke with all the strength of his persuasive magic. "Get out."

Roth swayed on the spot, while my heart pounded against my chest. I'd never seen one member of the Family pitted against another before, and I'd always assumed that like me, Adair was weaker than the other two. But he *did* have a talent they didn't share, and if Roth underestimated him, that might give him an edge.

Adair's face twisted in a grimace as Roth unleashed his own controlling magic, and the two fought a wordless battle, locked in a bitter power play. The remaining elves wisely retreated and disappeared into the surrounding woodland.

"They're going to kill each other," I whispered to Miles. "We need to find help."

I looked around the elves watching the carnage from within the bushes, and my gaze caught on one of the guards I recognised from last time.

Keeping an eye on the others, I made my way to his hiding spot and whispered, "Where are the Elders?"

"In the forest, protecting what's left of our power," he answered. "That man... he must have had direct contact with the Elders' Akrith recently. He's stronger than most of us."

Oh, hell. I hadn't realised that being in this realm would boost the Family's power, too, but they were still part elf, as well as having the Elders' own Akrith under their watch. I should have gone to find it first, but I'd been so sure at least one of them would be at the house—

A shout made my head snap up, and Adair fell prone to the ground, howling in agony. When Roth turned to me next, I froze for an instant. Then I threw the Akrith into Miles's waiting hands and stood directly in the path of Roth's attack.

A moment later, his magic hit me like a thunderstorm.

18

When I next came back to awareness, I found myself in a cage. Not a cage of interlocked branches in the elves' forest, but a manmade cell inside the Family's house. They had me right where they wanted me... and this time, there was no Tay to come to my rescue.

The irony? This was exactly where I'd needed to go if I'd wanted to find the Akirth the Family had taken and return it to the Elders, but right now, I could barely even move. Roth had seriously wiped me out. Even when I'd burned him and Lex to a crisp during my first escape, he'd never inflicted that kind of agony on me before. It was barely a glimpse of the pain he and Lex had inflicted on the elves and on his other enemies over the years, I knew, but if I didn't get the hell out of here, they'd do worse. The Akrith must be hidden inside this very building. I was so damn close, and yet it remained out of reach.

I'd managed to struggle into an upright position when Lex strode into view. She wore a surprisingly plain outfit, compared to her usual getup, jeans and a jacket and no makeup. While no traces remained of the damage the wyrm had inflicted on her at my command, her eyes narrowed with fury. "You're lucky I let you live."

"If you want me to thank you, you'll have to live with the disappointment." I shook my head, regretting the slight movement when more pain shot through my nerve endings. "Besides, by your own admission, I can't die. Thanks to what you did."

"I'm sure you know that isn't the case," she said. "Not with the tools we have at our disposal, which the elves will have told you about, I don't doubt."

Shit. The Elders' Akrith... could it undo *my* healing power? I bloody hoped not. "Is that the real reason you kept the Akrith for all these years, aside from wanting to maintain your longevity and youth? So you could dispose of anyone who disappointed you, even Adair and me?"

"Not initially, but it's vexing that both of you turned out to be such troublemakers," she said.

Both. So Adair must be imprisoned in here somewhere as well. While he'd undoubtedly fought against Roth, I still wasn't completely sure where he stood. He might have turned on him for selfish reasons rather than out of a desire to support the elves he'd been indifferent to for his entire life, and I couldn't count on his support.

Then again, what did I know? His behaviour was perplexing, and it wasn't like I could read his thoughts. Whatever the case, Lex clearly thought he'd betrayed her, and Roth did, too. Which at least gave me one fewer enemy to deal with.

I gave a faint shrug. "We were raised that way, weren't we? You shouldn't be surprised we ended up defying you."

"I'll give you the chance to surrender," she said. "It goes without saying that it'll be much easier for you if you comply with my commands. And for your allies, too, of course."

"Fuck you," I said. "You think I'll easily forget you're the reason the elves were cut off from their home? I bet that wasn't all you did in the last war, either."

"Of course not," she said. "When the mage council had their falling-out, we saw the opportunity and we turned our attention to developing cantrips which were designed for warfare. When the elves' Elders took issue with our actions, we decided that it would result in much less conflict if we simply severed the connection between their realm and ours."

"I take it you forced the elves to make cantrips for you back then as well?" I said. "They did all the work, as usual, just like the citadels and everything else you or the spirit mages have taken credit for."

"Oh, I wouldn't say it's inaccurate to call the citadels our creation," she said. "After all, it was our cantrip research which enabled some of their more recent developments. Like those ingenious machines, for instance."

Holy shit. My *family* had created those machines in the citadel, or at least the cantrips which fuelled them. The spirit mages might have been the ones who'd destroyed the Parallel during the last war, but the Family had the blood of the victims on their hands as much as their original creators did. "So you claim to have done more than the spirit mages did?"

"The spirit mages were gifted, but their skills were with the cerebral, the spiritual. Ours were more practical." She shrugged. "It was an even trade."

"You're sick."

"Maybe," she said. "But we're on the winning team. Soon the Houses of the Elements will fall the same way the Council did, and the former House of Spirit will be no more."

She means the Court of the Dead. Was the Death King under attack, too, if he'd even returned to the castle yet? I should be helping defend his territory, not stuck in a cage.

"I would advise you to think carefully about your choice, Bria," said Lex. "I'll give you the chance to decide whether you're going to cooperate or condemn your friends to a brutal death. Needless to say, there are no loopholes."

She turned away from the cage and walked out of sight, while I bit back tears of frustration. A throbbing pain centred in my skull, and no matter how hard I thought, I didn't see a way out of this situation without someone ending up dead. At least I'd helped Miles escape the elves before he could be captured, too. That was all the consolation I had left, because if she got hold of him… watching him die like Tay had would obliterate all the fight I had left inside me.

Maybe Lex had a point in that delaying my surrender would only condemn the people I cared about, especially Miles. The notion of swallowing my pride and making a deal with her in order to save my friends made me feel queasy and self-loathing, but what choice did I have? I'd exhausted all other options.

The sound of a faint groan hit my ears. I twisted around, ignoring the fresh shock of pain in my limbs, and spotted another cage further down the corridor from mine. So that's where they'd locked up Adair. From this angle, he looked like he was still unconscious, but he'd wake up in a world of pain soon, I didn't doubt.

Would Lex make him the same offer? It wasn't like he had friends or family for her to threaten. Aside from me, of course, and he'd already proved he didn't care if I came to any harm. I was pretty much on my own.

The idea of surrender dangled itself before my eyes again, but if I knew anything about the Family, it was that they were never satisfied with the bare minimum. They might let *me* go, but they'd never leave the elves alone, and I couldn't trust Lex or Roth not to harm them despite any promises they might make me. As for Adair? I couldn't believe I was considering depending on him to get me out of this mess, but I was out of any better options.

I scooted across the floor until I sat close enough to see his face through the cage bars. "Adair."

He didn't move.

"Hey. Adair."

His hand twitched. Then he let out a scream of agony, curling up in a ball as the remnants of Roth's magic jerked through him. My own nerve endings flared up in sympathy as he writhed and yelled. I covered my ears until he was done screaming and had sat up for long enough to figure out where he was—and to see me watching him from my own cage.

"Looks like they got both of us," I said to him.

He grunted. "Why are you so happy? You're locked up as well."

"I'm not happy," I said. "Not at all. Did you see where Roth went?"

"No, I passed out," he said. "The last thing I remember

was you throwing the stone at your friend and closing off the elves' realm."

At least Miles had got away. He probably knew they'd brought me here, but he'd be better off not staging a rescue mission, so I hoped the others kept him from risking his neck on my behalf.

"Are you surprised they locked you up as well?" I asked.

"No," he said. "You did see Roth use his power on me, didn't you?"

"Yeah, but nothing you did made any sense, to be honest," I said. "I figured you were challenging him for power, or something, not trying to stand up for the elves they betrayed."

He was silent for a long moment. "Guess that's more likely, huh. I've been a dick."

"That's the most honest sentence I've ever heard come out of your mouth."

"Hey, I wasn't lying when I surrendered to you," he protested. "I told you it was a bad idea to take me out of the castle."

"Roth already went after the elves," I pointed out. "And how do I know this isn't part of some elaborate plan on Lex and Roth's behalf to lure me into a false sense of security?"

"You don't."

At least *that* was honest. "If you really meant what you said, then hear me out."

He gave me a sharp look. "You have a plan?"

"Not much of one," I muttered. "Do you happen to know whereabouts Lex put the Akrith she stole from the

Elders years ago? Because that's what we need. Without it..."

"There's no chance of us taking them down," he finished. "Yeah. I figured that out when I first heard they took the elves' artefacts. They told you, too?"

"Yes." It wasn't exactly a secret anymore. "What I don't know is *where* they hid it. Have you seen anything that resembles an elven artefact in the house?"

"I reckon they put it in the mine," he said. "That's got to be the most secure place on the property."

"The mine?" Now I thought about it, the mine was one of the most well-guarded parts of the estate and was often the natural place to store anything valuable. The magical source inside the mine was valuable enough in itself, after all, and was the reason they'd kept a wyrm on the property in the first place.

"Yeah," he said. "I can try to use my ability on them for long enough to escape our cells. If you run, you can probably find your way through the mine by yourself."

"Using your ability on them is hit and miss," I reminded him. "Would you be able to persuade them to unlock both our cells at once?"

"Not both, but I bet I can convince Lex to hand over an unlocking cantrip," he said.

Hmm. If he *was* working against me, I'd need to leave enough leeway to get myself free without ending up in deeper trouble if he turned against me. As long as I had no other allies within reach, I'd remain vulnerable. Even if he was telling the truth, though, I'd seen his ability fail to work on Roth, and the Family would be on the lookout for trickery from both of us.

"I doubt it'll be that simple," I said to him. "Suppose one of us pretended to surrender…"

"You think they'd go for that?"

"Lex said she'd be willing to give me a chance to change my mind," I said. "She's dead set on me joining her of my own free will. Not sure she'd take my word for it, but she might take yours. Tell her I brainwashed you. Or the elves. Either works."

"You think?"

"Yeah, it's worth trying," I said. "If you can convince her you're on her side for long enough to grab the keys or a cantrip to get me out of here, then you might not need your persuasive magic at all."

That way, if he was already on her side and faking the whole thing, he'd have nothing to gain except an extra chance to taunt me. I, meanwhile, would have nothing to lose that hadn't already been taken away. Provided my allies didn't show up and end up getting caught too, of course.

"All right," he said. "I'll do it."

We sat in silence for a while, waiting for Lex to return. It was possibly the most amicable Adair had ever behaved towards me in our lives. We'd never been close even while growing up, more rivals than caring siblings, and while his cruelty had more often been directed at other people than at me, I'd never been able to trust him. Putting my faith in him at a critical moment like this was a weird feeling, and I wasn't sure I liked it.

When footsteps came down the corridor again, I caught Adair's eye and gave a brief nod.

Lex approached Adair's cell first, seeing he was awake. "Adair."

"Hey, Lex," he said.

"So it's true," she said. "Roth tells me that Bria led you astray."

"Did she hell," said Adair defensively. "I was trying a new strategy and you two both screwed it up for me."

"Excuse me?" she said. "A strategy for what, exactly?"

"To get back at the elves, of course," he said. "And to get close to Bria. I almost pulled it off, too, but Roth attacked me with his magic and then you locked me in a cage without even asking me any questions. I thought you had more faith in me than that."

I could almost believe the act, which said volumes for how little I trusted his word, but Lex was eating up every word of it. Unlike me, she'd never had any reason to doubt him until today.

"You attacked your father in front of the elves, Adair. What did you expect him to do?"

"I did it because *she* was there." He jerked his head in my direction. "I faked surrendering to her to manipulate her into bringing me to the Elders, since Roth ruined my first shot by breaking me out of the cage before I had the chance to lay a hand on them. Then he went and did the exact same again."

"What did you expect?" she said. "You didn't tell Roth or me a word of your plans."

"You disappeared," Adair said defensively. "And I tried to tell Roth, when he broke me out of the elves' jail the first time. Ask him. He refused to listen to me."

"I will," she said. "If you're lying to me, you'll be sorry, Adair."

And with that, she walked out of view. I waited for a few long seconds to ensure she was far enough away not to hear us before asking, "Is it true? Did you tell Roth you were planning on betraying me?"

"Yeah," he muttered. "Comes in handy when nobody expects you to keep your word."

"Guess so." *I'd better hope he does keep his word this time. Or we're both screwed.*

19

Lex returned within a few minutes and approached Adair's cage once again. "Roth confirmed you did tell him you intended to betray your sister."

"I'm glad you both trust me," Adair said, sarcasm dripping from his words. "Can you get me out of this cage now? I'm no use to anyone in here."

"Only if you promise not to run off alone this time," Lex said. "You can't go around forming your own plans without asking permission from either of us and expect not to end up in trouble, like you did with the elves the first time around."

"No need to rub it in," said Adair. "I'm not sitting in a cage while you two get to take part in the spirit mages' war."

"Didn't I tell you to stay out of the spirit mages' petty arguments?" she said. "They're welcome to finish one another off. *Our* goal is to clean up the aftermath."

So much for loyalty. She might have allied with the

spirit mages at the time of the last war, but everything the Family did was in their own self-interest. Question was, where was Roth? Was he still stalking around the elves' realm, terrorising them?

Adair stepped out of the cage, casting a brief glance in my direction. "What about her?"

"Since your sister hasn't seen sense yet, she'll be staying there until she does," Lex told him.

"All right." As she led the way out of the corridor, his gaze connected with mine, and he gave a slight nod before walking after her.

I can't believe I'm depending on Adair to get me out of here.

I couldn't trust him entirely, but I'd give him a little time to keep his word before devising a backup plan. Not that I had many options, so I settled for pacing in circles around my cage. Within a few minutes, more footsteps came from down the corridor. I halted my pacing as Adair rushed in, breathless. "I shook her off. We'll have to move fast."

"Only if you get me out first."

He held up a hand, revealing my pendant and the gleaming cantrips concealed inside it. "There's an unlocking spell in here, right?"

"Should be."

He found the right spell and unlocked the door to my cage. I stepped out and extended a hand for the pendant.

"Not going to thank me?" He pressed it into my palm.

"Only when I'm safely out of here," I whispered. "Where is Lex? And Roth?"

"Roth isn't here," he said. "As for Lex, she's talking to her team of assassins outside. I'm supposed to be minding my own business."

"Okay." I opened the pendant and retrieved an invisibility cantrip, which I used on myself. "Will they come looking for you?"

"Nah, Lex just told me to stay back here and not get in their way."

"Can you make sure she doesn't follow me to the mine?" I asked. "I might need a diversion if it turns out the Akrith *is* hidden in there."

"All right, but you know she and Roth will probably rip my head off if they find out I'm deceiving them."

"Welcome to the world of espionage," I said. "Let's go."

Outside, the sky was overcast, and there was no longer a spell concealing the rebuilt house where we'd been held captive. Behind, a huge chunk of gleaming golden metal lay half-submerged in the ground, and I trod in that direction, towards the maze of tunnels which had once comprised the mine. The earth mages must have spent weeks transporting all that material to the warehouse, but at the moment, the place looked out of use. My heart dropped. Had they already removed the Akrith from its hiding place? Had Roth been carrying it when he'd gone into the elves' realm? Their cantrip scheme had reached its end, and with the spirit mages' next power-grab on the horizon, for all I knew, they were willing to risk even their precious stolen artefacts to ensure their victory.

I turned back to Adair, seeing him watching the gates at the front of the estate. When I reached his side, I spotted Lex and her army heading towards the glowing node nearest to the Family's estate.

Is this it? Were they going to join Roth in searching the elves' realm until they found the Elders and wiped them out for good?

"The Elders' Akrith isn't in the mine," I whispered to Adair. "Did they take it somewhere else?"

"Might have," said Adair. "I don't see them carrying something that valuable to the battlefield, though."

"What if they think it'd assure their victory, though?"

"Not really their style. They're too dependent on its power to take the risk, I reckon."

True. I was surprised he'd noticed, but then again, he was observant. And smart, even if he didn't always act like it. It was kind of nice to have him on my team, even temporarily, rather than being on the receiving end of his mind games.

A flash of light drew my eyes back to the node. At first, I assumed the army was marching through to Elysium, but when the light blazed a familiar orange-red colour and a hot breeze rushed over me, I nearly tripped over my own feet.

"Was that an inferno cantrip?" I squinted at Lex, who'd crouched down near the blast of light. "What's she doing?"

Adair hissed a warning, but I'd already broken into a run towards the entrance to the estate. From there, I sprinted out into the wasteland and halted near Lex. Several round stones lay on the ground at her feet—or their charred remains did, anyway. *Holy shit, she set them ablaze.* I'd assumed the Akriths were all but impervious to damage, but the inferno cantrips had even burned through the elf-built machinery in the citadels. They'd scorched the Akriths until they were little more than rubble.

"The hell happened here?" Adair caught up to Lex, careful not to look directly at me.

Her gaze passed right over my invisible form. "I thought I told you to stay in the house."

"I saw a fire," he said. "What's this?"

"These are all the Akriths we were able to procure from the elves," she said. "I decided it was easier to cut off their realm again rather than risk them forming allegiances with the other elves in the Parallel behind our backs."

Oh damn. If the Family alone controlled the means of getting in and out of their realm, then it was a safe bet that the elves would have difficulty giving us any help during the upcoming conflict.

Adair frowned. "You don't have every stone in the Parallel in your possession, do you?"

"Of course not," she said. "But I doubt the elves will be able to replenish their own before the battle is over. We win."

But I still have my own Akrith. I'd given it to Miles before my capture, and now it might be my last remaining connection to their realm. Assuming they didn't wipe out the tree, too.

"Wow," said Adair. "I thought you wanted to convince the elves to fight at your side. Isn't that the whole reason you were hunting the stones down in the first place?"

"I underestimated how keen the Elders would be to avoid detection," she said. "Roth and I decided it was a waste of our time and resources to break past those pesky defences of theirs. Since our abilities are less effective on them even with their own Akrith on our side, it's better that we leave them alone."

Since what?

"Right." Adair's expression and tone betrayed nothing,

but he must have made the same observation as I had. "Do you want me to help?"

"Not yet," she said. "I'll call you when you're needed. Go on, get back into the house."

Adair made for the ruins of the estate again, as did I, since I couldn't think of anything else to do. When I was sure the two of us were alone, I swore under my breath. "I should have known they wouldn't make it easy for the elves to contact one another."

"Don't you have one of those stones?" he asked. "I did, but Lex took mine, and I assume she destroyed it along with the others."

I do. "That depends on how close the enemy's got to the Death King."

"You go back and warn your allies, then," he said. "I'll find Roth. If he isn't in the elves' realm, he must be somewhere else. I can get him to hand over the Elders' Akrith. I bet he's the one carrying it."

"But…"

"You don't really trust me, do you?" Adair said.

"I…" I didn't. I couldn't switch loyalties that fast, and besides, there were years of resentment and rivalry and fear that couldn't be bridged in such a short time. "I don't trust *him* not to see through the act and use his power on you again."

"You'd be surprised," he said. "Okay, Lex might have a few questions for me if she goes back to the jail and finds you aren't there…"

"There is that." But he was right—I needed to fetch my own Akrith if I wanted any chance whatsoever at warning the elves of the Family's latest scheme. "Try not to give me away, all right?"

I sprinted downhill, leaving the Family's estate behind me. I had to wait for Lex to turn away before hopping into the node and reappearing in front of the Death King's castle. When I reached the gates, it hit me that something was notably different about the swampland. For one thing, nobody stood on security duty. In fact, I didn't see anyone in the grounds at all, dead or alive.

Heart sinking, I ran through the gates, relief washing over me as I spotted Miles hovering near the fence. When I turned off the invisibility cantrip, he immediately ran over to my side and wrapped me in a bone-crushing hug. "Shit, Bria. What happened?"

"The Family captured me." I squeezed him back. "Adair helped me escape, would you believe it? But what's going on here?"

"It's not good," he said. "The Death King? He's gone."

"What do you mean, gone?"

"Not just him, but all the liches, too," said Miles. "Every single one of them. The enemy used some kind of spell that targeted every lich in his territory and made them start to… disappear."

"They vanished?" No. That couldn't be possible. "Even their King?"

"No, he went to search for a solution," said Miles. "Liv did, too. He ordered us to stay behind, and he took every one of the liches with him."

No way. "Do you have the Akrith I gave you?"

"Yeah, but I assumed it wasn't safe to go back to the elves' realm," he said.

"It isn't, but Lex destroyed all the other stones she had in her possession using an inferno cantrip," I said. "Worse, I'm pretty sure Roth ran off with the Elders' Akrith himself. Adair's gone to track him down, but I doubt he'll be able to overpower him."

"Adair? You mean your demented brother?" he said. "Is he still pretending to be on our side?"

"Believe me, I'm confused, too," I said. "But he faked surrender to get Lex to set him free, and then stole my pendant back and let me out of my cage without alerting Lex and Roth."

Miles blinked. "What does he have to gain from that?"

"Perhaps he was telling the truth when he said the elves made him realise how fucked up what Lex and Roth did to both of us actually is," I said. "Not that they're in any way discouraged. They think they've already won."

Trix ran out of the castle and brightened at the sight of me. "Bria! There you are. I thought the Family caught you."

"They did, but I escaped," I said. "The bad news is that they destroyed all the Akriths they could get their hands on."

"Not this one." Miles pulled the gleaming stone out of his pocket. "Just tell me what to do."

Trix's brow wrinkled. "Bria, did you have a plan?"

"Not much of one," I said. "Lex let something interesting slip when I was eavesdropping on her and Adair. She said her and Roth's abilities don't work on the Elders, or certainly not as effectively. Even with their own Akrith at their command."

"Oh, I know that," said Trix. "But in order for the Elders to stand a chance of overpowering them, they'd need to confront the Family in the elves' realm, which is only possible if they walk in willingly. And someone would need to take the Elders' Akrith away from them, too. From what I heard, it sounds like Roth took in as much of its power as possible before launching his attack on their realm."

"Evil bastard," I said. "I think he's carrying it himself, but I'm not sure he went. Lex implied she cut off the elves' realm to prevent the elves in the Parallel from forming alliances with them, so she must believe there's still a fighting force left among their number."

"Yes, you're right," said Trix. "The Family might have taken the Elder's Akrith, but their very realm is weaponised against those who wish them harm. No matter how hard Roth searches, he will not be able to find the Elders' hiding place. He was only able to attack the guards and the refugees from the warehouse because he took them off guard."

Good to know. Too bad that in order for my plan to work, there was a good chance we needed to get the Family back into the elves' realm and hope it didn't end fatally for everyone.

"You should know… your friend Drina was there as well," I told Trix. "In the elves' realm. I think she must have been taken to the warehouse, after she was captured."

"I thought so," he said. "I hope she's okay."

"She was alive, the last I saw," I said. "Adair seems to think he can convince Roth to hand over the Elders' Akrith if he catches him by surprise with his persuasive magic, but it's a major risk to take. I don't *think* he's in the elves' realm at the moment, but we can't afford to lose too much time."

Miles held up the Akrith. "Are you sure you want to go back there?"

"I am." I watched the light spinning around the stone's surface for an instant. "I'll see if any of the others are still willing to fight. Miles… can you wait here this time? We don't want the enemy mounting an attack on the castle when our backs are turned."

"Not many of us left here anyway," Miles said.

"I'll come with you, Bria," said Trix. "The Elders will listen to us."

After what the Family had already done, I had my sincere doubts we'd be able to find them at all, but I had to try. Miles didn't look happy, but he nodded and handed me the Akrith. "Please don't get captured again."

"I'll try not to."

After leaving him in the castle grounds, Trix and I headed through the node and landed outside the warehouse before walking over to the sprawling form of the elves' tree. To my relief, Lex was nowhere in sight, but she'd had an army of assassins to wrangle into line the last time I'd seen her. Besides, there was no reason for her to come back here now she'd destroyed all the Akriths aside from the one Roth himself carried.

I pressed the Akrith to the tree, and light flooded my sight before the path of the elves' realm extended in front of us. Trix and I stepped forward, and he exhaled in a pained noise when he saw the blood streaking the paths, though the bodies had been cleared away since my last visit. I looked around for any signs of the elves and saw two figures patrolling among the trees. The same two guards who'd escorted me to see the Elders pointed their weapons in our direction when they saw us. We were back to square one, apparently.

"Hey—don't worry, we're not here to attack you," I said. "I need to talk to the Elders."

"That's what you said before, yet you brought those *Vetran* here," spat the male elf.

"I didn't bring them with me," I said. "Roth and Lex captured me and dragged me to their prison, but I escaped. I need the Elders' help if I want to stop them from causing you further harm."

"How do we know you're not here to betray us?" said the female elf. "Again?"

"We aren't," Trix insisted. "Bria never betrayed you the first time around."

"Lex and Roth are destroying the other Akriths," I told the elves. "Except for the one they stole from the Elders, that is. I heard their powers don't work as effectively on the Elders as they do on the rest of us. Is that true?"

The two elves looked at one another. "Yes, but they've killed enough of us, and I would not risk the lives of our Elders. If you bring them here, you will face the same punishment as they do."

"We won't," I promised. "But we need your help. Lex and Roth have an army of assassins marching to Elysium right this instant. You promised the Death King you'd be willing to help him in the battle, and the time has come."

"And where is the King of the Dead?"

"Fighting." I hoped so, anyway. He'd taken the entire lich army with him, at any rate, and without them, our side looked awfully sparse at the moment. "The war is imminent. The enemy has already targeted the Court of the Dead, and... and the reason the Family destroyed the Akriths is to prevent you from allying with the elves in the Parallel. They're worried, scared you might get the upper hand, and I'm sure they have the Elders' Akrith with them out in the open. There won't be a better chance for us to take it back, but I can't fight them alone."

"We'll pass on your message to Elder Velkis and Elder Datra," he responded. "They refuse to leave the heart of the forest, understandably. If they do, and those *Vetren* come back, it would be catastrophic for all of us. They would destroy us entirely."

"We'll never allow them to do that," Trix said. "Would any of you offer your skills on the battlefield, to fight for the future of your realm? If you don't, I fear they will come here before long, and they will bring the Akrith they stole from the Elders to use against you."

Unless Adair steals it back first. But the odds of *that* happening were lower than Lex and Roth turning out to be nice, normal parents.

"We must ask our Elders' permission before sending anyone to fight outside of our realm," said the female elf. "If they agree, and if we have the adequate resources to join you, we will do so."

That would have to do, but until we got the Elders' Akrith away from Roth, beating them was a tall order. I suspected I'd only got lucky the time I'd set the estate ablaze because they'd been cocky enough not to keep the Elders' Akrith close at hand, and they hadn't seen my attack coming.

This time, though? They expected a war, and they had the Elders' Akrith in their hands to ensure their victory.

"Thank you," I said. "Tell you what... ask the refugees from the warehouse, too. I'm sure some of them will be more than happy to help us fight against the Family."

"I will pass on word to them," he said, turning away.

Trix and I left the elves' realm, landing in the same spot behind the warehouse we'd left from. We were lucky Lex hadn't employed an inferno cantrip here, too, though the tree might well be next on her list and we had no backup at hand. I didn't like to leave it unprotected, but I'd have to hope the Family was under the impression their purge had taken out all useable Akriths and left them with no point in destroying the tree as well.

I led the way back through the node, where we transported ourselves to the Court of the Dead.

Miles ran up to us at the gate. "Any luck?"

"The elves are asking the Elders if they can spare anyone to help us fight," I said to him. "Not sure if they'll get here in time if the battle's already kicking off. I did tell them Roth is likely carrying the Elders' Akrith, but I have no idea where he is."

"I do," said Miles. "At least, I'm pretty sure I know where he is."

"Wait, you do?" I frowned at him. "What did I miss?"

"They've taken Elysium," said Miles. "The Family is now in charge of all four Houses of the Elements."

hit. The Family had already taken over Elysium. That must have been where Roth had been while Lex prepared the assassins' army to join him, having no need to torment the elves any longer now they had a bigger target in their line of sight. "The elves are going to vote on whether to come and help, but if the army is already in Elysium…"

"They're not fighting," he said. "The Houses surrendered upfront without fighting back."

"Seriously?" Damn. "Why?"

"Why else?" said Ryan, approaching with the other Elemental Soldiers behind them. "They got hit so hard by those cantrips last time around that most of them surrendered without even considering putting up a fight. I think they're a lost cause, to tell you the truth."

"They can't be," I said. "Is the Death King there? I told the elves he was ready for war, but I know he disappeared and so did his army."

"I haven't a clue where he is," said Miles. "He told us

to stay behind while he and the liches went after the enemy and brought an end to whatever spell they used on him. I assumed that meant Elysium, but I think I'd have heard if he'd got between the Family and the Houses."

I shook my head. "We have to do something. There's got to be someone in Elysium who's prepared to help us force the Family to relinquish their grip on the Houses."

"We can look for dissidents who fled the Houses when the Family showed up," Ryan said. "There'll be some who'd have refused to join them, but hardly enough for an army, I wouldn't think."

"Better some than none," I said.

"Agreed," said Cal, to my surprise. "I know a few mages' hiding spots in the city."

"And me," added Felicity. "I was actually making progress with the House of Water before all this happened. I don't think every one of them would have turned their backs on their own House overnight. Maybe they're waiting for their chance to strike when the enemy's back is turned, but there's got to be some of them ready to fight."

"That'll be our next stop, then," I said. "We can't do much good from here, especially with the Death King gone."

"I agree," said Ryan. "I'm not staying here while our master fights to the death on our behalf and the Family undoes all the progress we made with the Houses. We can't let them bring back those cursed cantrips, either."

"No way," I said. "You're okay with leaving the castle, though?"

"The Death King didn't explicitly tell us *all* to stay

here," they said. "Besides, he's ready for all-out war and so are we. This is it."

"Then I think we should raid the Death King's cantrip stores first," I said. "In case any of us end up locked in the Houses' jail like I did last time."

The last thing I wanted was to get locked in the House of Fire *again, but we'd need to prepare for any eventuality.* While the others went looking for weapons, Harper accosted me near the doors. "You're leaving?"

"We have to fight for Elysium," I said. "Are you— bloody hell, Harper."

She looked awful, her shadowy form faded around the edges below the illusion of her human face. "What?"

"What's wrong with you?"

"I don't know." Harper's voice trembled, while her soul amulet dangled from her hand. "Whatever it is, it's affecting all the liches, including me. I hoped keeping hold of my amulet might help, but it didn't."

"Shit." Was *that* why the other liches had left? No wonder they'd all followed the Death King in a desperate attempt to find a solution. "Why didn't you go with the others?"

Her eyes filled with tears which swiftly disappeared as her illusion flickered at the edges. "I don't want to die in the darkness with a bunch of strangers. If I'm going to die, I'd rather be with my friends."

Tears stung my own eyes. "I don't know what's wrong, but if I can help, I will."

Mav, Harper's pet sprite, flitted into view. "Please help her. I can't lose her. I can't."

"I'll do my best." I turned around when Miles walked through the front door of the castle.

He eyed Harper in surprise. "I thought all the liches left."

"Something's wrong with her," I said. "Same as the other liches."

"Ah, crap." He handed me some cantrips and a pair of knives, too. "This is all I could get. The other Spirit Agents are with us, too, by the way."

"We have to leave if we want to stop the Family before they can do any more damage in Elysium," I said to Harper. "Can you hang on until we get back?"

"I don't want to die here," she said. "I'll come with you."

An argument rose on my tongue, but poor Harper looked to be at death's door already, and it wasn't like battle would be any worse for her. "All right. Let's go."

Once our group was fully armed, we made our way to the node and crossed over to Elysium, landing near the Spirit Agents' old house. The city was quiet enough that you wouldn't think it was under the enemy's control, but the Spirit Agents remained on edge as they walked past their old house. I kept a worried eye on Harper's fading form, a blue glow on her shoulder signalling the presence of her water sprite.

Miles peered over the fence to the Spirit Agents' house. "Hey… there's someone in there."

"Not the Family?" I backtracked to his side, trying to see through the slight gap in the curtains of the living room.

"It won't be," said Miles. "I wonder…"

He darted into the garden and approached the house. Before he could reach the door, it flew open, and a man appeared with fire blazing in his hands. "Get out!"

The stranger's curly hair was unkempt, his tawny skin

sprinkled with dirt, and he wore the red-and-black uniform of the House of Fire.

"You're in my house," Miles said.

"It's not your house, *or* hers," said the mage, spotting me standing behind him. "Unless the Death King owns this place now."

"Aren't you from the House of Fire?" In fact, he was one of Harris's fellow security guards. What was he doing hiding in the Spirit Agents' old house?

"Used to be," said a blond female mage from behind him, who wore the uniform of the House of Water. "We're hiding from those maniacs who took over the Houses."

So the others had been right and some of the mages hadn't taken the Family's side. That was one piece of good news. The bad news, of course, was that it couldn't be more obvious that however many people were in this house, they were vastly outnumbered by the mages who'd chosen to surrender to the Family. Only a few dozen people were visible inside the hall and the living room behind them, while judging by their uniforms, they represented all four Houses. Far from an army, though.

"Are there any other places where mages who escaped the Houses might have hidden?" I asked.

"I wish I knew," said the fire mage. "We all left after the talk of surrender began and grouped together when we realised we weren't alone. This was the only place in the middle of the city we could think of to shelter in where they wouldn't think to look for us. If anyone else is left inside the Houses who doesn't agree with the Family's take-over, they're trapped."

"That's what I was afraid of," I said. "We've come to see

who'll join us in challenging them, but if this is all we have…"

Miles cleared his throat. "I can think of one place you might find backup."

I rotated to face him. "Where's that?"

"Where in the city are there hundreds of mages imprisoned, most of whom are in full possession of their magical talents?" said Miles, an oddly calculating look in his eyes. "Enough people to make a real problem for the Family?"

"You mean criminals?" said the fire mage. "We can't set them loose in the city."

Oh. Now I got it… and it wasn't a bad idea at all.

"I think you and I both know that the majority of mages weren't jailed for committing anything which would count as a crime if the Houses weren't in charge of the city," said Miles. "Besides, don't you have records of which of them are dangerous murderers and which just made an enemy of the wrong person in the Houses? It shouldn't be too hard for you to leave the deadliest mages behind bars and free the rest."

"No," said the blond water mage from behind him. "It'd undermine everything we've achieved since the war."

"What, jailing innocent people?" I said. "I'm still not clear on what *I* was locked up for, aside from being in the wrong place at the wrong time. Lex and Roth are escaped criminals, yet the Houses let them take over anyway. Isn't that a good enough reason to throw the whole system out?"

Several of the mages murmured agreement, but others broke into arguing among themselves. I backed away from the doorstep to face the other Elemental Soldiers. "It's a valid idea, right?"

"I'm up for it," said Cal. "I wasn't locked up for any good reason, either."

"I'll help." Harper was barely visible, a shadowy smudge against the lawn. "The Houses are the reason the Family were able to get away with their crimes for as long as they did. They're the reason my brother died."

Yeah. The Family had hurt so many people, directly and indirectly. Their lies had crept among the Houses and ensnared the desperate, and Harper had only been one of their victims. If I had anything to do with it, we'd be the last people they ever hurt.

Miles raised his voice to address the bickering mages. "Look, the Houses are occupied by the enemy. The Family will probably set free anyone who's willing to fight for them anyway. Why shouldn't we get there first?"

"Exactly," I said. "Come on, guys, we can't waste all day arguing with one another. We have a city to defend, which is supposed to be your job, I might add."

The fire mage faced me. "Fine. But only if we can find a way to free them which doesn't involve us all getting killed."

"I'm sure we can come up with one."

Time for a mass prison breakout the likes of which had never been seen in the Parallel before.

———

Once we had a starting point, we broke into four groups to discuss strategies for tackling each of the four Houses. Cal seemed keen enough to take command of the earth mages, while Felicity spoke to the water mages. Ryan did the same with the air mages and Trix was happy enough to join them—which left Miles and me to deal with the House of Fire, along with the fire mage who'd let us into the house, who turned out to be called Xander.

"Don't forget the larger fortresses which belong to all four Houses collectively," said Shelley, who'd convinced the Spirit Agents to join our prison break plan. "In fact, the fortresses might even be easier to break into, because they aren't under the watch of the Family or whoever is acting on their behalf."

I glanced sideways. Miles's expression was deceptively calm, but I knew he must be thinking of his own family, imprisoned in the fortress in the north of the city. If we freed his parents along with the others, he'd be reunited with them, but would it really be as simple as that? "How many fortresses are there?"

"Four," said Ryan, overhearing. "Each of our four groups can go to one fortress before tackling the Houses. Think of it as a practise run."

"The fortresses have more security than the Houses do," said Cal.

"But they don't have the Family hovering outside their doors, do they?" I sais. "Their army will be gathered in the centre of the city, not the outskirts. If we divide into groups based on our magic type and walk in pretending the Houses sent us on behalf of their new leadership, they won't assume we're trespassing."

"Except for the spirit mages." Xander's gaze passed over me, Miles, and the other Spirit Agents.

"We can split up and keep watch, then," Shelley said, undeterred.

"We'll come to the northern fortress." I nudged Miles, who shook his head.

"They'd recognise my face," he said. "From the times I showed up asking them to release my parents. It's been a few years, but I bet their security remembers me."

"It doesn't matter," I said. "The guards at the fortresses won't actually be in the know about what's going on in the Houses, will they? They might not even have heard they surrendered to the Family. We can use that against them… or we can pretend to be in league with the Family ourselves. It's not like they'd know any better."

He gave a slow nod. "All right."

———

While the other three groups departed for the other prisons, our group headed for the northern fortress. Miles and I accompanied several fire mages, along with Harper. She'd managed to hold herself together so far, but worry prickled at me every time I caught sight of her shadowy form, which now appeared as pale as a sunbeam.

"I shouldn't come inside with you," she said. "I doubt having a lich with you would do you any favours. I'll wait outside."

"Sure," I said. "Give me a shout if you need me."

The northern fortress looked surprisingly ordinary from the inside, more like a hotel lobby than a magical prison. The mages had spared no expense, given the polished floors and wide staircases. I walked up to the two armoured mages staffing the long wooden desk which dominated the interior. "Hey, there. We're here on behalf of the new rulers of the Houses, Roth and Lex. You might know them as the Family."

"What?" said man on the right, a stocky mage wearing the green-and-black uniform of the House of Air. "You're lying."

"She isn't," said Miles. "The Family has officially taken command of the Houses of the Elements, and our first order is to free all the mages unlawfully locked up in your cells who haven't broken any of the major laws of the Parallel."

"No," said the second mage, a woman wearing blue-and-black, from the House of Water. "That's absurd."

"We have orders to use force if necessary," I added. "I'd prefer not to, but the Family's word is now law. Ask any other mage in the city if you don't believe me."

"She's right," said one of the fire mages, who'd entered the lobby behind us. "They surrendered. All four Houses."

The two guards looked at one another. "We can't allow you to free our prisoners."

"Either you will, or the Family will come here to do it in person," I said. "With the rest of their army. They're dealing with the Houses at the moment, but I'm sure they'll be interested if I tell them you're refusing to obey their commands."

The first mage paled. "No need for that."

The second mage fumbled behind the counter, then she pulled out a set of keys. "Take them."

"We need your records, too," added Miles. "A list of the prisoners and their crimes."

The first mage grabbed a heavy-looking book from the desk with shaking hands and pushed it over to him. Miles took it without a word, and our group split up to cover each floor. Since the vast majority of those incarcerated aboveground were imprisoned for petty crimes, if anything at all, we only needed to consult the book when we reached the lower levels, which were primarily full of murderers and other deadly magical criminals. By now, a large number of guards had come out to ogle us. As far as stealth missions went, it wasn't the greatest, but if we could get everyone out of here without any unnecessary bloodshed, they could stare all they liked.

"Which section are your parents imprisoned in, do you know?" I asked Miles, as he flicked through the book.

"Second floor." His voice was quiet. "I was never allowed to visit."

"We'll take that floor first, then."

Miles grew more visibly nervous as we climbed the stairs up to the second floor, finding ourselves faced with a plain corridor lined with barred cells. I stopped beside the first occupied one, checking on the resident. A mage lay on an uncomfortable-looking narrow bed inside the room, a fireball dancing between his palms. The flame went out when he spotted me and sprang over to the door. "Who are you?"

"Bria Kent," I said. "Former inmate of the House of Fire. The Houses are under new management, and we're here to set you free."

"What?" he said. "What management?"

"The Family." I dropped my voice, checking none of the guards were nearby. "But they aren't giving us orders, between you and me. We're just taking advantage of the Houses being distracted to let out anyone who was unlawfully imprisoned. It's your lucky day."

"You're joking, right?" he said. "You can't expect me to believe the Family took over the Houses?"

"It's true," said Miles. "Didn't you hear about their last attempt to start a war a few weeks ago, when hundreds of people died? They came back for round two and the Houses surrendered right away."

"I can't speak to what their plans are for you, but it wouldn't surprise me if they forgot you existed and left you to die in here," I told him. "Or forced you to fight in their army. We're not going to force you to do anything—we're offering you a choice. Either way, you walk free."

Miles unlocked the cell door. "We have a lot of prisoners to get through, so you can think about it and then decide whether you want to run now or wait until the Family's army is trampling through the city instead."

Leaving the door open, we went to the neighbouring cell. After a moment, the mage stepped out of his cell behind ys. "Where am I supposed to go?"

"Head down to the lobby," I said. "Our allies are down there, and the guards know we're here. You won't get arrested again."

We moved along the row of cells, going through the same routine with all the others—or the inmates marked as 'not dangerous' on their records, anyway. Even then, it was by no means straightforward. Some argued, while others refused to leave their cells for fear of punishment. I was painfully aware that the Family might show up at any moment, but with our allies occupying all four fortresses at once, they'd have a hard job figuring out where to go first. The corridor grew louder the more people we set free, and my apprehension built with every passing second.

Then Miles halted beside a cell containing a man with greying hair, who sat on a bench in front of the door. He looked up at Miles and me with dull eyes. "Who are you?"

Miles stepped closer to the cell door. "Don't you know who I am?"

The man blinked, dumbfounded, leaving me to try to cobble together an explanation. "The Houses of the Elements are under the control of the Family. We're here to set everyone free before they get here, too. I'm Bria, and… and this is Miles."

"The Houses?" Recognition dawned on his face. "You do look like my boy… but it's been years."

"It's true," I added. "He wanted to come here and free you in person."

"Yeah." Miles lifted his head, his eyes glistening. "Is Mum in here, too?"

"It *is* you." He was on his feet a moment later. I hastened to unlock the cell door, and the two embraced for the first time in what must have been years. My own eyes were stinging by the time they broke apart.

"I'll come with you to find your mother," said Miles's father. "I know she's on this floor somewhere."

I moved onto the next cell, while Miles and his dad walked ahead of me, their whispered conversation filling the background. After a while, there came several exclamations as they reached another cell. Miles unlocked the door and a frail-looking woman with Miles's straw-coloured hair walked out into the corridor and hugged them both.

We might not have won yet, but it felt like a victory to me.

21

It took less than an hour for us to clear the rest of the prisoners out of the second-floor corridor. I took over the job of guiding them to the stairs, giving Miles the chance to catch up with his parents.

He shot me a grateful look when I approached him after the last prisoner was freed. "Thank you."

"Come on." I smiled. "Let's get out of here."

The four of us headed down to the lobby, joining the steady flow of prisoners descending the stairs and walking out into the street. The guards watched them leave with wary expressions, but it seemed the others had managed not to give anything away about our real motives in freeing their prisoners. The mages hadn't got cold feet and turned us in either, but they were backed into a corner and they knew it. If they wanted to get the Houses back, we were their last hope.

When I caught up to Xander, I whispered, "Might want to take them a bit further off before we talk about who we're really working for."

"Fair point, but it's not like the guards can put them back in their cells now," he said. "That ship has sailed."

I paced outside the fortress while we waited for the remaining prisoners and mages to get outside, keeping an eye out for potential attackers. Logically, I knew the Family had put most of their attention on the Houses, but that didn't stop me wondering if some of them were patrolling the city looking out for interlopers. My gaze fell on Miles and his parents, who talked animatedly while the fire mages herded the prisoners down a side street out of earshot of the jail.

Harper drifted over to me. "I checked on the other fortresses. They're almost empty, too."

"Good," I said. "All three of them? Damn, the others move fast."

"Yeah, they're pretty efficient," she said. "They haven't got to the Houses yet either, though."

That's next. Once we were at a safe distance away from the fortress, Xander faced the gathering prisoners. "If you haven't already heard, we're not working with the Family. That was a cover story to give us a fair shot at letting you out before the Family got there first."

"You're a member of the House of Fire, aren't you?" said one of the prisoners. "I recognise you from when they brought me in. Your buddy shoved me in a cell."

Ah, crap. I hadn't realised the prisoners might not be thrilled at their new companions, but I should have guessed some of them wouldn't want to fight alongside people who'd once belonged to the Houses. Who could blame them? The Houses had wrought their own demise, in a way, but we needed as many as possible to stand a chance of driving the Family out of the city. The Houses would have to deal with the consequences of their prisoners' escape when the battle was over.

"And you were with the Houses, too." A ragged-looking prisoner pointed accusingly at another mage. "Is this a secret ploy to make us fight for you against the Family so you can gain the Houses back for yourselves?"

I hope not. He had a point, though, and I wouldn't trust the former House members either if I were in their position. It wasn't like the Houses' guards had ever lifted a finger to help them before.

Miles, clearly thinking the same, stepped forward. "Bria and I are the ones who decided to set you free, along with the Death King's Elemental Soldiers. These former members of the Houses agreed to help us, but they're not the ones calling the shots. Our main goal is to drive the Family out of the city. Afterwards, you're free. That's a promise."

"Exactly," I said. "If any of the mages here turns against you, feel free to let us know and we'd gladly make them pay for it. I'm a former inmate of the House of Fire myself, and Miles here has been a rogue for most of his life because his parents were imprisoned in this very building."

"I'm also the leader of the Spirit Agents," added Miles. "Several of my allies are helping free the prisoners in the other fortresses around the city along with the Death King's Elemental Soldiers."

"For what purpose?" said one of the ex-prisoners.

"To stop the Family from capturing you, killing you, or forcing you to fight on their side." I scanned the gathering mages. "If you want to help, you can come with us. We're going to break people out of the Houses of the Elements next, starting with the House of Fire. Then we're going straight to the Family."

Tension rippled through the crowd as my meaning sank in.

"If you don't want to fight, feel free to leave the city," added Miles. "But don't forget there's a war about to kick off, and most of you aren't armed."

"Then what the fuck are we supposed to do?" asked a burly mage.

"Come with me," Miles said. "We're using the Spirit Agents' former base as a safe house. I can't promise it'll stay that way, given how close it is to the Houses, but if you want weapons and supplies, we can help."

"Exactly," I said. "Go with Miles if you want to skip the jailbreak or join in the battle later. Anyone who wants to volunteer to help me break out the prisoners from the Houses of the Elements can come with me."

Miles and his parents led the mages who were undecided or didn't want to fight to the Spirit Agents' base. That left me and handful of former prisoners who eyed the House of Fire's guards on our team with open suspicion as we talked through our plan to infiltrate the Houses.

"This is going to be trickier," I said to Xander. "The Family might be there in person. Or if they aren't, the guards will be on the lookout for trouble."

In truth, I didn't know what we'd find at the House of Fire. I assumed Lex and Roth knew I'd broken out of their cage by now, though maybe they hadn't checked before coming here to put their plan into motion. Either way, the Family's real target had been the Houses, and while I'd escaped their capture, they'd already won in a way.

Thwarting them at this stage would take luck as well as skill.

"I think our best bet is for the former guards to go in and pretend we're still working for them," said Xander. "They might be angry with us if they thought we deserted, but it's the best we've got."

"Pretend you went to confront some deserters your-selves, then," I said. "Make all the excuses you like for taking off. The rest of us haven't a chance of fooling them, so it's on you."

"Then what are you going to do?" he asked me.

"I'll go into the jail," I said. "I'll use an invisibility cantrip to stay hidden. I know where they used to keep the keys. Not sure if they're in the same place, though…"

"I know where they are," said another ex-House of Fire guard. "I'll back you up."

"If you lock me in a cell, I'll punch your lights out."

"That won't be necessary."

The notion of depending on a bunch of strangers made me edgy, but I didn't want to leave the others to handle the Houses alone. Especially the House of Fire. It was entirely possible that some of the Houses' guards who'd left during the Family's takeover might have a moment of panic during our rescue and end up alerting them to our presence, but it was a risk the rest of us would have to take.

As we neared the node which would take us to the centre of Elysium, I spotted Harper lurking nearby, ghostly and semi-transparent.

"Are you okay?" I whispered to her. "You don't have to come with us. You can go back to join Miles if you like."

"I know," she said. "I'm going to the citadel instead."

"What?" I stared at her. "Why? Isn't the Family more likely to be in there than in one of the Houses' bases?"

"They can't hurt me while I'm like this," she said. "Besides… if you want to win, I think you'll need the Death King's help. If I go in there, I can search for him using the transporter."

I had an inkling she might be right, but that didn't make me any keener to send her into the eye of the storm. "Okay. If you're sure."

We used the nearest node to travel to middle of Elysium, where the citadel's piercing light illuminated the shadows of assassins perched on the nearby rooftops, all of them angled towards the tower. The light grew brighter, flickering like a living flame until the entire tower looked as though it was ablaze.

While Harper glided in the direction of the citadel, I used an invisibility cantrip to hide myself from sight before approaching the House of Fire along with the other mages. It helped that our companions were still wearing their guard uniforms, but I held my breath as the group of mages approached the doors to the House of Fire. I heard one of them exchange words with the guard nearest to the door, who then moved aside to let them pass. Silently triumphant, I trod into the hallway behind them, careful not to bump into anyone. The atmosphere seemed subdued, as opposed to chaotic, despite the light of the citadel visible through the windows and the assassins perched on the nearby roofs. They'd already surrendered, after all.

When Xander and some of the others went upstairs to fetch the keys to the jail cells, I held my breath as Harris walked into view. Of course the dickhead had decided to stay here and surrender to the enemy, no doubt planning to run at the first opportunity, or maybe take advantage of the Family's leadership for his own gain. In a feat of incredible patience, I resisted the urge to kick him as he walked by. Instead, I waited, invisible, for the other mages to return with the keys.

When we descended the stairs with the keys in hand, there were surprisingly few guards down near the jail cells. Come to think of it, the whole building seemed pretty quiet. Had the Family ordered the majority of the Houses' mages to come and join them in some other hide-out, or the citadel? Maybe. It wasn't like they even needed to use their persuasive powers now the Houses had surrendered, but the eerie silence set my nerves on edge.

My blood chilled when I reached the jail's first corridor and found that all the cells were empty. Every last one of them. After I'd searched the whole corridor, I backed up to the stairs, my heart sinking in my chest. We'd come here too late, and the Family must have already freed the prisoners in order to convince them to fight on their side.

I had to warn the others. Without a word to the other mages, I ran up the stairs until I reached the main corridor again. The front door was slightly ajar, and the loud commotion of a crowd came from outside. I walked out, hearing the voices echoing from the direction of the citadel. The light in the tower burned brighter, while assassins perched on the rooftops and mages from each of the Houses walked through the streets. Towards the citadel. Despite my urgency, I found myself turning in that direction, too. Had the Family called them? There must be hundreds out in the streets, walking towards the square as though drawn by a signal only they could hear.

As I came within view of the citadel's entrance, the door opened, and Lex and Roth walked out into the square.

I went still, my mind whirling, my plans evaporating on the spot. Lex and Roth were both here in person, and it didn't take a genius to figure out they'd worked their insidious magic on every mage who'd been left in the Houses. Our own numbers were far smaller, especially with Miles and the others at the Spirit Agents' base and the others scattered throughout the city. I could only hope Harper had managed to avoid them when she'd entered the tower, but I didn't see any signs of her—or of the Death King and his fellow liches.

I'd never felt more alone among the crowd of hostile mages approaching the square, where Lex and Roth both wore identical grins as they faced their army. "Are you ready to fight for us?"

Their magic rippled over the crowd, and I covered my eyes and ducked out of the way to avoid being caught in its web. At least a hundred mages from each House had gathered alongside the dozens of assassins waiting in the wings, and not a single voice rose to issue a challenge. Lex's and Roth's combined magic held them in its thrall. Most of the mages wore glazed expressions, as Roth's magic bled all the fight from them, and Lex's spell moved their limbs at her command. There was no sign of Adair, but they didn't need him to be there to have total domination over their followers.

It can't end here. Yet there could only be one outcome if

I showed my face in front of them. Where were my allies? Had they been caught in the spell, too?

Lex and Roth's grins vanished as a gust of wind swept several assassins off the roof, followed by torrents of water and soaring flames which forced everyone in their paths to duck out of range. The ground gave a tremor, which broke apart their army as the mages' attention turned to wildly scanning the area for their attackers. My heart lifted when the other three Elemental Soldiers came running into view, followed by a contingent of other mages, including Spirit Agents and ex-members of the Houses, who climbed the rooftops to take out the assassins and sowed confusion amid the army.

While Lex and Roth clearly had the advantage in numbers, my allies' assault had taken them by surprise. Weaving in and out of the chaos, I went to join them. As I flung a fireball and knocked an assassin off the nearest roof, my hands began to flicker. The invisibility spell was wearing off. *Ah, shit.*

I ducked out of sight around a corner, frantically grabbing for a replacement, but dodging around duelling mages made it impossible to halt for long enough to get into my pendant.

"I know you're here, Bria," said Lex, her voice ringing across the square. "Perhaps I can offer you an incentive to cease this pointless resistance."

I knocked down an earth mage with a punch to the jaw with my free hand, refusing to rise to her bait. The fight continued, brutal yet restrained, as the defecting mages had little desire to kill their former associates, and nobody could get near enough to the Family to land a hit on them.

Finally, a sudden blinding flash of light pierced the air. Everyone cringed, covering their eyes from the brightness that emanated from the direction of the citadel.

When the light dimmed, the square had cleared, the crowd pushed backwards as though by an invisible force. Lex and Roth remained in the centre, the former holding what appeared to be a sharpened tree branch. Green and white lights glimmered up and down its length, and unlike the smaller, stone-shaped Akriths, this one was vibrant, blooming, *alive.*

The Elders' Akrith.

"If you don't show your face right now, Bria," said Lex, "then I'll unleash this weapon on your allies. This entire city will be levelled to the ground."

22

My breath caught in my throat. While I'd known one of them must have been carrying the Elders' Akrith, I'd never expected them to openly use it on the battlefield, not when they relied on its magic to maintain their resilience. But they already believed they'd won, and I didn't doubt for a second that Lex spoke the truth when she said the weapon in her hands could unleash unspeakable damage. Even if the whole city was levelled to the ground, they'd survive... and so would I.

"Go on," said Lex. "Show your face, Bria. I know you don't want to watch them die."

As I prepared to reveal myself, another tall figure stepped out in front of Lex. *Adair*.

"Actually, it was me who brought the Death King's mages here," he told Lex and Roth.

"You?" said Lex.

"Yeah, is that so hard to believe?" said Adair. "It's not like you made any effort to help me out the last time I was locked up in the House of Fire. Thought that might get your attention."

"So you choose to oppose us, now of all times?" said Lex. "I thought I was right to give you a second chance, but perhaps I should have killed the both of you after all. Is your sister here?"

They hadn't seen me yet, but Adair must have guessed I was nearby. I didn't have time to ponder the risk he'd taken by pretending he'd been the one who'd launched the rebellion, because he looked Roth and Lex dead in the eyes and spoke clearly. "Stay there. Put down your weapons."

While Lex and Roth didn't put down their weapons, they didn't attack him either. Meanwhile, everyone in the surrounding area backed away, either recognising his hypnotic talent or else taking the opportunity to run. Not fast enough, however.

"Attack them. Fight among yourselves." Adair's words spread throughout the army, and a dozen elemental attacks rose into the air. None of them made contact with Lex or Roth, but whichever defences they'd used on themselves didn't completely protect them from the backlash of their army turning against one another all at once. Roth was forced to back against the wall of the citadel to avoid a torrent of flames propelled by the Air Element's magic, while Lex held the Elders' Akrith out of reach while she dodged a tidal wave from the opposite direction. As she raised her free hand, a dozen flailing bodies rose into the air, then flew down to earth, their limbs contorting, blood spurting out of deadly wounds.

I forced myself to ignore the carnage and focused on getting close to the Akrith. I ducked underneath arms and sidestepped trampling feet, only for Lex to release another deadly attack. More mages' bodies fell like skittles into my path, bones breaking, bodies spurting blood. She was attacking her own allies, too, and had no care in the world for who she hurt. The pile of bodies stymied my progress towards her—and that was when Adair reappeared. He slammed into Lex, and her eyes flew wide as her head struck the tower wall. With a dazed look in her eyes I'd never seen before, she scrambled to lift the branch into the air—and stabbed him in the chest. The branch speared him like a sword, straight through—and a blinding flash filled my vision.

"NO!"

My scream went unheard, while I flung myself flat as the dazzling light obscured my sight for a long few seconds. In the background, the sounds of fighting continued. The weapon hadn't levelled the city, or so it seemed. Had Lex lied, or had she been bluffing?

I lifted my head, blinking the glare from my eyes. The blast had knocked down everyone in the vicinity, but Adair had taken the brunt of the hit. Blood flowed from a gaping wound in his chest. His mouth parted in surprise, his face turning greyish. My whole body locked in place, horror rippling through me at the sight of Adair falling to his knees. His hands disintegrated as they hit the ground, his bowed head collapsed in on itself, until within a few seconds, nothing remained of Adair but a pile of clothes and ashes.

"How noble of him," said Lex, with a false laugh. "Let that be a lesson to you, Bria, wherever you're hiding. In the world after the war, it'll be easy to replace you."

Elements. He's... gone. The sinking feeling in my chest

warned me that I needed to run. The weapon had reduced Adair to ashes, and they wouldn't hesitate to do the exact same to me. There'd be no returning from death, no miracles... and yet surrender wasn't an option any longer.

As I pushed to my feet, Roth pointed in my direction. "There she is."

A sharp spasm of pain threatened to overwhelm my senses, but the agony lifted when Lex stepped in front of Roth, still wielding the Elders' Akrith. "Since you can't stand up to a bunch of pathetic humans, Roth, I'll do this myself."

My hands shot into the air in surrender against my will, and the mental pain became physical as Lex's power took hold of me. My feet walked by themselves, while my emotions muted to a faint quaver of fear deep inside my bones. I couldn't resist, not even when flames crackled between my fingertips and pointed directly at my allies and enemies alike. The crowd stilled, every one of them held under the same power as I was. I couldn't even shout out in warning, nor could they run away. Lex's grin was unbearable to look upon as I reached her side.

"Maybe I'll have you burn them," she whispered in my ear. "Or... maybe I'll make you use this instead."

She pressed the Elders' Akrith into my unresisting hands. I flinched, an involuntary movement which indicated a small percentage of me wasn't under her control. Too bad it wasn't enough. Try as I might, I couldn't lower my hands, not even to spare my friends from the growing flames.

The ground beneath my feet gave an almighty heave. A torrent of wind followed, along with a surge of water so high that it drenched me from head to toe and knocked the Akrith clean from my hands. Lex, also sopping wet, looked on in stunned disbelief as Ryan, Cal and Felicity approached, seemingly unaffected by Lex and Roth's combined magic… and wearing blindfolds.

Whoa. They'd figured out how to protect themselves, with the unfortunate side effect that they couldn't see where they were going either. Yet whenever someone tried to grab them, a wall of air and water pushed them back, while anyone who got too close found themselves knocked off balance by the trembling earth.

"You can't keep that up forever!" shouted Roth.

"Enough!" Lex grabbed the Akrith herself and pointed it at the Elemental Soldiers.

At the same time, the sound of pounding hooves echoed through the air and a group of zombie horses rode into the square, bearing wights and liches. The Death King's forces had arrived, and with them came a wave of darkness which scattered the already confused army of mages.

Better, every single lich was immune to Lex and Roth's magic. I spotted Harper amid their army, and she shot me a wave. *Yes. She found them in time.*

I seized my chance to run, only for Lex to bar my path. Her deranged expression turned to shock when Neddie the zombie horse ran through the carnage and crashed into me from behind, headbutting me into the air. I flipped over and crashed onto the zombie horse's back with a painful thud, my body trembling with the aftereffects of Lex's magic.

"Neddie, wait!" I groaned. "I need that weapon."

As per usual, the horse refused to listen and cantered away, carrying me through the growing forces of the

Death King's army and past the other Elemental Soldiers. As Lex and Roth struggled to fight their way through the melee, a tremendous screeching noise rose from above our heads.

Wyrms. Not just one of them, either, but at least five lithe reptilian creatures soaring through the sky to join the army. The one I'd set free must have gone in search of others of its kind, and it seemed they had their own grievances to inflict on Lex and Roth. For a moment, everyone stopped fighting, looking up at the new arrivals. Then panic erupted. Some of the mages tried to run, others hid inside the abandoned buildings or ran for the Houses of the Elements, no longer under the Family's control. When I spotted Miles among the confusion, I leapt from Neddie's back and landed at his side.

"You all right, Bria?" he said.

"Yes, but I need that weapon." I rotated on my heel, waiting for the path to clear, and my heart sank. Lex and Roth had disappeared from the square, along with the Elders' Akrith. If I had to guess, they must have run into the tower, which ignited from top to bottom in piercing white light.

"They're running away!" I shouted to the others. "They're going to escape through the portal, I bet."

"Not on my watch," said Ryan from behind me.

With a curse, I ran through the battlefield again, dodging limbs and bursts of elemental fire and water. Chaos erupted, mages duelling with one another, wyrms soaring overhead, and the Death King's forces too busy cutting through the remaining assassins to notice the missing Family. At least the other liches were still alive, relatively speaking, but where was the Death King?

Miles caught my arm. "What's going on?"

"Lex and Roth gave us the slip," I responded. "Where'd the liches come from?"

"Harper brought them here," he said. "She managed to get the Death King to help... ah, there he is."

The crowd on the battlefield parted as the Death King himself rode into view, with Liv riding another zombie horse at his side. She gave me a brief surprised glance before the enemy closed in around them. I began to move through the crowd again, fighting my way through to their side.

Liv peered at me from her horse. "Got rid of that Family of yours, did you?"

"Not yet," I said. "I need to get into that tower. Then I'll have them."

"We need to get into the tower, too," said Liv. "We have to shut down the spell that's affecting all the liches."

"All right." The Death King climbed off his horse and strode up to the citadel, simply pushing aside anyone who got in his way. He then reached the tower door first and opened it on the lower floor.

Several assassins waited on the other side, but I turned them to ashes in one sweep of lethal fire and sprinted around the spiralling stairs to the top. There, I shoved the door open, skidding to a halt in the centre of the room. The fading light of the transporter confirmed my suspicions.

The Family had fled through the portal... along with the Elders' Akrith.

23

I turned to Miles. "Where do you think they went? Because if it isn't somewhere we've already been, I'm not sure we'll be able to follow them."

"I can," Miles said, with certainty. "I can use my spirit magic to track them down. It's usually hard to do that with someone who isn't a spirit mage, but that weapon of theirs left a hell of a trail behind them."

"Are you sure?" I said. "Where are your parents?"

"Helping anyone who can't take part in the battle stay hidden at the Spirit Agents' house," he answered. "They'll be fine. I'm coming with you, Bria."

I didn't stop to argue. We needed to catch up to Lex and Roth—and get that weapon back, preferably into the elves' hands. While the Death King and Liv examined the machinery, I hopped onto the platform. "Anyone who wants to chase down the Family, come with us."

Harper drifted in behind us, while Miles faced the Death King. "Is the spell here?"

"No. We'll look elsewhere." The Death King's gaze slid over to me. "Good luck, Bria."

In a flash, Miles transported us away. We landed in a familiar room, identical to the one we'd left except for the door at the back which led to a room which had once contained trapped sprites. *We're in the middle of the old elvish town.*

Except this time, a larger cage surrounded the platform, preventing us from walking into the room. On the other side of the bars, Lex and Roth watched us, the former still holding the Elders' Akrith in her hands.

"I wondered if you'd have the sense to come alone," said Lex. "Apparently not."

She swivelled in my direction, and I ducked my head to avoid eye contact. "Your promise to level the city fell pretty flat."

"Oh, I was holding back, she said. "The Elders' Akrith works best in conjunction with the elves' other technologies. Like this very tower, for instance."

My gaze went to the machine and then to the weapon in her hands. "I don't follow."

I had an inkling I knew exactly what she meant, though. The machinery had an amplifying effect on any cantrips placed inside it. Would it have a similar effect on the Elders' Akrith, too? The citadels had certainly played a part in the devastation caused during the last war, and only now did I wonder if the elves' creations had held a bigger role than I'd ever imagined. The Akrith was almost a template for the modern-day cantrips, in a way, and even Lex and Roth weren't immune to its effects. Given what they'd done to Adair, I had little doubt that its magic was lethal—and whatever they planned, I had no chance of stopping them as long as I was stuck in this cage.

But Harper could. Her shadowy form drifted straight through the cage bars, unseen by anyone but me, and I did my best to keep my gaze from flickering in her direction as she approached Lex and Roth from the side.

Lex, however, spotted her right away. "You brought a lich?"

"I know that lich," said Roth. "She's the one who gave us the slip last time."

"*She's* the reason Bria beat you?" said Lex in incredulous tones. "I think she ought to be our first test subject."

"Perfect." A vicious smirk appeared on Roth's face. "I think that's fitting, Bria, don't you? We'll test our weapon on your friend."

Lex pressed a button on the machine. Lights flashed along its surface, and a smile identical to Roth's curled her lip as she pointed the Elders' Akrith straight at Harper.

"No!" I flung myself at the cage bars, to no avail.

A moment later, a blinding flash came from the weapon, and a resounding crash echoed around the room. I heard Miles say something in my ear, but I couldn't make out the words—and then the crashing of metal and stone filled the background. My teeth rattled in my skull, and a blinding light seared my vision. I squeezed my eyes shut and crouched on the floor of the cage, waiting for the end.

When I raised my head, the source of the light became apparent. The roof of the citadel had *gone*, opening the room to the heavens, while the walls gaped open to show the ruins surrounding the citadel. Lex and Roth remained untouched, but the back of the room had been torn to pieces.

Nothing of Harper was left.

"You fuckers." I clawed at the bars, then the cage's odd emptiness hit me. The light I'd seen… damn, Miles had vanished through the transporter. If he'd told me where he was going, I hadn't heard him over the sound of the blast.

"So everyone on your side has abandoned you," said Lex. "Except for that lich, and it didn't do her much good, did it. That spirit mage of yours isn't as noble as you thought, but who can blame him?"

A hollow sensation filled my chest. "I'd have done the same if I wasn't the only person who can destroy you."

"I beg to differ." She gestured at the ruins of the town now visible through the gaping hole where the back room used to be. "This is all that remains of the former elven stronghold. The elves would do well to remember it."

"You can't seriously want to cause the same destruction as the spirit mages did in the last war?" I indicated the town's ruins at the foot of the tower. "There's nothing left of it. You don't build new things. You steal, and you destroy."

They'd killed Harper. They'd even killed their son for daring to stand up to them. *I won't let this be the end.*

"You're nothing," said Roth. "You were always nothing, Bria, as long as you refused to allow yourself to be what you were created to be."

"You mean what *you* created me to be," I said. "You've never had the right to dictate who I am. Only I get to choose that."

Harper had befriended me despite all the crap that'd

come to light about my past. She wasn't the only one, either. The other Elemental Soldiers had welcomed me among them, the Spirit Agents had done the same—especially Miles, who'd seen the good in me when I hadn't been able to see it myself. I refused to believe they'd all truly abandoned me.

"We'll make you see sense," said Lex. "But it's going to be a slow and bitter struggle. One you'll lose, like the poor fools who lived in this town."

An odd flickering light caught my eye somewhere in the wasteland. *Phantoms.* Drawn to the carnage, maybe, knowing more blood would soon be shed. They were inside the tower, too, judging by their close proximity. I stiffened as two of them glided past my cage, and Lex and Roth noticed them, too.

"Go away," said Roth.

The phantoms swarmed closer, and when they did, the transporter lit up again. Lights flared around the platform, shining beneath my feet.

"Duck!" yelled Miles's voice.

He appeared behind me, and a cantrip flew from his hand. With his other, he caught my shoulder and yanked me backwards as the bars on the cage burst open under a torrent of flames. Lex and Roth ducked behind the machinery to avoid the spell, while the phantoms continued to drift throughout the room, apparently oblivious to the blast.

Miles released me, pushing to his feet. The crumpled remains of the cage bars lay scattered from the impact of the inferno cantrip. As I climbed upright, a bright light shone from my pocket, dazzling my eyes. The Akrith—*my* Akrith. Why was it glowing like that?

"Stop her!" Lex poked her head out from behind the machinery, her hair full of ash and bits of splintered metal and wood. Roth didn't look much better, crouching out of sight as though he could hide from the phantoms surrounding the pair of them. The Elders' Akrith was still in Lex's grip, but from the way she squinted, the light from my pocket had dazzled her as well.

My Akrith. Was it resonating with something in this room?

Miles gripped my arm. "The transporter."

Shock froze my hand on the stone in my pocket as its vibration fell into tandem with the humming from the platform below my feet. The stone was resonating with the *transporter*… a spell powered by a cantrip. Would it be possible to use the Akrith to open the elves' realm from *here*? I'd never have considered the possibility before, but the elves had built this very citadel, and the humming sensation from the stone matched the vibration of the transporter.

Before I could second-guess my decision, I leapt over to the bank of machinery and pressed the stone to the surface.

The light brightened, spiralling around the room like a white flame shining from the heart of the citadel. A torrent of light spread from the Akrith in my hand to the one Lex held, and she released the weapon with a startled cry as several elves appeared in the middle of the room.

Lex and Roth stared openly into the portal to the elves' realm which now lay open on the platform. Their momentary shock gave me the pause I needed to snatch up the Elders' Akrith from the floor.

"I believe this is yours." I held out the weapon towards the elves. "The Elders' Akrith."

More elves appeared behind them, outlined in light, and the Family shrank away with horrified expressions. Thanks to their impromptu getaway plan, whatever was left of their army was back in Elysium. Nothing remained here but drifting phantoms, ruins… and us.

One of the elves took the Akrith from me. "Thank you for returning our property."

As all eyes turned to Lex and Roth, the pair of them froze to the spot. I waited, breath held, certain I was about to watch an execution. Instead, the elves passed the Akrith among themselves, none of them making a move to use it on them.

"There's no need for bloodshed," said Elder Veksis's voice. "Without our Akrith, they will no longer be immune to damage, and eventually, they will age and die."

My mouth went dry. Both Elders appeared among the crowd, standing on a path which somehow went *through* the citadel's platform, transplanted on top of the ruined town below. The phantoms ignored the elves entirely, continuing to drift around Lex and Roth until they both shuffled out from behind the machinery

"Do you want *me* to kill them?" I asked uncertainly. "Because—they're still immortal. Or long-lived, anyway, until you take the Akrith away from them. And they're dangerous."

"They will be put on trial before our council," said Elder Datra. "Come with us."

"Do I not get a choice in that?" Not that I wanted to let Lex or Roth out of my sight, but who knew what I might miss if I left my allies on the battlefield?

"You want to see them punished, do you not?" said Elder Veksis.

Yes. I did. Lex and Roth might appear harmless, shivering and terrified of the phantoms circling them and whispering in their ears, but I wouldn't rest easily until they were put behind bars forever. My friends would understand.

The elves walked down the path through the citadel's centre, herding Lex and Roth between them, and I walked into the light along with them.

24

The elves hauled Roth and Lex along the path and into the forest. Instinct told me to turn back, not to leave my allies behind, but I had to see this through. If I didn't ensure the Family was unable to ever hurt anyone again, I knew I'd regret it. Without them, their army would have no direction, so my allies should be able to take them apart with ease.

The trial took place in the same clearing where I'd first met the Elders. I felt distinctly out of place, standing among a contingent of elves, but since I couldn't sneak off, I zoned out for the duration of their long speeches. The upside was that everyone was in agreement that Lex and Roth deserved to be punished for their crimes, though they didn't necessarily agree on the nature of that punishment. Understanding elven legal speech in a language I was barely fluent in was beyond my comprehension, so I left them to it and focused on trying not to fall asleep.

It wasn't until Lex and Roth were carted away to jail

that the other elves began to disperse, at which point I went to talk to the two Elders.

"They're not going to stay immortal, are they?" I asked.

"Not without the Akrith," said Elder Veksis. "Which they will never set eyes on again. They'll fade soon enough during their imprisonment."

Not as fast as a swift execution, but then again, it'd be fitting for them to perish while slowly losing the immortality they'd fought so hard for.

"The Family destroyed most of the Akriths," I said, "but I still had mine, and I used it to open a way here via the citadel. Did you know that was possible?"

"I suspected, but our towers have been out of our hands since long before the last war," he said. "The tower will be linked to this realm for as long as the transporter remains active."

"That means I can get back now, right?" I said. "Because I need to check up on my allies."

"Yes," said Elder Datra, raising the Akrith from its spot next to their thrones. "You may leave."

The Akrith flashed, and an instant later, I landed on top of the platform in the empty upper room of the tower. While the sun was high, indicating at least a day had passed, the room itself remained a smouldering wreck—the ceiling and walls blasted open, the wrecked cage's twisted remains littering the ground, and the gleaming form of my own Akrith sitting atop the machinery.

I left it there, descending the stairs with the intention of hunting down a node somewhere in the ruins. As soon as I walked out of the citadel doors, a group of phantoms came to surround me, whispering my name. This time, the whispers didn't sound sinister to my ears, though part of me was still too dazed with shock and relief to take anything else in.

"They're gone," I said to the phantoms. "They won't hurt anyone again."

I didn't know if they understood my words, but the phantoms continued to drift around me as I walked through the ruins until I found a node. I stepped into its path, travelling through the light and landing outside the castle. My nerves prickled as I walked closer to the gates, and towards the two Elemental Soldiers patrolling the grounds.

Felicity's eyes brightened at the sight of me. "There you are, Bria."

"Thought you'd show up when all the hard shit was over," said Ryan.

"Hey, it's not my fault the elves' realm doesn't run on the same time schedule as this one," I said.

"That was a joke," they said. "Not a good one, I'll admit."

A joke was an improvement on their former hostility towards me, so I decided to let that one slide. "Are you still trading shifts on guard duty?"

"Not exactly." Cal strode up to join them. "It's complicated."

"How so?" I looked between them. "What's going on with the Houses? Did they kick up a fuss about us freeing their prisoners even after we saved them from the Family?"

"We told them to direct all their complaints to the Death King," said Felicity. "So far he's ignored all of them."

"Good." I saw no signs of the Spirit Agents inside the grounds, but Trix the elf was visible nearby, feeding something to the vampire chicken. He bounded over the instant he saw me. "Bria! You're back."

"I am," I said. "Sorry I took so long. I had to watch the Family's trial."

"And?" Ryan gave me an expectant look, as did the others.

"They've been jailed for life," I said. "Which will be shorter than they think, since the Elders' Akrith will no longer have any effect on them. They'll start losing their powers and ageing soon enough, I'm sure."

"Good," said Trix vehemently. "I'm glad of it."

"Yeah."

They deserved worse, really, but I wasn't about to question the Elders' decision. The Family had destroyed so many lives over the years, and they'd even taken Adair's future from him as well. Maybe he'd have ultimately reverted to his old ways, but there was no way any of us would ever know that now he was gone. They'd taken away his chance at proving himself a better person.

They'd killed Harper, too. My chest tightened like a vice, and I swallowed, my eyes swimming.

"You okay?" asked Trix. "Are the elves?"

"Yes," I said. "I think they are. Their trial took a while, so I didn't get the chance to talk to all of them, but the pathway to their realm is still open in the citadel where I left it."

"In the citadel?" echoed Felicity.

"Turns out the Akriths work like cantrips," I explained. "I put my Akrith into the transporter and it created a link, so their realm will remain open as long as the Akrith is active."

"So that's how you did it." Trix gave a nod of understanding. "And you're going to leave it open?"

"They didn't tell me not to," I said. "Is that okay?"

"It's brilliant!" said Trix, beaming. "I'll be sure to let the other elves know."

"Better warn the Elders they're coming first," I added hastily. "Anyway, I think the Elders will want to keep the path open so the elves can travel back and forth the way they did before."

"Of course," he said. "The Family is no longer a danger, so there's no reason to keep the realms apart."

"Exactly." I looked around the castle grounds. "Where are the Spirit Agents?"

"They went back to their old base in Elysium," said Ryan. "Miles took them back home once the aftermath of the battle had died down. I think he wanted to make sure none of the runaways from the Houses stole anything."

"Right... and his parents are free, too." Things would change for the Spirit Agents, that was for sure. "What does the Death King think of all this?"

Ryan looked over my shoulder. "Speak of the devil."

The Death King himself walked out of the castle, looking down at me from the top of the stairs.

"Bria," he said. "I wondered when you'd come back."

"Sorry I ditched you." Did his voice sound different than usual? His expression was hard, distant, but it was difficult to tell if that was due to his face being an illusion. "Guess you need your Fire Element back."

"I won't need any Elemental Soldiers any longer," he said. "I've disbanded the Court."

My heart missed a beat. "You... you what?"

"Yeah," said Cal from behind me. "That's the complication."

I frowned at the others. "You're all still here, though."

"We're stubborn." Felicity shrugged. "And it's what we're good at."

"Damn." I turned back to the Death King. "You want us to give up our jobs?"

"I think it's the right decision," said the Death King. "The Houses are restructuring, and so too is the House of Spirit. You're welcome to apply to join the security team if I end up starting a new one. For now, though, consider the Court disbanded."

My mouth parted. "That's putting a lot of stress on *if*."

"It's up to you," he said. "You can check in with the Spirit Agents if you want to hear their own ideas for how to work with the Houses as they reform."

I just blinked at him. Losing my job was the last thing I'd expected of my return from the elves' realm, but I'd have time enough to question the other Elemental Soldiers about this unexpected new development later.

Had it really only been a day or two since the war? It felt longer, and not just on my end. Everyone seemed to be figuring out their shit, yet I felt like I'd left part of myself out there on the battlefield. The Family were no longer a threat to me. Adair was dead. So was Harper, and Tay, and everyone I'd wanted to protect. Which left me at a loose end. A fire mage without a job, half elf and half human without a home to call her own.

Yet.

———

I went back to Elysium. It seemed the sensible thing to do, though my nerves skittered at the thought of seeing Miles. He and his family had been reunited at last, but I didn't know if there was any place for me in his new life. Or vice versa. We'd already pulled off one miracle by beating the Family, but after the loss of my Elemental Soldier status, I didn't dare hope for anything to be the same as it was before.

Before leaving the castle, I took the time to change out of my muddied clothes. The Death King hadn't said I couldn't use my quarters, and besides, I wasn't about to pass up the opportunity for a warm shower and a clean outfit. I did elect to leave my Fire Element cloak behind, since it didn't feel appropriate anymore. I ditched my pendant, too, leaving my elf ears on full display.

Only when I stepped through the node and landed in the winding street did the relief hit me that the city had made it through the war. Elysium was the first place I'd chosen as my home, and maybe, if I couldn't stay in the castle, it would become home again.

My pulse spiked as I approached the Spirit Agents' base. The house looked none the worse for wear, including the vampire chickens roaming around outside. As I knocked, the shadow of a wyrm flew overhead. I assumed they'd been left to roam free after the battle, given that it just seemed to be flying around, not dive-bombing anyone. A relation of the other wyrm? Maybe. It would explain their loyalty to one another.

Miles answered my knock, and we looked at one another across the threshold for a moment. Then I hugged him, greeting him with a kiss that sent the blood pumping through my nerve endings and healed some of the numb disbelief which had battered me since the Death King's revelation.

"Thank the Elements," he said. "I know you went off with the elves, but I was starting to worry you weren't going to come back."

"Nah, they just took forever to get to the point in the Family's trial," I said. "The pair of them are jailed for life, on pain of… well, pain."

"That's good enough for me," he said. "I don't care what happens to them as long as they never walk free again."

"They won't, and the path between our realms is going to remain open for the foreseeable future," I said. "Which will at least give me something to do with my time, because I just got fired."

"Oh." Miles's expression dimmed a little. "Yeah. The Death King told me before I left the castle that he was disbanding the Court. If it helps, I know a lot of people in Elysium are looking for a new cantrip supplier."

I groaned. "Yeah, I need a job, but that definitely isn't for me."

"I thought not." His mouth tilted up at the corner. "If it helps, I don't exactly have gainful employment either. I've spent the last few days wrangling spirit mages, escaped convicts and other… people."

I frowned in confusion at the emphasis on the word *people*, wondering if there was something he hadn't told me. Then a door opened behind Miles, and Harper walked out of the living room. *Walked.*

"Hey, Bria," she said.

"Harper." My mouth fell open. "How are you here? How—you're—"

"Human." She beamed. "You're not the only one who pulled off a miracle. We have a lot to catch up on."

"No kidding." I looked her up and down, hardly believing she'd survived. Not just survived, but come back to life, which was supposed to be impossible. "How?"

"You know that weapon the Family used on me?"

"The Elders' Akrith?" I said.

"Yeah, it… kinda had the opposite effect than it would have had on a human," she said. "When I woke up, I was lying in the ruins draped in my weird lich cloak as if I'd never died at all."

Holy shit. I hadn't even considered that using the weapon on a dead person might have the reverse effect to using it on a living one. I doubted it had ever occurred to Lex or Roth, either. Did the *elves* know? Maybe they did. Given what I'd seen in the citadel, it was pretty clear they were more in tune with the intricacies of magic than I'd ever imagined.

"I'm glad." I ran forward and hugged her. "I'm so glad."

"I know." She smiled as Mav flew over her shoulder, the water sprite's blue glow as vibrant as ever. "I think that kind of miracle happens once-in-a-lifetime, though this is technically my second life, so who can say?"

"There might be hope for the Court of the Dead, then." Or whatever they'd decide to call themselves in their new incarnation. "So… you're staying with the Spirit Agents now?"

"I didn't really have anywhere else to go," she said. "Since I'm not a lich, and I wasn't a spirit mage before I died. I have my fire magic back now, but I don't want to work for the Houses either."

"Can't say I blame you for that," I said. "You got your magic back?"

"No spirit magic anymore, but I always preferred being a fire mage," she said. "As for the Houses, they're going through reforms."

"I heard," I said. "I also heard they're sending complaints to the Death King about their escaped prisoners."

"Speaking of prisoners..." Miles retreated into the living room without finishing his sentence, so I hovered in the doorway with Harper, wondering what future awaited two misfit fire mages like us. I might have considered going to live with the elves, given that they'd doubtless be happy to welcome the person who'd helped save them from the Family, but even with the two realms linked once again, I couldn't imagine moving there myself. The gulf between us was too big, and in the end, Elysium was my home. It always had been.

I looked for Miles and saw him talking to someone inside the living room. Several mages had gathered around him, presumably ex-prisoners or maybe defectors from the Houses. Or new spirit mages, even. I hadn't asked if any of *them* had been among the freed prisoners, though it wouldn't surprise me if they were

"Did the others from the Houses come here?" I asked Harper.

"Oh, I'm not from the House," said the man talking to Miles, overhearing me. He was maybe Harper's age, eyeing me warily from beneath a mop of dark hair. "I was given an enhanced cantrip when I was a kid which gave me... weird abilities. So they locked me up. Not sure I count as a regular mage, so I came here. Hope that's okay."

Oh, damn. Someone had experimented on him. Like Tay. Like… the other people the Family had sold their illicit cantrips to.

"He isn't the only one," said Miles. "Tons of other victims were among the other prisoners in the Houses' jails. We didn't figure it out until after the battle."

Damn. Of course there were others who'd had their lives ruined by the Family's magic, who'd been arrested and then abruptly freed. They'd be in desperate need of direction, that was for sure.

"So this is like… a safe house for all kinds of mages now?" I asked.

"You've got it." Miles shot me a smile. "Fair warning, it's kinda chaotic in here."

Fair warning… as if he knew I wanted to stay.

And I did. I really did.

"I'm used to it." My fingers moved to fiddle with the pendant around my neck, except of course I'd left it behind at the castle.

Miles's gaze went to my neck, then my ears. "You're not wearing the cantrip anymore. I like it."

I smiled. "I decided I wanted a change. The rest of my stuff is still at the castle, but if there's a spare room—"

"You don't even need to ask." With a grin, he pulled me one-handedly over the doorstep and into a room swarming with mages, all of whom walked free for the first time in months or years.

It wouldn't be easy for any of us. I was under no illusions that moving forward would be without its challenges, but now the Family had gone, we were free to carve our own paths.

I'd write my own future.

ABOUT THE AUTHOR

Emma is the New York Times and USA Today Bestselling author of the Changeling Chronicles urban fantasy series.

Emma spent her childhood creating imaginary worlds to compensate for a disappointingly average reality, so it was probably inevitable that she ended up writing fantasy novels. When she's not immersed in her own fictional universes, Emma can be found with her head in a book or wandering around the world in search of adventure.

Find out more about Emma's books at
www.emmaladams.com.